STRAWBERRY SHORTCAKE MURDER

Hannah stared at the hammer glistening in the light. It was out of place, but perhaps Boyd had been doing some repairs and had forgotten to put it away.

"He's . . . He's over here," Danielle whispered.

As Danielle led her toward Boyd's Grand Cherokee, Hannah spotted the plastic cover of her cake carrier. It had rolled under his car and was peeking out by the rear wheel. They rounded the side of the Jeep, and Hannah gasped. Jordan High's head basketball coach was sprawled out on the cement floor of his garage, lying in a gooey pile of cake, whipped cream, and crushed strawberries.

Hannah stepped closer and swallowed the lump that rose in her throat. The red splotches on the concrete weren't from the crushed strawberries; they were from Boyd's crushed skull. He was dead; there was no doubt in Hannah's mind. No one could lose that much blood and live. . . .

Books by Joanne Fluke

CHOCOLATE CHIP COOKIE MURDER

STRAWBERRY SHORTCAKE MURDER

BLUEBERRY MUFFIN MURDER

LEMON MERINGUE PIE MURDER

FUDGE CUPCAKE MURDER

SUGAR COOKIE MURDER

PEACH COBBLER MURDER

CHERRY CHEESECAKE MURDER

KEY LIME PIE MURDER

CANDY CANE MURDER

CARROT CAKE MURDER

CREAM PUFF MURDER

PLUM PUDDING MURDER

APPLE TURNOVER MURDER

Published by Kensington Publishing Corporation

STRAWBERRY SHORTCAKE MURDER

 A Hannah Swensen Mystery

JOANNE FLUKE

KENSINGTON BOOKS
Kensington Publishing Corp.
http://www.kensingtonbooks.com

KENSINGTON BOOKS are published by

Kensington Publishing Corp.
850 Third Avenue
New York, NY 10022

All Kensington Titles, Imprints, and Distributed Lines are available at special quantity discounts for bulk purchases for sales promotions, premiums, fund-raising, and educational or institutional use. Special book excerpts or customized printings can also be created to fit specific needs. For details, write or phone the office of the Kensington special sales manager: Kensington Publishing Corp., 850 Third Avenue, New York, NY 10022, attn: Special Sales Department, Phone: 1-800-221-2647.

Kensington and the K logo Reg. U.S. Pat. & TM Off.

ISBN-13: 978-0-7582-1972-5
ISBN-10: 0-7582-1972-5

First Hardcover Printing: March 2001
First Paperback Printing: February 2002

20 19

Printed in the United States of America

For my kids.
You asked for your favorite recipes.
Here they are in novel form.

Chapter
One

The sound of a crash startled Hannah Swensen awake. It was the middle of the night, she lived alone, and someone was in her condo. She sat up and grabbed the first thing handy, her goose-down pillow, before her sleep-numbed mind realized that it wasn't a very effective weapon. She had to wake up and take action. Then she heard a second noise, coming from the direction of her kitchen. The intruder was dragging something across the linoleum floor.

Hannah peered into the darkness, but all she could see was the dim outline of the window. She knew that turning on her bedside lamp would only make her a more visible target, and she quickly dismissed that option. Hannah slid out of her warm bed to retrieve the baseball bat she'd kept in the corner of her bedroom ever since the night she'd suspected that Ron LaSalle's killer was staking out her home. Thankfully, all that was in the past, now that the murderer was behind bars.

The noises from the kitchen continued as Hannah crept

down the hallway, bat grasped firmly in both hands. A less courageous person might have stopped to dial nine-one-one on the bedroom extension, but the concept that someone had invaded her home made Hannah see red. There was no way she was going to cower in the closet, waiting for someone from the sheriff's department to arrive. She had the advantage of knowing every inch of her condo in the dark, and her bare feet were soundless on the thick-pile carpet. With a little luck and a better swing than she'd had in Little League, she could bash the intruder over the head before he even knew what had hit him.

The dim light filtering in through the miniblinds at the kitchen window revealed no dark shape pressed against the walls, no threatening figure crouched beneath the table. But there was a curious chewing sound that didn't cease as she stepped through the doorway. What kind of burglar would break into her home and take a break for a late-night snack? Hannah moved closer, bat at the ready, and gave a relieved sigh as she spotted a pair of startled yellow eyes near the bottom of the refrigerator. Moishe. She should have known better than to leave a pot of catnip out on the kitchen counter.

Hannah turned on her heel and headed back to the bedroom, leaving her orange-and-white feline chewing and purring simultaneously. There was no sense in reprimanding Moishe. The damage was done, and he'd simply ignore anything she said. He was a cat, and Hannah had learned that it was just the way cats were. She'd clean up the mess in the morning.

It seemed as if she'd no sooner climbed back in bed and closed her eyes, than the alarm went off. Hannah glanced at the dial, it was six in the morning, and she swore with more vehemence than usual as she reached out to shut it off. She flicked on the lamp next to her bed and yawned widely as

she massaged the back of her neck. Moishe was back in her
bed, hunkered down on her pillow and purring loudly. No
wonder her neck was stiff. He'd stolen her favorite pillow
again.

Hannah sighed deeply and began the painful process of
mentally preparing herself for the million and one things she
had to do today. It had been a late night. Mike Kingston, the
supervisor of detectives at the Winnetka County Sheriff's
Station, had taken her to a party at the Lake Eden Inn, and
she hadn't gotten home until after midnight.

"Move it, Moishe." Hannah roused the disreputable tom-
cat she'd rescued from the streets and reclaimed her pillow.
Then she slipped her feet into the fur-lined moccasins by the
side of her bed and made her way to the kitchen. Coffee was
a necessity at this hour of the morning, and she'd set the
timer on her coffeemaker so that it would be ready when she
woke up.

It was December in Minnesota and the morning sky was
masquerading as night. Daybreak wouldn't come for another
hour and a half. Hannah had no sooner switched on the
banks of fluorescent tubes that gave her gleaming white
kitchen the luminescence of an operating room, than the
phone rang. There was no one else who'd call this early and
Hannah groaned as she reached for the receiver. "Good
morning, Mother."

Of course Delores Swensen wanted to know all about her
date with Mike. Hannah gave her a brief description as she
poured her first cup of coffee and gulped it, scalding hot.
What was a little pain compared to the blessings of caffeine?
Once she'd reported that Mike had driven her out to the Lake
Eden Inn, they'd enjoyed a buffet dinner with the contestants
who'd arrived for the Hartland Flour Dessert Bake-Off, listened to the after-dinner speech by Clayton Hart, the owner
of Hartland Flour, and gone back to her shop to mix up the

cookie dough for today's baking, there was nothing else to say. "That's it, Mother. Mike was really nice, and I had a good time."

Hannah tucked the phone between her shoulder and her ear and grabbed the broom to sweep up the dirt and shards of pottery from the catnip pot. There were no leaves left. Moishe had scarfed up every one. Then she opened a new box of kitty crunchies for Moishe, who was insistently and none too gently rubbing against her ankles, and answered her mother's question. "No, Mother. Mike didn't mention marriage. The subject's never come up."

Hannah rolled her eyes as she dumped dry cat food into the Garfield ceramic bowl she'd found at Helping Hands, Lake Eden's thrift shop. Delores believed that a woman who was almost thirty and still unmarried just wasn't trying hard enough. Hannah disagreed in principle and especially in her own case. She didn't want to get married at this time in her life. Actually, she wasn't sure she *ever* wanted to marry.

"Look, Mother . . ." Hannah made a conscious effort to keep her tone pleasant. "There's nothing wrong with being single. I'm running a successful business, I own my own condo, and I have plenty of friends. Can you hold on a second? I have to get Moishe some water."

Hannah placed the receiver on the counter and turned on the faucet, filling Moishe's water bowl to the brim. She set it down next to his food bowl, and whispered an aside to him, "She'll start in on the baby thing next. I'd better head her off at the pass."

"It's not like I'm dying to have children, Mother." Hannah settled the phone against her ear again. "I've got Tracey and I see her almost every day. Between the shop and catering, I wouldn't have time to be a good mother anyway."

Delores launched into her predictable argument and Hannah half listened while she poured herself a second cup of coffee. It was nothing new; she'd heard it all before.

Hannah's niece, Tracey, couldn't possibly take the place of Hannah's own child, Hannah didn't know what she was missing, and there was no joy like holding your own baby in your arms. When Delores got to the part about ticking biological clocks, Hannah glanced up at her own kitchen clock, shaped like an apple and another acquisition from Helping Hands. It was time to end the conversation, and that wouldn't be easy. Delores didn't like to be stopped short in the middle of one of her lectures.

"I've got to run, Mother. I promised to be at the school in less than an hour."

Just saying that she was in a hurry didn't sway Delores from her purpose. She had to give one last warning about Mike Kingston and how she didn't think he was interested in marriage. Hannah was forced to agree with that assessment. Mike's wife had been killed two years earlier, and Hannah knew that he was in no hurry to remarry. But then Delores brought up the subject of Norman Rhodes, Lake Eden's bachelor dentist, and Hannah let out an exasperated sigh. Her mother had been in league with Norman's mother, Carrie, in trying to promote their romance ever since Norman had come to town to take over his father's practice.

"I know you're close to Carrie, but you're both trying to make something out of nothing," Hannah responded quickly, before Delores could go into her litany of Norman's virtues. "I like Norman. He's nice, he's intelligent, and he's got a great sense of humor. But we're just good friends, and that's all there is to it."

Delores still wasn't through, so Hannah used a trick she'd learned from her younger sister, Andrea. She clicked the disconnect button a couple of times, and said, "I think there's something wrong with my phone. If we get cut off, I'll call you back later when I get to the shop." Then she started to say something else and cut herself off in the middle of her own sentence.

Hannah replaced the receiver and stared at it for a minute. The phone didn't ring again, and she gave a smile of satisfaction. Andrea had sworn that no one would suspect that you'd deliberately hung up on yourself.

Twenty minutes later and freshly showered, Hannah pulled on a pair of worn jeans that were a little tighter around the waist than they'd been when she'd bought them, and a long-sleeved beige pullover that bore the legend "GOT COOKIES?" on the front in red block letters. She loved the color red, but she'd never been able to find a shade that didn't clash with her hair.

After refilling Moishe's food bowl and tossing him a couple of kitty treats that were supposed to be made from real salmon, Hannah hurried down the steps to the underground garage and climbed into her candy-apple red Suburban. She'd bought it when she'd first started her business over two years ago, and she'd found a local sign painter to letter the name of her shop, The Cookie Jar, in gold script on both doors. It even had a vanity license plate "COOKIES," and it was a mobile ad for her business. At least Stan Kramer, Lake Eden's only accountant, claimed that it was when he filled out her tax forms.

Hannah was about to back out of her parking space in the underground garage when she heard a shout. Her downstairs neighbor, Phil Plotnik, was waving his arms and pointing at something near the front of her truck. He held up one hand in a gesture to stay put and walked over to unplug her head bolt heater cord from the strip of electrical outlets that lined the garage wall. Hannah nodded her thanks and gave him the high sign as he wound it around her front bumper. She always snapped a couple of extension cords each winter, before she got used to the fact that her truck was plugged in. Phil had saved her the cost of one replacement.

It wasn't snowing as Hannah drove up the ramp and

emerged into the icy predawn darkness, but the wind was whipping up the loose flakes that had fallen during the night. When she rolled down her window to use her electronic gate card to raise the wooden bar at the exit of the complex, the frigid air whistled into her truck. Hannah turned up the fur collar on her parka and shivered. It couldn't be more than twenty degrees outside.

The heater didn't kick in with its welcome burst of hot air until she'd turned north onto Old Lake Road. It would be a full five minutes before it could warm the cavernous interior of her truck, and Hannah kept her collar turned up. But she did pull off one of her leather gloves to reach back and grab a bag of cookies.

Hannah never sold day-old baked goods, and the cookies were leftovers from the previous day's baking. She packed them up in bags after she'd closed her shop for the night and stowed them in the back of her Suburban. They never went to waste, and Hannah's generosity was legendary in Lake Eden. The younger children called her the "Cookie Lady," and they were all smiles when she pulled up in her truck and passed out samples. One free cookie could turn into a sale, especially if a child went home and clamored for Mom to go down to The Cookie Jar to buy more cookies.

Hannah was munching a leftover Old-Fashioned Sugar Cookie as she approached the Cozy Cow Dairy and stopped for the light at the intersection of Old Lake Road and Dairy Avenue. Pete Nunke was standing by his truck, checking his orders under the bright lights of the loading dock, and Hannah gave a polite beep on her horn as the light turned to green and she drove on by. Pete was a good deliveryman, but she still missed Ron LaSalle.

Ten minutes later, Hannah pulled into the parking lot at Jordan High. It was seven in the morning, much too early for either the teachers or the students, and she found a prime parking spot right in front of the auditorium. A huge green banner hung over the double doors, declaring that it was the site of the Hartland Flour Dessert Bake-Off.

"Morning, Hannah." Herb Beeseman, Lake Eden's marshal and the only law-enforcement officer on the city payroll, greeted her with a smile as she pushed through the door. "You're right on time."

Hannah grinned back and handed over the small bag of cookies she'd brought in from her truck. "This is like bringing coals to Newcastle, but they're your favorites, Molasses Crackles."

"Coals to Newcastle?" Herb looked puzzled for a moment, then he laughed. "I get it. You think the contestants will want me to be their official taster?"

"I wouldn't be surprised. After all, you're the only one here."

"That's right." Herb looked pleased at the thought. "I can't leave my post, but Mr. Hart said you could go right in. I turned on the lights for you."

Hannah was surprised as she stepped through the inner doors. She'd graduated from Jordan High and had been in the auditorium more times than she could count. Today, it looked completely different. The raised wooden stage, which was used for school plays and programs, had been converted into four individual kitchen sets with temporary waist-high partitions between them. All the electrical wires and plumbing pipes had been enclosed in large conduits that ran into a space below the kitchen counters and could be easily removed when the contest was over. One of the stipulations Jordan High's principal, Mr. Purvis, had made was that nothing could damage the stage floor.

Once she'd climbed the steps to the stage, Hannah examined each of the kitchens. They were identical, with new appliances and working sinks and dishwashers. Refrigerators hummed softly, stovetops glistened, and there was a full complement of kitchenware on each set. Once the contest was over and the grand prizewinner had been declared, Mr. Hart would donate all of the equipment to the home economics department at Jordan High. He'd also promised to completely renovate the cafeteria and the school kitchen over the summer, a gesture that had the head cook, Edna Ferguson, singing his praises all over town.

It took a while to test the appliances and inspect each of the four kitchen sets. As the senior judge on a panel of five, it was her responsibility to make sure that the kitchens were identical in every way. Once she was satisfied that everything was working, Hannah said good-bye to Herb and hurried back out to her truck. It was seven-thirty, and she had to help her assistant, Lisa Herman, get ready for the morning crowd that would be waiting at The Cookie Jar when they opened at eight.

When Hannah pulled into her parking spot in back of her bakery, Lisa's old car was in the adjoining spot. There was a heavy coating of ice on the windshield, and it took at least a couple of hours for that amount of ice to build up. Lisa had come in very early this morning.

Lisa was in the process of removing two trays of cookies from the ovens when Hannah walked in. She slid them onto the bakers' rack and wiped her hands on the towel that was looped to her apron. On Hannah, the same apron would have come to a spot just above her knees, but Lisa was petite and she'd folded it several times at the waist so that it wouldn't trip her when she walked. "Hi, Hannah. Did you remember to plug in your truck?"

"Of course. How long have you been here, Lisa?"

"Since five. I figured you'd be busy with the contest, and I wanted to have everything ready to go. The cookies are all baked, and the coffee's made, if you want some."

"Thanks, I could use it." Hannah hung her coat on the strip of hooks that ran along the back wall and walked toward the restaurant-style swinging door that led into the shop. Then she remembered what had happened with the catnip that Lisa had sent home for Moishe, and she turned back. "Moishe loved your catnip. He ate it all up in the middle of the night."

"Did you leave it out where he could get at it?"

"Yes. My mistake." Hannah decided not to tell Lisa how she'd crept down her hallway in the middle of the night, armed with a baseball bat. "How about the strawberries? Are they ripe, or should I use frozen for tonight?"

"They're ripe. Now that I know how to do it, I'm going to grow them every winter. They're in a bowl in the cooler if you want a taste."

"No thanks," Hannah declined. "I'm only allergic to one thing, and that's strawberries. So that greenhouse gardening really works?"

"It works on strawberries and tomatoes. That's all I grew this year. Dad loves BLTs, and he doesn't remember that you can't buy good tomatoes in the winter."

"It's nice of you to grow them for him." Hannah turned and headed off to the coffeepot. Jack Herman had Alzheimer's, and Lisa had given up her college scholarship to stay home and take care of him. It was a shame, but it had been Lisa's decision, and Hannah knew that she didn't regret it.

Once Hannah had switched on the old-fashioned overhead fixtures and poured herself a cup of coffee from the giant urn that sat behind the counter, she went back to the bakery to check the cakes she'd baked two days previously. There were four cakes, each wrapped in plastic wrap and covered with a layer of foil. She grabbed a sharp knife and went to the walk-in cooler to cut two thin slices from the test cake. Then she rewrapped it and carried one of the pieces out to Lisa, who was sitting on a stool at the stainless-steel work island.

"I love cake for breakfast. It makes me feel rich." Lisa took a bite and chewed thoughtfully. "It's wonderful, Hannah. What do you think?"

Hannah tasted her slice and nodded. "It doesn't get any better than this. Two days is the perfect settling time."

"It was great fresh, but it's better now. It's almost like cheesecake without the cheese."

Hannah was pleased with Lisa's assessment. The cake for the strawberry shortcake she'd agreed to make on camera tonight was close to perfection. "You're reacting to the density. This cake gets heavier each day it sits in the cooler."

"It's going to be a huge hit with the newscasters." Lisa finished her slice and stood up. "It's time, Hannah. Do you want me to open the door?"

"I'll do it. You can finish decorating the cookies for the Dorcas Circle Christmas party."

Hannah walked through the swinging door and into her cookie shop. She was still a little nervous about appearing on television tonight, but it had been Mr. Hart's idea, and everyone in town, Hannah included, wanted to please Mr Hart. This was the first Hartland Flour bake-off, and they were all hoping that it would become an annual affair.

The bake-off had reawakened Lake Eden from its winter's sleep. The town's population, which dwindled when the summer people closed their lake cottages and moved back to the city, had swelled again with the arrival of the bake-off contestants, their families, and the spectators. Sally and Dick Laughlin, the owners of the Lake Eden Inn, had been delighted to open their doors in the off-season, and almost every shop in Lake Eden had experienced an influx of new business. Lake Eden was booming at a time when most residents were struggling to make a living, and Mr. Hart had hired locals for everything from carpentry and plumbing to ushering the audience into the auditorium. The mayor had called Hannah only yesterday and said he hoped that Mr.

Hart would make Lake Eden the permanent site of the bake-off.

To advertise the four-day event, Hannah had agreed to act as a live backdrop for KCOW Television's local news, done on-location at the school auditorium. Mason Kimball, a Lake Eden resident, was KCOW's producer, and he'd advised Hannah to bake something colorful, like strawberry shortcake. Hannah had taken his suggestion literally and decided to assemble Strawberry Shortcake Swensen on camera tonight. There wasn't time actually to bake the cake, but Hannah would mix up the batter, pour it into pans, and stick them into a cold oven to be baked after the show by Edna Ferguson, the school cook. Hannah would substitute the cakes she'd already baked, and after she'd presented her strawberry shortcake to the newscasters, a number would be flashed on the screen so that viewers could call the KCOW switchboard for a copy of her recipe. The number of requests would indicate how many people had watched Mason's broadcast.

Just after she'd flipped the "Closed" sign to "Open," the phone began to ring. Hannah knew that Lisa would pick it up in the bakery, and she ignored the insistent ringing as she unlocked the door and greeted the line of customers that awaited her.

First in the door were Bill Todd, Hannah's brother-in-law, and Mike Kingston, his supervisor. Mr. Hart and Mason Kimball were right behind them, and Andrea was next, with Hannah's niece, four-year-old Tracey. Andrea's blond hair was pulled back in an intricate knot this morning, and she was dressed in a smart little navy blue suit that must have cost her a week's salary. She looked as if she'd just stepped out of an ad for women executive fashions, and Hannah felt a small stab of envy that she quickly covered with a warm, welcoming smile. Hannah had never been able to compete with Andrea in the looks department, and she'd stopped trying when they were both in high school. Andrea and Michelle, Hannah's youngest sister, resembled their mother, who was still a strikingly beautiful woman. Hannah was the only one who'd inherited her father's gangly height and his frizzy red hair. Luckily, Tracey had received her mother's beauty genes, and she was a pint-sized version of Andrea, right down to her shining blond hair.

Tracey was Hannah's first priority, and once she'd gotten her favorite and only niece settled on a stool with milk and cookies, she turned to her other customers. She'd just begun the process of filling their orders when Lisa walked into the coffee shop. Hannah finished serving Mr. Hart, who had ordered a cup of black coffee and two of her Regency Ginger Crisps, and then she stepped over to Lisa. "Is something wrong?"

"I think so." Lisa lowered her voice so they wouldn't be overheard. "Norman Rhodes is on the phone, and he says it's an emergency. I can take over for you here."

Hannah moved aside so that Lisa could take her place behind the counter and hurried back to the bakery. Norman was levelheaded. He wasn't the type to use the word "emergency" lightly.

Lisa had left the wall phone off the hook, and Hannah took a deep breath before she picked it up. "Hi, Norman. Lisa said there's an emergency?"

"Mr. Rutlege came in with an impacted molar, and I've got some really bad news." Norman sounded very worried.

Visions of disaster raced through Hannah's mind. Norman knew that she'd helped Bill solve two murders already, and she was an old hand at dealing with death. Had Mr. Rutlege died in the dental chair? And who was he? Hannah knew she'd heard the name before, but she couldn't quite place it. "Who's Mr. Rutlege?"

"You must have met him at the Lake Eden Inn last night. He's tall and thin with silver hair, and he looks a little like Ricardo Montalban."

Hannah had met dozens of strangers last night. The names were a blur, but she remembered the man that Norman had described. He was one of the out-of-town judges for the bake-off. "What happened to Mr. Rutlege?"

"It started out as a simple extraction. There was no way I could save the tooth. But he had a negative reaction to the anesthetic, and to make things even worse, I discovered that his blood didn't clot properly."

Hannah's fingers tightened on the receiver. "He's not . . . *dead,* is he?"

"Dead?" Norman sounded shocked at the question. "Of course he's not dead. But Mr. Rutlege can't judge the bake-off. There's no way he'll be eating anything that doesn't come out of a blender for at least a week."

Strawberry Shortcake Swensen

Serves 12 *(or 6 if they ask for second helpings)*

To make this dessert, you will need: ***Pound Plus Cake ****, three boxes of ripe strawberries, and a bowl of ***Hannah's Whipped Crème Fraiche.*** *(Pronounce it "Cremm Fresh" and everybody will think you speak French.)*

Pound Plus Cake

Preheat oven to 325° F.,
rack in the middle position.

1 ½ cups softened butter *(3 sticks)*
2 cups white sugar
4 eggs
1 cup sour cream *(you can substitute unflavored yogurt for a lighter cake)*
½ teaspoon baking powder
1 teaspoon vanilla
2 cups cake flour *(DO NOT SIFT—use it right out of the box)*

** **Pound Plus Cake** must chill for 48 hours. Make it 2 days before you plan to serve. You can also bake it, cool it, wrap it in plastic wrap and then in foil, and freeze it until you need it. This recipe makes 2 cakes. Each cake serves 6 people.*

Generously butter and flour two 9-inch round cake pans. *(Don't use Pam or spray shortening—it won't work.)*

Cream softened butter and sugar in the bowl of an electric mixer. *(You can mix this cake by hand, but it takes some muscle.)* Add the eggs, one at a time, and beat until they're nice and fluffy. Then add the sour cream, baking powder and vanilla. Mix it all up and then add the flour, one cup at a time, and beat until the batter is smooth and has no lumps.

Pour the batter into the pans and bake at 325 degrees F. for 45 to 50 minutes. *(The cakes should be golden brown on top.)*

Cool in the pans on a rack for 20 minutes. Run a knife around the inside edges of the pans to loosen the cakes and turn them out on the rack.

After the cakes are completely cool, wrap each one in plastic wrap, sealing tightly. Wrap these packages in foil and store them in the refrigerator for 48 hours. Take them out an hour before you serve, but don't unwrap them until you're ready to assemble the dessert.

The Strawberries

(Prepare these several hours before
you serve.)

Wash 3 boxes of berries and remove stems. *(The
easiest way to do this is to use a paring knife to cut off
the top part of the berry.)* Slice all but a dozen or so,
reserving the biggest and best berries to top each portion. Taste the berries and add sugar if they're too tart.
Stir and refrigerate, covered tightly.

Hannah's Whipped Crème Fraiche

*(This will hold for several hours.
Make it ahead of time and refrigerate it.)*

2 cups heavy whipping cream
½ cup white sugar
½ cup sour cream *(you can substitute unflavored yogurt, but it won't hold as well and you'll have to
do it at the last minute)*
½ cup brown sugar *(to sprinkle on top after you assemble the dessert)*

Whip the cream with the white sugar. When it
holds a firm peak *(test it by dipping in your spatula)*,
fold in the sour cream. You can do this by hand or by
using the slowest speed on the mixer.

Assembling Strawberry Shortcake Swensen

Cut each *Pound Plus Cake* into 6 pie-shaped wedges and place on dessert plates. Top with the sliced strawberries. Put several generous dollops of *Crème Fraiche* on top and sprinkle with the brown sugar. Garnish with the whole berries you reserved. Serve and receive rave reviews.

Made this for Norman, Carrie, and Mother. Used only one *Pound Plus Cake* and froze the other—Reduced *Crème Fraiche* recipe by half and used only two boxes of berries.

Chapter Two

Hannah added sugar to a bowl of heavy cream and finished whipping it during the weather report. It was hot under the lights, and she hoped it wouldn't turn to soup. When it was stiff enough to hold a peak, she folded in the sour cream. In addition to adding a new taste dimension, the sour cream helped the sweetened whipped cream keep its shape. Just as she was about to dip her finger into the bowl, she remembered that she was on camera and settled for tasting it with a spoon. Then she ladled a big scoop of Lisa's homegrown strawberries onto the slice of cake, put on generous dollops of her whipped cream mixture, popped a perfect whole berry in the center, and sprinkled brown sugar over the top. Her original creation, Strawberry Shortcake Swensen, was ready to serve to the newscasters.

The stage manager, a short, heavyset man who possessed more energy than anyone Hannah had ever met before, gave her a signal to get ready. The weather report had concluded and Chuck Wilson, the handsome, chisel-faced anchorman, was just winding up with a reminder for the viewers to stay tuned for the Hartland Flour Dessert Bake-Off, right after the network "World News."

Hannah's heart started to pound as she picked up the serving tray. She'd practiced all this in rehearsal, but carrying an empty tray wasn't the same as managing a serving platter loaded with cake, plates, and forks. Careful not to trip over the heavy cables that were taped to the stage floor with something Mason Kimball called "gaffer's tape," but looked like plain old duct tape to her, Hannah put on the brightest smile she could muster and made her way to the long curved news desk, where the four newscasters sat. Careful not to let her smile slip, Mason had warned her about that, she presented her dessert to each of them in turn.

Hannah stood by while they oohed and aahed and then tasted her dessert. Chuck Wilson, the anchorman, made a comment about how expensive out-of-season strawberries could be. Where did Hannah find them this time of year? Hannah smiled and replied that her assistant, Lisa Herman, had grown them in her greenhouse. Dee-Dee Hughes, Chuck's anorexic co-anchor, asked how many calories were in each slice of shortcake. Hannah said she really didn't know, but she didn't think it mattered because people on diets usually passed when it came to dessert. Wingo Jones, the sportscaster, said he thought pro athletes should use Strawberry Shortcake Swensen to carb up before each game. Hannah's smile was wearing a little thin by then, but she managed to say that she thought it might be a good idea. The only member of the news team who didn't make some sort of insipid comment was the weatherman, Rayne Phillips, who continued forking shortcake into his mouth until he'd finished every bite.

The moment the news was over, Hannah went back to the kitchen set to pack up her supplies. She opened the oven and found it as bare as Old Mother Hubbard's cupboard. Edna had already whisked the unbaked cakes away to the school kitchen. Rather than juggle all the half-filled bowls, Hannah decided to assemble the dessert and carry it home that way. She dumped the rest of Lisa's strawberries over the top of the cake, frosted with the whipped cream mixture, added the whole berries she'd reserved for a garnish, and sprinkled on the extra brown sugar. Then she clamped the domed lid on her cake carrier, stacked the utensils and bowls she'd used in the cardboard carriers she'd brought, and lugged everything backstage.

"You were great out there, Hannah." Andrea was waiting for her in the wings, and she helped Hannah carry her things to the metal shelves that had been set up against the back wall.

"Thanks," Hannah acknowledged the compliment, and looked around for her niece. When Hannah had repeated Norman's conversation and Mr. Hart had learned that one of his judges had to be excused, he'd asked Tracey to choose the fifth member of the panel from a glass bowl containing the names of the Lake Eden Town Council. "Where's Tracey?"

"She's still in makeup. Bill's bringing her here just as soon as she's through."

"She's not nervous, is she?"

Andrea shook her head. "She thinks it's fun. You're taping it, aren't you, Hannah? Bill set our VCR before we left the house, but I need a backup copy."

"You'll have two. I'm taping it, and so is Mother."

"Mother?" Andrea's eyebrows shot up. "She still hasn't figured out how to set her VCR. When our cable was out, I asked her to tape a movie for me and she got two hours of Richard Simmons."

Hannah reached out to pat her sister on the shoulder.

"Calm down, Andrea. Lisa's taping it, and so are most of my customers. You'll have dozens of backups. I can almost guarantee it."

"I hope so. This is Tracey's very first television appearance, and you never know when a big-name producer might be watching. That's how they discover child stars."

Hannah managed a smile, the same smile she'd used when she'd been forced to listen to the idiotic comments three of the four newscasters had made about her shortcake. She wasn't about to tell Andrea how unlikely it was that any big-name producer would be watching KCOW local television.

"I'd better go see what's keeping Tracey." Andrea took a step toward the door, then turned back. "You should try to do something with your hair before the contest starts. It's all frizzy from the lights."

Hannah felt awkward and self-conscious as the cameraman panned the judges' table. At least she didn't have to worry about being discovered. No big-name producer would look twice at a too-tall, slightly overweight woman pushing thirty with a perpetual dusting of flour on her face. But Tracey looked beautiful, and Hannah was proud of her niece. Tracey's blond hair resembled spun gold under the lights, and she was poised as she dipped her hand in the large crystal bowl and drew out the name of the replacement judge.

"Thank you, Tracey." Mr. Hart beamed at her as she presented him with the slip of paper. "You didn't draw your daddy's name, did you?"

Tracey shook her head. "He's not on the city council, Mr. Hart. My daddy's a detective with the Winnetka County Sheriff's Station."

"Do you know what a detective does, Tracey?" Mr. Hart asked.

"Yes. A detective investigates crimes. If someone gets murdered, my daddy collects all the evidence, catches the killer, and keeps him locked up in jail until they have the trial."

It was obvious that Mr. Hart was startled, but he managed a smile. "That was a very good answer, Tracey. I'd ask you to read the name of the new judge, but you're not in school yet, are you?"

"I'm in preschool, Mr. Hart. That's where you go if you're not old enough for kindergarten. But I know how to read. If you give me the paper, I can tell you what it says."

The camera zoomed in on Mr. Hart's surprised face as he handed the slip of paper back to Tracey. Hannah watched as Tracey unfolded it and silently sounded out the words. Then she looked up at Mr. Hart and announced, "The substitute judge is . . . Mr. Boyd Watson."

The lights came up in the audience and everyone applauded as Boyd Watson, Jordan High's winningest coach, stood up. Hannah could see that Boyd's sister, Maryann, was seated next to him, but his wife, Danielle, wasn't present. She hoped there wasn't a sinister reason for that. Several months previously, Hannah had discovered that Coach Watson battered his wife. Danielle hadn't been willing to press charges, but Hannah had confided in Bill, and he'd promised to keep an eye on Boyd to make sure it didn't happen again.

Once Boyd had taken a seat in the empty chair next to Hannah, Mr. Hart introduced the night's contestants and sent them off to the kitchen sets to add the finishing touches to their desserts. While the contestants were slicing, decorating, and arranging their creations on plates, he explained the mechanics of the contest.

There were twelve semifinalists in the Hartland Flour Dessert Bake-Off, all winners of local and regional contests. The first four contestants had baked this afternoon, and samples of their desserts would be presented to each judge. While the panel was tasting and critiquing the entries, there would be a montage of the contestants and their families for the viewers and the audience to watch. When that segment was over, the scores would be tallied and each judge would comment on the entries. A winner would be chosen, and that lucky contestant would advance to the finals on Saturday night.

Hannah waited until the contestants had presented their samples and the montage was on the screen. Then she turned to Boyd, and asked, "Where's Danielle?"

"She's home." Boyd raised a forkful of cherry pie to his mouth and tasted it. He didn't look happy as he swallowed. "Just like my mother used to make, so sweet it makes your teeth ache."

Hannah tasted her own piece of pie and decided that Boyd was right. "She didn't want to come tonight?"

"My mother?"

"No, Danielle." Hannah wrote down a score and moved on to the second offering, a slice of nut-filled pastry.

"Danielle's sick."

"Is it serious?" Hannah watched for signs of guilt on Boyd's face, but he was perfectly impassive.

"It's just a winter cold. She's taking a bunch of over-the-counter stuff for it." Boyd tasted a piece of the nut-filled pastry and made a face as he chewed. "My mother used to make this, too. I hate things that are loaded with this much cinnamon."

Hannah tasted her own slice and found she had to agree with Boyd again. The cinnamon and nutmeg overpowered the flavor of the nuts. She wrote down her score and turned to the third dessert, a slice of orange cake. "Has she seen a doctor?"

"She says she doesn't need one. Danielle hates to go to the doctor."

Rather than make any comment, Hannah tasted the orange cake. She could understand why Danielle was afraid to get medical attention. Doctors asked questions, and they were required to report anything that indicated possible abuse.

"This is too bitter." Boyd pushed the orange cake away and moved on to the fourth dessert.

Hannah swallowed her bite of orange cake and sighed. Boyd was right again. The contestant had grated in too much white with the orange zest.

"Not bad," Boyd commented as he tasted the last dessert, a lemon tart. "As a matter of fact, it's the best one here. Of course, there wasn't much competition."

Hannah moved on to the lemon tart. The crust was tender and flaky with butter, and the filling was both tangy and sweet. It was definitely the winner. Boyd had been right about all four entries, and his objections mirrored hers exactly. She still didn't like him—he was arrogant and brutal—but he did have an educated palate.

The red light on the camera covering the panel of judges came on again, and the interviewing began. As the lead judge, Hannah was the last to be interviewed, and she listened to her colleagues with interest. They were very tactful in critiquing the desserts, and the first three judges liked the lemon tart best.

Then it was Boyd's turn and Hannah winced inwardly as he repeated the same comments he'd made to her. She'd heard one of his team members remark, "Coach calls 'em like he sees 'em," but Hannah thought that Boyd's criticism could have been sweetened with a few compliments.

Hannah wasn't a tactful person herself, but she did her best when her turn came. She praised all the contestants for their efforts and reminded the audience that all four of them had won local and regional contests. She found something nice to say about each dessert, but the damage had been done, and Hannah could tell that there were hurt feelings. After the winning contestant had received her blue finalist ribbon, the program ended and Hannah filed out into the wings with Boyd.

"You could have been a little kinder, Boyd," Hannah chided him the instant they were backstage. "There wasn't any reason to make the contestants feel bad."

Boyd stared at her, obviously confused. It was clear he had no clue why Hannah was upset. "But feelings have no place in a competition like this. Either you win, or you don't. There's no sense in sugarcoating it. If you don't come in first, you're a loser."

Hannah was speechless for a moment, an unusual circumstance for her. She knew she had to try to change Boyd's attitude before the next night of the contest, but she wasn't sure how to go about it. She'd have to think it all out when she got home and call him in for a talk in the morning. For the time being, it was best to keep the peace.

"I saw you making that strawberry shortcake." Boyd changed the subject. "Too bad you couldn't enter the contest. I bet it would have won, hands down."

That gave Hannah an idea. Danielle was sick, and she might like something she didn't have to cook. "Boyd?"

"Yeah?"

"I've got some leftover shortcake. Would you like to take it home?"

Boyd looked surprised at the offer. "Sure. Strawberry shortcake's our favorite."

"Good. You have a discerning palate, and you can critique it for me." Hannah walked over to retrieve the cake carrier and handed it over to him. "I'm expanding my menu at The Cookie Jar to include some desserts."

Boyd grinned as he spied the fresh berries through the plastic top of the cake carrier. "I'll make sure Danielle gets most of the strawberries. Fresh fruit is good for a cold. Thanks, Hannah."

Hannah just shook her head as he walked away. There was no doubt in her mind that Boyd loved Danielle, but he still lashed out at her physically. And Danielle loved Boyd, in spite of the injuries she'd suffered. Hannah doubted she'd ever understand their abusive relationship, and she wasn't sure she wanted to try. She just hoped that it wouldn't end in the kind of tragedy that was splashed all over the papers.

"I'm home, Moishe," Hannah announced, bending down to catch the orange streak that hurtled itself at her ankles the moment she opened her condo door. Moishe was always glad to see her when she came home, especially when she'd gone out at night. She preferred to think that he'd missed her, but perhaps it was only because he couldn't fill his food bowl by himself. She gave him a scratch under the chin, then she said, "Just let me change into my sweats, and I'll get your bedtime snack."

Once she'd hung up the lovely mocha brown dress Claire Rodgers had provided from Beau Monde Fashions, Hannah changed into her oldest sweatpants and top and walked to the kitchen, the room she considered the heart of a home. She filled a cut-glass dessert dish with vanilla yogurt for Moishe, poured herself a glass of white wine from the gallon jug in the bottom of her refrigerator, and settled down on the couch to watch the tape she'd made of the news and the contest.

The local news, which she'd heard before, was of little interest. Seeing herself in the background, however, was a bit of a shock. She didn't look half-bad. Her white bib-style apron, with "THE COOKIE JAR" printed in red block letters on the front, showed up well on camera. Stan Kramer would be pleased, since he'd deducted the cost of her aprons as an advertising expense.

Hannah assessed her performance and found nothing to criticize. She was efficient, she didn't drop any of the ingredients, and she juggled the mixer and the spatula like a pro. Of course she *was* a pro, a fact that always gave her a pleasant jolt of surprise.

Moishe showed no interest in the program until he heard Hannah's voice, answering the question that Chuck Wilson, the anchorman, had asked her. He looked up from his empty dessert dish and stared at the television with his ears laid back. Hannah reached out to give him a reassuring scratch, but he backed up just out of her reach. Moishe stared at her for a moment, the tip of his tail flicking, and then he began to make a sound like a growl, deep in his throat.

"It's just a tape, Moishe." Hannah picked up the control and put the tape on pause, freezing Dee-Dee Hughes's perfect face and catching her with her mouth open.

The moment the audio stopped, Moishe made a flying leap to the top of the television where he assumed the Halloween Cat position, his back stiffly arched and his tail puffed up to three times its normal size. Something had obviously upset him. Hannah thought about it for a minute and hit on a possible reason.

"Come down, Moishe," Hannah called him, patting the cushion next to her. "I'm not *in* the television. I'm right here on the couch."

But Moishe refused to be coaxed, and Hannah started the tape again to see if her theory was correct. The moment her voice reemerged from the speakers, Moishe yowled loudly, swiveling his head to look at her and then back, to stare at the television. She wasn't anthropomorphizing. Moishe was truly reacting to what he viewed as an immutable breach of physics.

"I give up," Hannah muttered, muting the sound and giving in to her pet's peculiar reaction. If Moishe yowled through the whole program, she wouldn't be able to hear the dialogue anyway. She was about to fast-forward through the World News, to make sure she'd taped the bake-off, when the phone rang.

Hannah glanced at the clock as she answered. It was ten o'clock, and it was probably Andrea, checking to see if she'd gotten a good tape of Tracey's television debut.

"Hannah! I'm so glad you're home! It's . . . it's Danielle Watson."

"Hi, Danielle." Hannah caught the furry orange-and-white bundle that landed in her lap. Moishe had obviously forgiven her for confusing him with the tape. "How's your cold?"

"Hannah . . . please! Can you come over right away? I . . . I didn't know who else to call."

"What's wrong, Danielle?" Hannah imagined the worst. The last time she'd gone to Danielle's house, she'd found her nursing a black eye. "Is it Boyd?"

"Yes. I can't say anymore. Please, Hannah?"

"Relax, I'm on my way." Hannah hung up the phone, tipped Moishe off her lap, and grabbed her purse and her parka. Danielle had sounded very upset, and perhaps, this time, she'd be willing to press charges against the man who had broken his promise to love, cherish, and protect her from harm.

In less than fifteen minutes, Hannah was ringing Danielle's doorbell. If Boyd was home, it would be an awkward situation, and it might even be dangerous. Bill had told her that domestic violence calls were a deputy's nightmare, ranking second only to "officer down." The door opened, and Danielle pulled her in, clutching at her like a drowning person.

"What's the matter, Danielle?" Hannah shut the door. The neighbors didn't need to see Danielle in this state. She was crying, she had a black eye, and her face was so pale, Hannah wondered if she was going to faint.

"It's . . . it's Boyd," Danielle choked out the words. "He's . . . he's . . . in the garage."

"Show me." Hannah took Danielle's arm, half-supporting her as they walked through the kitchen and into the attached garage.

At first glance, Hannah didn't see anything wrong. Both cars were parked in their usual places, and the fluorescent light over Boyd's workbench was on. The garage was as neat as a pin, if you didn't count the oil spots on the floor. Hannah figured that one of their cars must have a leak. Each tool had its own place on the pegboard over the workbench, and the outlines of the tools were painted in blue. All the outlines were filled except one, and Hannah noticed a shiny ball peen hammer lying on the floor by Danielle's car.

Hannah stared at the hammer, glistening in the light. It was out of place, but perhaps Boyd had been doing some repairs and he'd forgotten to put it away.

"He's . . . he's over here."

As Danielle led her toward Boyd's Grand Cherokee, Hannah spotted the plastic cover of her cake carrier. It had rolled under his car, and it was peeking out by the rear wheel. Then they rounded the side of the Grand Cherokee and Hannah gasped. Jordan High's head basketball coach was sprawled on the cement floor, lying in a gooey splotch of cake, whipped cream, and crushed berries.

Hannah gave a fleeting thought to her dessert. What a waste. Danielle would have loved it. Then she stepped closer and swallowed past the lump that rose in her throat. The red splotches on the concrete weren't from the crushed strawberries; they were from Boyd's crushed skull. He was dead. There was no doubt in Hannah's mind. No one could lose that much blood and live.

Danielle's hands began to tremble... she set... her water... glass down... the cold med... up to bed.

Chapter
Three

Bill was out in the garage, helping Doc Knight load Boyd
Watson's body onto a stretcher for the trip to the
morgue. Doc Knight doubled as the town physician and the
Winnetka County Coroner. It didn't leave him much time for
anything else, and he always bristled whenever anyone mentioned how doctors were supposed to have golf days.

Hannah was in the living room with Mike and Danielle,
listening as he interviewed her. She'd twisted Mike's arm for
that privilege, insisting that she should be present. She was
Danielle's friend, and Danielle needed a friend right now.

"I watched the contest on television while I was taping
it." Danielle's hands began to tremble, and she set her water
glass down on the coffee table. "Then I switched to cable
and started to watch a movie, but I fell asleep. The cold medicine I'm taking makes me sleepy, and I really wanted to go
up to bed."

Mike nodded. He was being very solicitous of Danielle,
and Hannah was glad. "But you stayed on the couch?"

"Yes. Boyd expects me to wait up for him. I always do. If I don't, he gets . . . upset. But I guess you know that."

Hannah glanced at Mike, and he caught her eye, giving her a slight nod. They both knew what happened when Boyd was in a bad mood. The black eye Danielle was sporting was ample proof of that.

"When did he blacken your eye, Danielle?" Mike asked. His voice was tight, and Hannah could tell he was barely controlling himself. They'd discussed Danielle's problem shortly after she had confided in Hannah, and Mike had admitted that he had no patience with men who battered their wives.

"It happened yesterday. Boyd came home from school for lunch and he got . . . upset with me."

"Did you see a doctor?"

"No. I knew what to do. And it's not as bad as it looks. It hardly hurts at all anymore."

Mike gave Hannah a warning look, one that said *Don't interfere.* Then he turned back to Danielle. "If someone gave me a black eye, I'd be pretty angry at them. Were you angry with Boyd?"

"No. I know how frustrated he gets, and he was really sorry afterward. He got me an ice pack and took care of me."

Mike shot Hannah another warning glance, and she clamped her lips together. Boyd Watson had been a brute and a wife beater. And Danielle had refused to press charges against him, preferring to accept the abuse he dished out rather than making it public. Hannah knew that most battered wives were at a terrible disadvantage emotionally; they usually believed that they'd done something to deserve the abuse. Now that Boyd was dead, Danielle wouldn't have to live in fear of her husband any longer. And while Hannah wouldn't have wished such a violent and bloody death on anyone, she found she couldn't summon up much grief for the man who'd beaten and terrorized her friend.

"Let's get back to what happened tonight." Mike's voice was soft, inviting Danielle's trust. "You said you fell asleep on the couch?"

"That's right."

"What time did you wake up?"

"I'm not sure. The movie was over, so it must have been after nine-thirty. I turned off the television and called out for Boyd, but he didn't answer. I thought maybe he'd come home and gone up to bed. That's why I went out to the garage to see if his car was there."

Mike frowned slightly. "You didn't go upstairs to see if he was there?"

"No, I was just too tired. I didn't want to climb the stairs and then have to come down again. It was easier to check the garage."

"Tell me exactly what you saw when you opened the garage door."

"Well . . . it was dark, so I turned on the light over Boyd's workbench. His car was there, so I figured he'd come home and gone up to bed. Then I noticed that the garage door was still open, so I closed it."

"The garage door was open, but the light wasn't on?"

Danielle shook her head. "It burned out yesterday. Boyd was going to replace it, but he hadn't gotten around to it yet. And then I saw the hammer, and I knew that something was wrong."

"Why?" Mike asked.

"Boyd's very particular about his tools. They all have a place on the pegboard, and he's really careful about putting them back after he uses them. That's just the way he was brought up."

"Do you ever use his tools?"

"Never." Danielle looked surprised at the question. "He bought me a kit with my own tools for the house. I keep it in the kitchen drawer."

Hannah nodded, imagining what Danielle's punishment would have been if she'd used one of Boyd's tools and hadn't returned it.

"How about Boyd's hammer? Did you touch it?"

"Yes. I knew I hadn't used it, but I didn't want Boyd to get upset when he saw that it wasn't hanging up in the right place. He . . . he might have blamed me. So I picked it up and it was . . . sticky." Danielle shivered slightly. "I looked down at my fingers and then I . . . I dropped it."

"Did you realize that the hammer had blood on it?"

"I don't remember. I guess I must have or I wouldn't have dropped it. I walked over to his car and then . . . I saw him. Down there on the floor."

"What did you do next?"

"I knelt and felt for a pulse. But there wasn't any. And then I tried to give him CPR. He was still warm, and I thought maybe . . ." Danielle stifled a sob and drew a deep shaky breath. "But it didn't work. I just sat there staring at him for a minute. I . . . I just couldn't believe it! And then I got up and went to the kitchen to call Hannah."

Hannah provided the answer before Mike could ask. "I looked at the clock when the phone rang. Danielle called me at ten. When she asked me to come over, I drove straight here, and it was ten-fifteen when I rang the bell."

"Got it." Mike wrote the time in his notebook and turned back to Danielle. "Is there anything else you can remember? A sound that woke you? A car that you heard in the alley?"

Danielle thought about it for a minute, then shook her head. "I don't think so. Maybe something woke me up, but I don't remember what it was."

"There's one other thing, Danielle." Mike looked very sympathetic. "I know what your husband did to you, and I'm sure there were times when you were afraid of him. Isn't that right?"

"Yes," Danielle admitted, and a tear rolled down her cheek.

"Did you ever strike back at Boyd after he'd hit you?"

"Oh, no!" Danielle looked alarmed at the suggestion. "It would have made things even worse. I knew that Boyd didn't mean to hit me. He loved me, but he just couldn't help himself."

Mike slipped his arm around Danielle's shoulder. "Maybe he did love you, but he also hurt you very badly. A lot of abused wives reach a point where they just can't take it anymore. Some of them leave, but others find the courage to fight back. If your husband threatened you, and you picked up that hammer to defend yourself, you'd be perfectly justified."

"I know," Danielle swallowed hard, "but that's not what happened. When I found Boyd in the garage, he was already dead. I know someone killed him, but it wasn't . . . it wasn't *me!*"

Danielle stifled a sob, and Mike handed her a tissue from the box on the coffee table. "Okay. I just wanted to make absolutely sure you understood that no one would blame you if you struck out at him to defend yourself. That's all."

Hannah felt sick as she added it all up in her head. Danielle's prints were on the murder weapon, Boyd's blood was all over her clothing, she'd admitted that Boyd had battered her at noon on Tuesday, and she had a black eye to prove it. Hannah knew that it wasn't unusual for an abused wife to strike back hours, weeks, and even months after being injured. There were no witnesses to Boyd's murder, at least not yet, and every shred of circumstantial evidence pointed to the fact that Danielle had snapped and bashed Boyd's head in with his ball peen hammer.

"You . . . you believe me, don't you?" Danielle asked, looking up at Mike.

Mike gave her a little hug before he stood up. "Yes, I do."

Hannah gave a deep sigh of relief. Mike was one of the most honorable men she knew. He didn't lie, and she was sure that he believed what Danielle had told him. But what about Sheriff Grant? This was an election year, and Coach Watson's murder was what the *Lake Eden Journal* would call a high-profile case. If Sheriff Grant believed that Danielle was guilty, he might discourage his detectives from investigating further. She looked up at Mike and found him watching her. Had he guessed what was running through her mind? She had to talk to him, and the sooner, the better.

"This has been a terrible shock for you, Danielle." Hannah moved over to take Mike's place on the couch. "I think that you should try to rest."

Danielle dabbed at her eyes with the sodden tissue. "I . . . I can't. I have to . . . to call Boyd's relatives and . . ."

"It's too late to do anything tonight," Hannah interrupted her. "I'll help you with all that in the morning."

Danielle seemed relieved as she sagged back against the cushions. "Thank you, Hannah, but I don't think I can rest. Every time I shut my eyes, I see Boyd's face with all that . . . that blood!"

"Don't think about it." Hannah knew her advice was useless, but she had to say something. Once someone said not to think about something, you couldn't think about anything else. "I'll go make you a cup of hot chocolate. That'll make you feel better."

"That's nice of you, Hannah, but I don't have any hot chocolate mix."

"Do you have cocoa?"

"I . . . I think so. There should be some in one of the cupboards."

"How about sugar? And milk?"

"The sugar's in a canister, and there's milk in the refrigerator."

"Then I'll make it from scratch. It's better that way."

"I . . . I'm not a very good cook. How do you make hot chocolate from scratch?"

Hannah smiled. At least she'd gotten Danielle's mind off finding Boyd's body. "I'll show you sometime. Right now I want you to stretch out on the couch and try to relax. You have to keep up your strength."

"All right." Danielle's voice was shaky, and her face was a sickly shade of gray. "Thank you, Hannah."

Hannah unfolded the afghan that was draped over the back of the couch and tucked Danielle in. "Rest, Danielle. We'll be back in a couple of minutes."

Mike took Hannah's cue and followed her out to the kitchen. He sat down in a chair and watched while she opened cupboard drawers and located the ingredients. Danielle hadn't been overly modest when she'd admitted that she wasn't a very good cook. Almost everything in her cupboards was a mix. There were instant potatoes, Hamburger and Tuna Helper, instant pudding, Minute Rice, scalloped potatoes in a box, and even instant coffee and tea.

"What was all that about?" Mike asked her.

Hannah looked up from the pan she was using to heat the milk. "What was *what* about?"

"The hot chocolate."

"It's simple." Hannah used a wire whisk to stir the milk so it wouldn't burn on the bottom of the saucepan. "Danielle's got a terrible cold, and she probably hasn't been eating right. The sugar's pure carbohydrate, and she needs the calories. And the caffeine and endorphins in the chocolate will keep her from getting too depressed."

"Not that. I mean, why did you want me to follow you into the kitchen?"

"Oh." Hannah mixed the sugar and cocoa together in a bowl and poured in some of the hot milk. "I needed to talk to you alone, and it was a good excuse."

"What about?"

"I'm worried about Danielle. She's hanging on by her fingernails. You don't have to drag her out to the station tonight, do you?"

Mike shook his head. "I've got what I need for now, and she's too sick to answer any more questions."

Hannah stirred the mixture in the bowl until the sugar melted and the cocoa turned into a paste. "I'd better stay with her. Her mother lives in Florida, and she doesn't have any other family close by. She shouldn't be alone at a time like this."

"Danielle won't be here. I checked with Doc Knight, and he's got room at the hospital. I'm going to move her there."

Hannah added the chocolate paste to the heated milk in the saucepan and blended it with the whisk. Doc Knight had examined Danielle right after he'd arranged to have Boyd's body transported to the morgue. "Does Doc think Danielle's that sick?"

"No, but I don't want her talking to anybody, and the hospital's a good place for her. I'll question her again tomorrow morning."

Hannah turned to him in alarm, her hand stopping in mid-whisk. "Is Danielle a suspect?"

"The spouse is always a suspect." Mike didn't quite meet Hannah's eyes. "You'd better stir that before it burns."

As Hannah started to whisk again, she thought about what Mike had said. She needed more answers, but she preferred to get them in private, after Danielle had been settled in a room at the hospital. "Do you want me to drive Danielle to Lake Eden Memorial?"

"No, I'll have Bill take her in the cruiser."

Hannah turned to him in surprise. "In the back? Like a prisoner?"

"Of course not. Danielle's not under arrest. I could call for an ambulance, but I think she'll be more comfortable riding with Bill. I'm just following procedure, Hannah."

Hannah poured the hot chocolate into the biggest mug she could find. "I'd better take this in so she can drink it before she leaves."

"Good idea. Bill should be back from searching the alley any minute now."

Hannah stopped, turning back at the kitchen door. "Will you have time to drop in at my place after you finish up here?"

"It might be late." Mike's eyebrows quirked up, and he gave her a devilish grin. "Just what did you have in mind?"

"I want to pump you for information, of course."

"Oh." Mike's eyebrows settled back down. "I'll try to be there by one at the latest, but there's not a whole lot I'll be able to tell you. The investigation's confidential."

"That's okay. I'll stop by Lake Eden Liquor and pick up some beer for you. Cold Spring Export, right?"

"Right."

Hannah picked up the mug and walked into the living room, hiding a rather smug smile. Mike would tell her what she needed to know so that she could help Danielle. He just didn't realize it yet.

"What are you feeding him? Bricks?" Mike stared down at Moishe, who had just plunked down in his lap.

"A lot of kitty crunchies. He's always hungry." Hannah reached over to pick up her pet and move him to a pillow. "Is Danielle okay?"

Mike took a swallow of his beer. "She's fine. Doc says it's just a bad cold, but he's keeping her under observation for a couple of days. He gave her a sedative so she could sleep through the night."

"A good night's sleep is just what she needs." Hannah took a small sip of her wine. She passed Mike the bag of hard, onion-flavored pretzels she'd bought at Lake Eden Liquor, and asked, "Did you find any witnesses?"

"Not yet."

"Was there anything in the alley?"

Mike shook his head and chomped down on a pretzel. "These are good."

"They're Bavarian." Hannah took a deep breath and got to it. "Tell me the truth, Mike. It doesn't look good for Danielle, does it?"

"Well . . . there's a lot of circumstantial evidence against her."

"Her prints on the murder weapon, Boyd's blood on her clothing, and the black eye he gave her?"

"All that plus her lack of an alibi. She didn't even talk to anyone on the phone until she called you. You heard me try to give her an out. If she admits that she killed him, she can plead self-defense. No jury in the world would convict her."

"But that only applies if she killed him." Hannah bit down on a pretzel. There was a reason they called them "hard" pretzels. Perhaps she should mention them to Norman. If he gave his patients Bavarian pretzels for Christmas, it could promote return visits. "What if she didn't kill him?"

"Then someone else did." Mike stated the obvious.

"I thought you believed her when she told you that she was innocent."

"I *do* believe her." Mike chewed thoughtfully for a moment. "I think she's telling the truth . . . as she sees it. But it's possible that she blocked it out and doesn't remember."

"Are you saying that Danielle could forget killing her own husband?"

"It's possible, Hannah. She told us that she was sleepy, and she took some pretty strong cold medicine. She could have been woozy and disoriented, almost in a dream state."

"No way." Hannah shook her head. "Danielle was upset when she called me and asked me to come over, but she was perfectly lucid. And when I got there, what she said made sense."

"Maybe."

Mike didn't sound convinced, and Hannah sighed deeply. "Let's just assume for a minute that Danielle didn't kill Boyd. You're going to look for other suspects, aren't you?"

"We'll do a routine investigation. If nothing turns up, Sheriff Grant will want us to wrap this up quickly."

"That figures." Hannah rolled her eyes. "He won't want an unsolved murder on the books in an election year. It's much easier to say that Danielle did it, even if she didn't. But Sheriff Grant can't close the case if new evidence turns up, can he?"

"No." Mike began to frown. "Look, Hannah. I don't want you to start nosing around and asking questions. Leave that to the qualified professionals."

Mike was patronizing her, and Hannah knew it. She curbed the sharp retort she wanted to make and did her best to sound calm and reasonable. "But the *qualified professionals* aren't going to do anything more than a routine investigation. You said that yourself. Danielle needs someone to prove that she's innocent."

"That's easier said than done, Hannah." Mike still sounded patronizing to Hannah's ears. "I don't want you to get involved in this. If Danielle didn't kill Boyd, the real killer is still out there."

"That's right. So what?"

"What if you stumble across a clue? And what if the real killer suspects that you're on his trail? You could wind up in real danger." Mike reached over and took her hand. "You're important to me, Hannah. You're my best friend in Lake Eden, and I don't know what I'd do if something happened to you. Promise me that you'll stay out of it."

Hannah was silent for a long moment. She didn't want to lie to Mike, but she wasn't going to stay out of it, not when Danielle needed her help. She had to think of some way to make Mike *think* she was going to follow his advice without actually promising that she would.

"Hannah?"

Hannah gave him what she hoped was a guileless smile. "You don't have to worry, Mike. I'm not bucking for your job."

"My job?" Mike began to grin. "Do you really think that you could handle it?"

"Of course not. I wouldn't take it on a bet. Think about your dress uniform."

Mike gave her a look that said he thought she was losing it. "What's wrong with it? The maroon shirt with the tan pants looks sharp."

"It does on you. But with my hair?"

Mike stared at her, then he started to chuckle. "You've got a point. A maroon shirt and red hair don't mix."

"That's right. You can have your job, Mike. I'd much rather bake cookies. At least I don't have to worry about finding murder victims in my ovens. And speaking of ovens, Boyd brought Maryann to the bake-off. Did you find out what time he took her home?"

"Yeah. We went over there to tell her about her brother. I think that's the only part of the job I really hate."

"It can't be easy, telling people that someone they love is dead."

"It isn't. Bill warned me to ask about the time before I gave her the bad news. It's a real good thing we did it that way."

"Why?"

"She got hysterical, and we had to take her to the hospital."

"Oh-oh." Hannah groaned. Maryann and Danielle had never gotten along. The fact that they were both at Lake Eden Memorial was a lot like stuffing a mouse and a cat in the same gunnysack, especially if Maryann suspected that Danielle had killed Boyd. "Tell me they're not in adjoining rooms."

"They're not. Doc Knight put them on opposite ends of the hall. And just to make sure there's no trouble, I posted a deputy outside Danielle's door."

"For her own safety? Or because it's police procedure?"

"A little of both," Mike admitted.

"That's what I thought. What time did Boyd leave Maryann's apartment?"

"Eight-twenty. She offered him coffee, but he told her he had to be home by eight-thirty because Danielle wasn't feeling well."

"If Boyd left Maryann's place at eight-twenty, he must have been killed between eight-thirty and ten."

"That's right. Doc Knight did a liver temp, but he couldn't narrow it down any more than that."

"How does he do a liver . . . ?" Hannah stopped in mid-question. "Don't tell me. I don't want to know. What happened with the neighbors? Did anyone see or hear anything?"

"Not a thing."

"And you didn't find anything in the alley?" Hannah asked.

"A lot of tire tracks, but all the neighbors use it. It's impossible to tell which ones are fresh. And the only thing we found in the garage was the murder weapon and your cake carrier. You can have it back just as soon as the lab checks it for prints. Do you have any more of those pretzels? They're really good."

Hannah went to the kitchen to get the other bag and brought it back with a cold beer. "Here you go. These are garlic-flavored."

"Great! I'm crazy about garlic." Mike reached for the bag, but he didn't open it. "You're going to have some, aren't you?"

"I guess so." Hannah thought she knew which path his mind was taking, but she wanted to find out for sure. "Why?"

"Garlic's strong, especially if the other person doesn't eat any."

"That only applies if you're angling for an invitation to sleep with me."

Mike threw back his head and laughed. "That's what I like about you, Hannah. You always say exactly what you mean."

Hannah wished that she could call back her words. She didn't sleep around; she never had. Casual sex just didn't work for her. She'd had one brief affair with a professor in college, and she'd loved him deeply. It had ended badly, and before she took that particular plunge again, she wanted to make sure that history wouldn't repeat itself. "Why don't we just chomp down those pretzels, have another drink, and get some sack time."

"Sounds good to me."

"In our own beds," Hannah corrected his false assumption.

"Oh," Mike said, frowning a bit. "Okay Hannah, if that's the way you want it."

Hannah curbed her impulse to say more. It wasn't exactly what she wanted either, but that's the way it was going to be. Sleeping with the opposition was a no-no, and right now, Mike was the opposition.

When Mike left, thirty minutes later, Hannah was pleased with herself. She hadn't lied to him, but she hadn't promised *not* to nose around and investigate Boyd's murder either.

Chapter Four

When Hannah got up the next morning and padded into the kitchen to find her coffee brewed and ready, she gave thanks to Thomas Edison for her electric coffeemaker and timer. Coffee was essential for someone who'd gotten only four hours of sleep. She gulped down the first scalding cup and smiled. There was nothing like a caffeine jolt in the morning. She was just pouring her second cup when the phone rang.

"Wonderful. Just what I need," Hannah muttered, shooting a baleful look at the phone. As she crossed the floor to answer it, she reminded herself that the telephone was a convenience, but that didn't keep her from moving Alexander Graham Bell to the bottom of her favorite inventors list. It was probably Delores. Her mother was the only one who called this early. But it could also be some sort of emergency, and a ringing phone at six in the morning had to be answered.

"Hannah?"

"Yes, Mother." Hannah made a face. She should have let the answering machine get it.

"I just heard the morning news on KCOW. Did you know that Boyd Watson is dead, and they suspect foul play?"

"Yes, Mother." Hannah stretched out the phone cord and walked over to the cupboard that held Moishe's food. She unclipped the bungee cord that held the door closed and took out his box of kitty crunchies. The bungee cord was a necessity. Moishe had learned to open the cupboard door the day after she'd adopted him, and he wasn't exactly tidy when it came to getting his own breakfast.

"I thought you didn't listen to the radio in the morning." Delores sounded surprised.

"I don't. I knew about it last night."

"Oh? Did Bill tell you?"

"No." Hannah knew exactly how Delores would react when she found out that her oldest daughter had been at the scene of another murder, and she wasn't ready to deal with it yet. "Hold on, Mother. I have to feed Moishe."

"Can't it wait?"

"Not if I want my ankle intact." Hannah set the phone down and pushed Moishe aside with her foot. It was probably the result of being on the streets for so long, but he tended to be a bit overenthusiastic when it came to getting his food. Once she'd filled his bowl with kitty crunchies and given him fresh water, she retrieved the phone. "I'm back."

"How did you know about it if Bill didn't tell you? Was it Mike Kingston?"

Hannah sat down at the table and caved in to the inevitable. She'd stuck her big foot in her mouth by mentioning that she'd known about the murder, and now she'd have to pay the price. "Mike didn't tell me either. Danielle called me last night."

"Why did she call you?" Delores sounded surprised.

"Because I'm her friend, and she didn't know what else to do."

"Did she tell you that Boyd was dead?"

"Danielle was in no shape to tell me anything. She just asked me to come over, and once I'd seen Boyd, I called in Bill and Mike."

"So you found another body." Delores pronounced the words like a curse. "You have *got* to stop doing this, Hannah. If you're not careful, the men in this town will think that disaster hovers over you like a storm cloud."

"And no one wants to *court* disaster?"

"That was very clever." Delores gave a little laugh at Hannah's joke. "You've got a good sense of humor, Hannah. And you can look very attractive if you put your mind to it. I just don't understand why you haven't found . . ."

"Give it a rest, Mother," Hannah interrupted her. "Don't you want me to tell you about last night?"

There was a brief silence, and Hannah imagined her mother switching gears. Delores had been all primed for a lecture, but the prospect of hearing some fresh details that she could repeat to her friends was too much for her to resist. "Of course I do. Tell me, dear."

"He was down on the garage floor next to his Grand Cherokee, and his head was bashed in with a hammer. There was blood all over the place."

"There's no need to be so graphic," Delores objected, but Hannah knew her phrases would be repeated word for word. "Is Danielle taking it badly?"

Hannah bit back a sharp retort. How did her mother think a wife would react when she saw her husband with his skull split open? "She's in pretty bad shape. She's got a winter cold, that's the reason she wasn't with Boyd at the bake-off, and the shock of seeing Boyd like that was too much for her. Bill took her to the hospital last night."

"The poor dear! And how about Maryann? She was so close to her brother. Their mother was working, and she practically raised him, you know."

"Maryann's in the hospital, too. Mike said she got hysterical when they told her about Boyd."

"Do you think I should visit them? Maryann's in my Regency Romance Club, and I sat with her at the last Dorcas Circle meeting." Delores named two of the dozen or so clubs she'd joined after Hannah's father had died. "I really don't know Danielle that well, but I'd like to offer my condolences."

Hannah cringed at the thought of her mother room-hopping at Lake Eden Memorial, carrying tidbits of gossip back and forth from Maryann to Danielle. "I don't know if they can have visitors, Mother. Why don't you just send sympathy cards?"

"Of course I'll do that. I would have anyway. But cards are so impersonal."

"Then why don't you ask some of your clubs to send flowers? I'm sure Danielle and Maryann would appreciate that."

"That's an excellent idea. I'll do it right away. By the way, you looked nice on television last night. I set my VCR, but it didn't work. There must be something wrong with it."

Hannah started to grin. There was nothing wrong with her mother's VCR that a different operator couldn't fix. "How did you know I looked nice if your VCR didn't work?"

"Carrie recorded it. When we got home from the bake-off, she brought her tape over and we watched it together. Tracey was just darling."

"Yes, she was." Hannah took a bracing gulp of her coffee and wondered how she could end the conversation.

"I still can't believe that we've had another murder in

Lake Eden! I think television's to blame. All that violence is a bad influence. Do they have any suspects yet?"

Hannah crossed her fingers, an old habit that had survived her childhood, and prepared to lie through her teeth. "I don't know, Mother."

"Well, let me know if you hear anything. I've got to go, dear. I need to call Carrie and ask her to help me with the flowers."

Hannah hung up the phone with a smile on her face. She'd just stumbled on an excellent tactic to cut her mother's phone conversations short. All she had to do was give Delores something to do, and her mother couldn't wait to hang up and get started.

Ten minutes later, Hannah was showered and almost dressed. She glanced at the thermometer outside her bedroom window and shivered. The mercury was hovering under the ten-degree mark. It would be a cold day. She pulled on a pair of clean jeans and opened the closet to choose a long-sleeved pullover. She had plenty of selections. Most of her friends liked to give her gifts with a cookie theme, and she had a whole section of tee shirts and pullovers with legends on the front. Some were witty, others were sweet, and a couple were just plain silly. Hannah settled for a vivid blue one with gold block lettering proclaiming, "Happiness is a Chocolate Chip in Every Bite."

Hannah shut her closet door and glanced at her reflection in its mirrored surface. She looked tired, and there were dark circles under her eyes, but that couldn't be helped. She brushed her hair back, clamped it with the gold barrette that Andrea had given her for her last birthday, and headed for the kitchen and the last cup of coffee in the pot.

Moishe hopped off the bed, where he'd been watching her dress, and rubbed up against her ankles as she walked down the hall. Hannah knew that meant his food bowl was empty again. When she'd taken him in, he'd been a scrawny orange-and-white shadow, but now he weighed in at twenty-two pounds. The town vet, Bob Hagaman, said he was healthy, and that was all Hannah cared about. With his torn ear and one blind eye, she certainly wouldn't be entering him in any Lake Eden Cat Fanciers' Club contests.

Once Moishe's food bowl had been refilled, Hannah left her pet crunching happily and poured herself the last cup of coffee. She still had fifteen minutes before she had to leave for work, and this was her favorite time of the morning. Delores had called, there would be no more interruptions, and she had time to plan out her day.

Hannah sat down at the white Formica table she'd found at the thrift shop and reached for the green-lined stenographer's notebook that was a twin to the ones in every other room in her condo. There was something wonderful about a blank sheet of notepaper. The lines were there, just waiting to be filled, and the page could turn into anything from a grocery list to the opening of The Great American Novel. The possibilities were endless.

She remembered her very first notebook, the red-covered tablet that she'd carried off to kindergarten with fondness. There had been a picture of an Indian chief on the front, a black line drawing of a regal, chiseled face wearing a feathered headdress.

They didn't make Big Chief tablets anymore. Hannah knew because she'd tried to buy one recently. It probably had something to do with the new political correctness campaign. If the politicians had their way, the Indian chief on the tablet would now be called a "Native American Community Leader." In Lake Eden, Minnesota, "Indian" wasn't a racially biased word. Jon Walker, the full-blooded Chippewa who manned the prescription counter at Lake Eden Neighborhood Pharmacy, had explained that "Native American" was a mis-

nomer. He'd done some research and he believed that his an-
cestors had come to North America from Siberia and con-
quered the indigenous people.

Hannah reached for a pen from the cracked coffee mug
that had taken on new life as a penholder. Today was going
to be a very full day. With her judging duties at the bake-off,
her television appearance to promote Mr. Hart's contest, and
her work at The Cookie Jar, there wasn't going to be a moment to spare.

Hannah wrote the date at the top of the page. Now that
Boyd was dead, they'd have to choose another judge for the
contest. She doubted that any of last night's contestants
would shed any tears over his death. They might even think
that he had deserved his fate, since he'd made such nasty
comments about their desserts.

What if one of them was an incredibly sore loser?
Hannah chewed on the end of her pen. Was it possible that a
contestant or a family member had followed Boyd home,
confronted him in the garage, and bashed in his head? It
seemed unlikely, but she couldn't dismiss it summarily.
Since all the bake-off contestants were staying in Lake Eden
until Saturday night, she'd have plenty of time to check out
that theory.

Hannah jotted down a note on the top line, *Check Alibis
of Contestants & Family.* The winner wasn't a suspect, but
she'd investigate the three who'd been eliminated. Boyd's
murder hadn't been premeditated, Hannah was certain of
that. If the assailant had gone to Boyd's house, intending to
kill him, he would have carried his own weapon and not
grabbed a hammer from Boyd's pegboard.

The second line was waiting to be filled, and Hannah
wrote down the time frame, *Wednesday night 8:30–10:00.*
She thought about it for a moment and then she added, *Re-
interview Neighbors.* Deputies from the sheriff's department
had already talked to them, but it couldn't hurt to do it again.

Sometimes people didn't want to get involved and told the authorities as little as possible.

A glance at the clock told Hannah that it was time to leave, but she took time to add one last item to her list. *Local Grudge,* she wrote. It was possible that the murder wasn't related to Boyd's nasty comments as a substitute judge. Someone had been angry enough to pick up his hammer and bash in Boyd's skull, and she needed to find out if anyone else in Lake Eden had a compelling reason to want him dead.

Lisa had come in early again and had everything under control by the time Hannah arrived at The Cookie Jar. Hannah did a few things in the bakery, then went into the coffee shop to enjoy twenty minutes of unexpected downtime. She didn't turn on the lights. That would have invited early customers. She just poured herself another cup of coffee and sat at one of her little round tables, enjoying the customer's view of her gleaming mahogany counter and the shelves that held glass cookie jars filled with the day's offerings.

Opening The Cookie Jar had been Andrea's idea. When Hannah had come home from college to help her mother cope with her father's death, she'd been at loose ends. Though her family had urged her to go back to finish her thesis, the prospect of teaching English literature to a class of uninspired students had lost its appeal. There was another, private reason, one she hadn't mentioned to her mother or her sisters; the campus was simply too small for Hannah, her former lover, and his new wife.

Hannah sighed and cupped her hands around her coffee mug. The old platitude was true, and time did heal. On the rare occasions she thought about Bradford Ramsey and their time together, she experienced only a slight twinge of regret.

It had been his first term teaching, and he'd been young,

handsome, and brilliant. Hannah had been passionately in love and just about as naïve as a woman her age could be. She should have suspected that the reason Brad could never spend any holiday with her had less to do with his aged parents and more to do with his fiancée, who'd been staying with them at the time.

Hannah had grown up a lot since she'd come back to Lake Eden. She loved her work, had much more self-confidence, and had managed to establish a warm relationship with Andrea. She'd even learned to cope with her mother, which took some doing. The only area of her life that still gave her problems was romance. Once slammed in the face by that particular door, she was going to be careful about opening it again.

The sight outside the huge plate-glass window was spectacular, and Hannah began to smile. The winter sun was peeping over the horizon, and pale golden rays touched the snow-covered roofs, making them glisten as if they were made of bits of colored glass. The huge old pine, directly across the street from her shop, resembled a perfectly flocked Christmas tree with its snow-laden branches. Several brilliant blue jays and bright red cardinals were perched on its branches like avian ornaments.

As Hannah sat there enjoying the picture-perfect view, a car pulled up in front of her shop. Plumes of white exhaust rose up from the tailpipe, and Hannah got up and moved closer to the window to see who was inside. She didn't recognize the car. It was a new Grand Am in a sporty red color and had dealer plates. In a town the size of Lake Eden, new cars gave their owners bragging rights, and Hannah hadn't heard anyone say that they'd bought a new vehicle.

The driver's door opened and a woman emerged. She had short black hair, stylishly cut, and was wearing the expensive teal-colored winter coat that Hannah had seen in the window of Beau Monde Fashions. The woman turned and walked toward the front door of The Cookie Jar, and Hannah's eyebrows shot up in surprise. It was Lucy Richards, a reporter for the *Lake Eden Journal,* and she had a whole new look.

Mentally, Hannah added up the cost of Lucy's new acquisitions. The coat had cost four hundred dollars. Hannah knew because she had priced it when she'd first seen it in Claire Rodgers's window. The fur-lined leather boots that Lucy was wearing hadn't come cheap, and Hannah couldn't even begin to speculate on the cost of the fancy Grand Am. Lucy lived rent-free in the attic apartment of her great aunt, Vera Olsen, but that couldn't account for all those new things. Rod Metcalf, the owner and editor of their small weekly paper, didn't pay much over minimum wage. There was no way that Lucy could have saved up enough for a new coat, new boots, *and* a new car!

Hannah sat back against the wall, hoping she wouldn't be spotted. There was no way she'd open early for Lucy Richards. They'd crossed swords last week after Lucy's story about the Hartland Flour Dessert Bake-Off had run in the paper. She'd put words in Hannah's mouth that she hadn't said, and Hannah was still doing a slow burn about it.

Lucy hammered on the door and stood there, tapping her foot impatiently. Hannah let her tap, knowing full well that it was freezing outside. She was due to open in less than fifteen minutes, and perhaps Lucy would give up and go away.

Then Lucy started to shiver, and Hannah took pity on her. Perhaps she'd come to apologize for the misquote. Hannah got up from her chair, hit the light switch, and headed for the door to unlock it.

"It's cold out there!" Lucy waltzed in and stamped her feet on the mat by the door. "Is the coffee ready?"

"Of course." Hannah gestured toward a stool and moved behind the counter to pour Lucy a cup.

"Thanks. I'll take a couple of those Oatmeal Raisin Crisps."

Lucy laced her fingers around the mug, shivering slightly. Then she took a deep breath, and said, "Sorry about the story. My recorder didn't work, and I was writing it from memory."

It wasn't really an apology, but the fact that Lucy had offered any kind of excuse was a first.

"But that's not what I came about."

"Oh?" Hannah served Lucy two oatmeal cookies on one of her white napkins with red block letters that advertised the name of her shop. Then she picked up a cloth and wiped down the already spotless counter. Lucy wanted something, and Hannah wasn't about to ask what. She'd just outwait her and force Lucy to make the first move.

"I wanted to talk to you privately, Hannah." Lucy finished her first cookie and started in on the second. "I know we don't see eye to eye, but I want you to understand that I have a job to do."

"It must be a very *good* job." Hannah gestured toward the new Grand Am. "That car must have cost a bundle."

"It's a lease. And I didn't earn the money for it at the paper. Rod pays me only a fraction of what I'm worth."

It was a perfect straight line, and Hannah could think of several appropriate rejoinders. She had to bite the inside of her cheek, but she didn't give voice to any of them. Instead, she said, "I see you have a new coat. Very pretty. And new boots."

Once that comment was delivered, Hannah leaned back and waited. After six years of college and standing in the interminable registration lines each semester, she was very good at waiting.

"Yes." Lucy looked a bit uncomfortable. "Actually, my advance paid for that."

"Advance?"

"For my book."

"Really?" Hannah was curious. "I didn't know you'd written a book."

"Oh, I haven't, not yet. That's why they call it an advance. It's going to be an exposé about a rich and famous person."

"That sure leaves out anybody in Lake Eden!"

"True." Lucy gave a little laugh. "I can't tell you any details, Hannah. My publisher doesn't want me to detract from the shock value when my book comes out."

"When will that be?"

"I'm not sure yet. It all depends on when I finish writing it. They're in a big rush, but I told them I didn't want to let Rod down at the paper. He depends on me for all the big stories."

"That's very loyal of you." Hannah had all she could do not to hoot out loud. Rod had hired Lucy as a favor to Vera Olsen, and Hannah knew that he didn't let Lucy write anything he considered important news.

Lucy preened a bit, warming to her subject. "They think it's going to be the smash hit of the year. That's why I got such a big advance."

"I see." Hannah took that with several grains of salt. Lucy had never mentioned knowing any rich and famous people before, and Hannah suspected she'd fabricated the whole thing to explain her new car and her new wardrobe. Either Lucy had run up her credit cards to the max, or the money had been a gift from a lover with plenty of spare cash. Hannah suspected the latter. Vera had once told Delores that her great-niece Lucy had been kicked out of college for being "wild."

Lucy pulled out her notebook and flipped it to a blank page. "Tell me what happened last night. I'm doing the story."

Hannah hesitated. She wasn't about to let Lucy misquote her again. "You don't need me to tell you anything. You were right there."

For some reason that comment seemed to rattle Lucy because she set her coffee mug down on the counter with a thump. "I was *where?*"

"At the bake-off. I saw you talking to some of the contestants."

Lucy rolled her eyes. "Don't play dumb, Hannah. This isn't about the bake-off."

"It's not?" Hannah assumed a perfectly innocent expression. "What is it then?"

"I talked Rod into running a banner headline, 'Local Coach Murdered,' and I need details about how you found Boyd Watson's body."

Hannah had all she could do not to groan. People would be upset enough as it was about the murder. Sensationalism would just add fuel to the panic flames. "What makes you think I was there?"

"One of my sources saw your truck. Give, Hannah. I really need to know."

Hannah shook her head. "I can't tell you, Lucy. It's part of an ongoing sheriff's department investigation."

"Big deal." Lucy waved away that concern. "How did he look? And what did Danielle say? That's what people want to read about."

"Then they'll have to wait for an official press release." Hannah stood firm. "If you want the details, you'll have to drive out to the sheriff's station and ask."

"They won't tell me anything. They never do. Come on, Hannah. I'll let you read my story before it goes to press, and you can edit out anything you don't like."

Hannah didn't believe it for a second, but that wasn't the point. "I told you before, Lucy. I can't say anything until the sheriff's department okays it."

"Then you're working with them to solve the crime?"

Lucy scribbled something in her notebook and Hannah started to frown. "I didn't say that!"

"But you had something to do with solving their last murder case, didn't you?"

Hannah knew she was skating on thin ice. It was true that she'd helped Bill solve Ron LaSalle's murder, but no one was supposed to know about that.

"Didn't you?" Lucy repeated.

Lucy was zeroing in, and Hannah knew she had to say something. She settled for, "I didn't do much, Lucy. I just passed on information that came my way. Any concerned, law-abiding citizen of Lake Eden would have done the same."

"Oh, sure." Lucy rolled her eyes. "Okay, if that's the way you want to play it. Let's get back to Coach Watson. Do you have any suspicions about who might have killed him? You were first on the scene, after all."

"No."

"No, you weren't the first on the scene?" Lucy held her pen poised over the paper. "Or no, you don't have any suspicions?"

"No to both." Hannah salved her conscience by reasoning that she wasn't exactly lying. Danielle had found Boyd, and that meant she hadn't been the first on the scene. And she didn't have any *real* suspects, at least not yet.

"How about Danielle? Did she have any reason to kill her husband?"

Hannah bit back a sharp retort about Lucy's parentage. "I really don't know, Lucy. And I certainly can't speculate. You're asking the wrong person. You should be talking to Bill or Mike Kingston."

"I'd like to do more than talk to Mike Kingston." Lucy reached up to fluff her short hair. "But I guess I shouldn't be telling *you* that."

Hannah gritted her teeth. Lucy was trying to goad her into slipping some information, and she refused to play that game. "Sorry, Lucy. I told you before, I can't tell you a thing. As a matter of fact, I shouldn't even be talking to you."

"Does that mean you know more about the case than you can tell me?"

"No. It means I should be getting ready to open for business. You're wasting your time, Lucy. And you've outstayed your welcome. That'll be a dollar and a quarter for the cookies and coffee."

"Catch me later. I'm in a hurry." Lucy stood up and headed for the door. When she got there, she turned, and said, "Since you're so uncooperative with a respected member of the Fourth Estate, I'll just have to talk to Danielle!"

Hannah groaned as Lucy stormed out and slammed the door behind her. She reached for the phone, punched in Mike's number at the sheriff's station, and hoped that he'd come in early.

"Kingston." Mike picked up on the third ring.

"It's Hannah. I'm at the shop, and Lucy Richards just left. She tried to pump me for information about Boyd Watson's murder."

"That figures." Mike chuckled. "She called Bill at home the minute the news broke on KCOW and didn't get a very warm reception."

"I'll bet." Hannah began to smile. "Bill's a real bear in the morning."

"Andrea answered. It's her day off, and Bill was in the shower."

"Uh-oh." Hannah's smile grew wider. Anyone who woke Andrea at six in the morning on her day off got an earful. "When Lucy left here, she said she was going to talk to Danielle. Is there any way you can keep her away?"

"No problem. Rick Murphy's guarding her room, and I told him not to let anyone in."

"Good." Hannah was pleased for a moment, but then she

realized the full implication of what Mike had said. "Danielle can have *some* visitors, can't she?"

"At this time, it's not advisable."

"For medical reasons?"

"No. She still has a bad cold, but Doc Knight said she's not in any danger." Mike was silent for a moment and then he sighed. "Look, Hannah. Like it or not, Danielle's our prime suspect."

"But even prisoners in jail can have visitors," Hannah objected. "You've already taken Danielle's statement, haven't you?"

"Yes."

"Then it's not like anyone can influence her, or tell her what to say."

There was silence for a moment, then Mike sighed. "That's true."

"Danielle's not under arrest, is she?"

"No, not officially."

"Then you should let me visit her." Hannah marshaled her arguments. "She's all alone, Mike, and she's probably scared half out of her mind. It's not right to keep her locked up and isolated from her friends when you haven't officially charged her with anything."

"Okay."

"I can visit?"

"Yes, but just you. I'll call Rick and tell him to let you in."

Hannah drew a deep breath of relief. "Great! I'll go this morning and take her some cookies."

"Hannah?"

"Yes, Mike."

"You're just going as a friend, aren't you?"

"Of course I am."

"You haven't decided to ignore my advice and get involved?"

"You should know better than that, Mike. I'd never ignore your advice." Hannah answered him truthfully, not voicing the other half of her thoughts. *I considered your advice for a long time last night, and I came to the conclusion that you were wrong and I was right. And since Danielle doesn't have anyone else on her side, you bet your buns I'm getting involved!*

Chapter Five

Hannah had just served the last of her early-morning customers when Lisa stuck her head around the swinging door that led to the bakery. "Hannah? I need you back here for a minute."

"I'll be right back," Hannah excused herself to Bertie Straub, the owner-operator of the Cut 'n Curl Beauty Parlor, and headed for the back room. As she pushed through the door, she was surprised to see Delores sitting at the stainless-steel work counter, clutching her purse in her lap. She was dressed in a cranberry red wool skirt and sweater set that would have looked far too young on most of the matrons in Lake Eden, but it suited Delores perfectly. Her glossy dark hair was styled in a flattering layer cut, and her makeup was flawless. Hannah didn't delude herself by thinking that Delores had dressed up to visit her at work. She knew that her mother had never set foot outside her door without being perfectly groomed and coifed. Delores Swensen always endeavored to be a perfect photo op, just waiting for the cameras to roll.

"Mother?" Hannah was puzzled. On the rare occasions that Delores had visited The Cookie Jar, she'd always come in through the front door. "Is something wrong?"

"No, dear. It's just something I forgot to tell you on the phone this morning." Delores turned to Lisa. "You can take over for Hannah in the shop for a minute, can't you, Lisa?"

Lisa smiled, catching the none-too-subtle hint that their conversation would be private. "Of course, Mrs. Swensen. Would you like a cookie? These Molasses Crackles just came out of the oven."

"No thank you, dear. They smell delicious, but I'm watching my calories. Christmas is coming, you know."

Hannah's lips twitched. Delores had been a perfect size five when she'd married Hannah's father and she was still a perfect size five. Most Lake Eden women who were past the half-century mark had relaxed a bit about their appearance, but Delores was determined to look as attractive as diet, professional hairstyling, specially formulated makeup, and cosmetic surgery could make her.

The moment that Lisa had disappeared through the swinging door, Delores turned back to Hannah. "I was so rattled this morning when I heard about Boyd, I completely forgot the reason I called you."

"Oh?" Hannah picked up a warm cookie and tasted it, knowing full well that they were her mother's favorites. "Are you sure you won't have just one cookie, Mother?"

Delores wavered. "Well . . . just one. But don't tempt me with more. I have a lovely new dress for Christmas Eve, and it's not going to fit if I gain weight."

"Here, Mother." Hannah handed her a cookie. "What did you want to tell me?"

"I don't think you should put all your eggs in one basket."

"What?"

"I just want you to be careful, dear. I know you're attracted to Mike, but it would be a real shame to let a good prospect like Norman get away. Lucy Richards is after him, you know. Carrie told me last night."

"Lucy Richards? And Norman?" Hannah had trouble believing her ears. Sweet, funny Norman and the reporter who thought of herself as a female Bob Woodward were as unlikely a mix as oil and water. "Are they dating?"

"Not yet, but Carrie said she dropped in at the clinic last week, and Norman was in his office with Lucy and the door was closed. After Lucy left, Carrie asked him about her, and Norman acted very secretive."

"Secretive?"

"Carrie asked him why he was in his office with Lucy, and he refused to tell her. There's something going on, Hannah, and Carrie doesn't like it one bit. I think you'd better start paying more attention to Norman before Lucy snatches him up on the rebound."

Hannah's mouth dropped open. What rebound? She'd gone out with Norman three times, and there was nothing romantic about it. But saying that would only lead to a longer discussion, and she needed to get back to work. "Consider me warned. I'll talk to Norman today, I promise."

"Make sure you do." That seemed to satisfy Delores because she stood up and smoothed down her skirt. "I've got to run, dear. I told Carrie I'd pick her up in ten minutes."

"Christmas shopping at the mall?" Hannah guessed.

"Of course not." Delores looked slightly affronted. "I do my shopping the day after Christmas. The bargains are simply amazing. I've had all my presents wrapped and stored for almost a year."

Hannah saw her mother off and went back into the front of her shop. Delores had always been incredibly organized.

Hannah admired that quality in her mother, but she knew it wouldn't work for her. If she bought next year's presents the day after Christmas, she'd forget where she'd stored them and have to run out at the last minute to buy them all over again.

During the next two hours, Hannah served coffee and cookies nonstop. On her forays to the tables, carrying cookies and coffee refills, she heard at least a dozen different theories about Boyd Watson's murder. Kathy Purvis, the principal's wife, thought that Boyd had interrupted a burglary in progress. Lydia Gradin, a teller at First National, was sure that a carload of gang members from Minneapolis was to blame. Mrs. Robbins and her friends from the Lakewood Senior Apartments thought that the killer must have escaped from the state reformatory for men in St. Cloud, while Mr. Drevlow, Lisa's neighbor, insisted that he must have been a homicidal lunatic from the state hospital in Wilmar who'd been released owing to budget cuts. Only one person mentioned the Hartland Flour Dessert Bake-Off, and that was in passing. "Digger" Gibson, the local mortician, speculated that an old enemy of Boyd's had recognized him on television while he was judging the bake-off and driven to Lake Eden to kill him. Hannah hadn't heard anyone mention Danielle's name without following it with the phrase, "the poor dear," and she assumed that, so far, Boyd's shameful secret was safe. She also knew that the sympathetic thoughts that were wafting Danielle's way could change to suspicion in an instant. If the residents of Lake Eden found out that Boyd had battered Danielle, they'd be convinced that she'd killed him either in self-defense or as retaliation.

By the time eleven-fifteen rolled around, there was only

one customer left. It was too late for a breakfast cookie, every-one's midmorning coffee break was over, and the cookie-after-lunch crowd wouldn't appear until noon or later. Hannah had just finished putting on a fresh pot of coffee to prepare for the noon rush when Andrea came in the door.

"Hi, Hannah." Andrea hung her coat on the almost-empty rack and slid onto a stool at the counter. She glanced over at old Mr. Lempke, whose daughter had left him in Hannah's care while she'd run down to the drugstore, and frowned slightly. "Does he have his hearing aid turned on?"

Hannah shook her head. "Roma took his batteries to the drugstore to get replacements."

"Good. I need to talk to you about Danielle. Bill told me all about it, and I want to do something to show my support. I don't believe for a second that she killed him, but if she did, he deserved it!"

"I know." Hannah poured a mug of coffee from the carafe she'd filled before she'd emptied the urn and shoved it over to her sister. Andrea's color was high, almost matching the coral pink of her expensive cashmere sweater, and her blue eyes were snapping. "You're really upset, aren't you?"

"You bet I am! Bill says Sheriff Grant is sure that Dan-ielle is guilty, and you know what *that* means."

"I'm afraid I do." Hannah started to frown. "They're just going to go through the motions?"

"That's right. Bill says he doesn't dare go out on a limb about it. He's been a detective for less than two months and they won't listen to him anyway. And he doesn't think that Mike will buck Sheriff Grant, either."

"Because he just transferred here?"

"That, and because he's not sure Danielle *didn't* do it."

Hannah was so shocked she couldn't speak for a moment. When she did, her voice was hard. "What is he, stupid? I *told* him that Danielle wasn't capable of killing Boyd!"

"You can't blame him, Hannah. He doesn't know Danielle like we do, and he's still got that big-city-cop mentality. I'll bet that in Minneapolis, lots of abused wives kill their husbands."

"But this is Lake Eden," Hannah reminded her. "It's different here."

"I know." Andrea blew on the surface of her cup and took a tentative sip. "How does your carafe keep things so hot? We've got the same kind, and our coffee's always lukewarm."

"Do you fill it with boiling water and let it sit for a couple of minutes before you pour in the coffee?"

"No, but I'll try that tomorrow morning. So what are we going to do first, Hannah?"

"About what?"

"About Danielle. It's up to us to prove she didn't kill Boyd."

Hannah reared back and stared at her sister in surprise. *"Us?"*

"You didn't think I'd let you tackle something like this alone, did you?" Andrea gave a smug little smile. "I'm not quite as good at snooping as you are, but I'm learning."

Hannah wasn't quite sure she liked being categorized as a snoop, but she let it pass. "Bring your coffee and let's go in the back. I need to pack up my box of ingredients for tonight."

Once the switch was accomplished and Lisa had taken Hannah's place behind the counter, Andrea sat down at the work island with her coat in her lap and watched Hannah fill a box with ingredients for the dessert she planned to bake on television.

Hannah worked efficiently, measuring ingredients and putting them into plastic containers. Once she'd assembled everything she needed, she began to store them in the box. There was a container of sugar, a pound of butter, and a plastic bag filled with diced apricots. Hannah added a loaf of sliced white bread, stuck in her handwritten recipe, and walked to the cooler to make sure she had plenty of eggs and cream. When she'd clamped the lid on the box, she turned to find Andrea staring at her curiously. "What?"

"I was just trying to figure out what you're baking to-night."

"Apricot Bread Pudding. It was one of Great-Grandma Elsa's favorite recipes, but she used raisins instead of apricots. I like it better this way."

"So do I. Apricots are a lot better than raisins. So what are you going to do, Hannah?"

"There isn't time actually to bake it during the news, so I'll make it ahead of time and prepare another one on camera. That's what I did with the Pound Plus Cake for Strawberry Shortcake Swensen."

"Not that. I mean, what are we going to do about Danielle? We've got to help her."

"I know. But how about Bill? He's not going to like it if you get involved in another murder investigation."

Andrea waved off that concern. "He's so busy, he won't even notice. Let's go and visit Danielle at the hospital. We need to get all the facts we can before we start."

"You can't visit her, Andrea. I talked Mike into letting me see her, but I'm the only one."

"I know. Bill told me. But Rick Murphy's guarding her door, and I know him from high school. If I keep him busy talking to me, he won't be able to overhear what you and Danielle are saying."

"That's brilliant." Hannah was impressed.

"Thanks. So you're going to let me help, aren't you, Han-nah?"

Hannah hesitated, taking time to fill a bag with cookies

for Danielle. "Bill may kill me when he finds out, but I could really use you."

"That's great!" Andrea was obviously delighted. "You know, I really like to do things with you, Hannah. It's just a pity it took Ron LaSalle's murder to bring us together like this."

Hannah thought about that as she went to tell Lisa to hold the fort until they got back. It *was* a pity that her relationship with Andrea hadn't smoothed out into friendship until they'd investigated their first murder together. Before that it had been a competition between the two sisters, each feeling the other had the edge.

Andrea had been the popular sister, the one who'd never lacked for a date. Pretty and petite, the picture of the quintessential prom queen, she'd been at ease in any social situation, especially when it had involved boys. Andrea had been a younger version of Delores, and her popularity proved it. Hannah, on the other hand, had resembled her father. She'd been tall, lanky, and extremely capable, with an unfortunate tendency to indulge her wicked sense of humor. The boys had liked Hannah well enough as a study partner or a wisecracking pal, but she certainly hadn't made any male teenage palms turn sweaty. That had been Andrea's forte. Bill always said that Andrea could charm the birds right out of the trees, and it was true. And Hannah knew that the only way she could achieve the same effect was to load a shotgun and shoot them down.

When Hannah came back into the bakery, she grabbed her winter parka and the box of ingredients, and turned to find Andrea frowning. "What is it now?"

"You're not going to the hospital like *that,* are you?"

"Like what?" Hannah was puzzled.

"In that ratty old parka."

"My ratty old parka was new last year," Hannah informed

her. "And it's a lot warmer than that silly trench coat of yours."

"My coat's not silly. It's a perfect knock-off of the leather trench coat that was featured in *Vogue* last month!"

"That's New York. This is Minnesota. You don't wear an unlined coat that barely covers your knees when it's in the low teens outside."

"I do." Andrea slipped into her coat and headed for the back door. Once she'd stepped out, she turned back to Hannah. "Just because it's cold doesn't mean you have to look like an Eskimo. My coat is a fashion statement."

"It's a fashion statement that's going to give you frostbite from the knees down." Hannah led the way to her truck. "At least wear some wool slacks with it."

"But that would defeat the whole purpose. Really, Hannah. You just have no fashion sense."

Hannah was getting ready to give her sister a piece of her mind when she realized that what they were fighting over was ridiculous. She started to grin as she unlocked her truck, climbed behind the wheel, and waited for Andrea to get in. Perhaps they'd always bicker the way they'd done in high school, but that bickering no longer had to escalate into a fight.

Hannah waited until Andrea had buckled her seat belt, then backtracked with as much grace as possible. "Forget what I said, Andrea. I know my parka isn't exactly attractive. And I agree that I could use a little of your fashion sense."

"And I could use a little of your common sense. It's a lot colder than I thought it was going to be today."

"I've got a blanket." Hannah reached in back to retrieve the old quilt she'd stuck in her truck for emergencies. "Wrap up, Andrea. This truck takes forever to get warm."

Andrea took the quilt and draped it over her lap. "Thanks, Hannah. Maybe we should go out to the mall sometime and advise each other."

That suggestion just floated on the icy air for a moment. Then both sisters started to laugh, imagining the fights they'd have if they ever went on a shopping trip together.

Lake Eden Memorial Hospital was on Old Lake Road, five miles from The Cookie Jar and well outside the downtown area. It had been built on a rise that overlooked the frozen surface of the lake, and it was Doc Knight's pride and joy. The V-shaped cinder-block building had been painted a cheerful shade of yellow, and it was completely surrounded by small pines that had been planted so that each of the two dozen rooms would look out on perpetual greenery and a view of Eden Lake.

Hannah drove around to the back of the building and entered the parking lot. There weren't many cars this time of the day, and she pulled up next to Doc Knight's new Explorer. There were posts with electrical outlets on the far row for the nurses and the staff, but Hannah decided that she didn't need to plug in her truck. They wouldn't be staying more than an hour and probably less.

"Ready?" Hannah turned to her sister.

Andrea nodded and removed the quilt. "I hate hospitals."

"Me too." Hannah waited for Andrea to get out and locked up her truck. They fell into step together and when they reached the front of the hospital, Hannah pulled open the heavy glass door, and they stepped into the foyer. They stomped off their boots, wiping them on the mat, then went through the set of double doors that led into the large lobby.

Visiting hours were posted on a sign above the reception desk. They were from two to four and seven to nine. It was almost noon, and the desk was deserted. Hannah didn't bother to press the buzzer for assistance. How hard could it be to find Danielle's room? It would be the only one with a uniformed sheriff's deputy stationed outside.

The hospital corridor smelled like disinfectant and cauli-flower. At least Hannah hoped that it was cauliflower. The mixture made her wrinkle up her nose and wish for the soothing aromas of vanilla and chocolate.

"It smells bad in here," Andrea spoke in a hushed voice.

"I know." Hannah wondered if anyone had ever done a study of which smells made sick patients sicker. She'd be willing to bet that cauliflower would be right up near the top of the list.

"I think it's the food," Andrea commented, as they neared a food cart and she spotted a lunch tray. "You brought Danielle some cookies, didn't you? Nobody should have to eat food like that."

"Of course I did." Hannah held up the bag she was carry-ing, filled to the brim with Cocoa Snaps, Pecan Crisps, and Chocolate Chip Crunches.

"This food is all white." Andrea made a face. "I knew it would be bad, but not *this* bad."

Hannah stared down at the tray. Andrea was right. The food had no color. There was a glop of vanilla pudding in a little plastic cup, an entrée of poached fish with some sort of white cream sauce on top, a scoop of mashed potatoes, a compartment filled with limp-looking steamed cauliflower, and a piece of white bread with a pat of butter. Hannah would have passed on lunch even if she'd been hungry. And from the look of the barely touched trays, so had most of the patients at Lake Eden Memorial.

"That must be Danielle's room." Andrea pointed toward the far end of the hallway. "There's Rick."

Hannah recognized the tall, lanky figure of Cyril Mur-phy's oldest son. "How long do you think you can keep him talking?"

"As long as you need. All I have to do is ask about his new baby. It's their first."

Hannah stepped forward with her cookies, a smile pasted on her face. Rick reported directly to Mike, and if he suspected that this was any more than a friendly visit, he'd mention it. Hannah didn't even want to think of what Mike would say if he realized that the Swensen sisters were on a mission to prove him wrong and catch Boyd's real killer in the bargain.

Apricot Bread Pudding

Do not preheat oven yet. The
bread pudding must settle for 30
minutes before baking.

8 slices of white bread *(either homemade or "store
    bought")*
½ cup melted butter *(1 stick—¹/₄ pound)*
⅓ cup white sugar
½ cup chopped dried apricots *(not too fine, you want
    some chunks)*
3 beaten eggs *(just whip them up with a fork)*
2 ¼ cups top milk* *(you can use light cream or Half
    'n Half)*

Heavy cream, sweetened whipped cream, or vanilla
    ice cream for a topping

* *"Top milk" is Great-Grandma Elsa's word for the
cream that floated to the top of old-fashioned milk bot-
tles.*

Generously butter a 2-quart casserole. Remove the
crusts from the bread and cut each slice into 4 triangles. *(Just make an "X" with your knife.)* Melt the butter in a large microwave-safe bowl and put in the bread
triangles, tossing them lightly with a spoon until
they're coated with butter.

Arrange approximately a third of the triangles in
the bottom of the casserole. Sprinkle on a third of the
sugar and half of the chopped apricots.

Put down half of the remaining bread triangles, sprinkle on half of the remaining sugar, and add ALL of the remaining apricots.

Cover with the rest of the bread triangles. Scrape the bowl to get out any butter that remains in the bottom of the bowl and put that on top. Sprinkle with the last of the sugar and set aside.

Whip up the eggs in the butter bowl and whisk in the light cream. Pour this over the top of the casserole and let it stand at room temperature for thirty minutes. *(This gives the bread time to absorb the egg and cream mixture.)*

Preheat the oven to 350 degrees F., rack in the middle position. Bake the bread pudding uncovered, for 45 to 55 minutes, until the pudding is set and the top is golden brown.

Let it cool slightly *(five minutes or so)* and serve in dessert dishes with heavy cream, sweetened whipped cream, or a scoop of vanilla ice cream on the top.

You can make this with any dried fruit, including currants or raisins. Andrea likes apricots, Mother prefers dates, and Michelle thought it was "yummy" with dried pears. We didn't try it with prunes. Carrie Rhodes is the only person I know who likes prunes. (And I'm not going to comment on that!)

Chapter
Six

"**O**h, Hannah! You came!"

"Of course I did. I said I would." Hannah tried for a cheerful smile, but it was difficult. Danielle was sitting up in bed, there were traces of recent tears on her cheeks, and she was wearing the expression that Hannah thought of as the "whipped puppy look."

"I didn't think they were going to let me have any visitors." Danielle's voice quavered slightly.

"They weren't, but I did some fast talking." Danielle had "victim" written all over her, and Hannah knew she had to do something or they'd be defeated before they even started. Danielle needed a shot of courage and the belief that she controlled her own fate.

"Have a Cocoa Snap." Hannah reached into the bag and handed her a cookie. Then she placed the bag within easy reach on Danielle's bed stand. "The chocolate will cheer you up and give you some energy."

Danielle bit into the cookie and the ghost of a smile

crossed her lips. "Thanks, Hannah. These are good. I couldn't eat my lunch. You should have seen . . ."

"I did. I wouldn't have eaten it, either." Hannah interrupted her. A discussion of hospital food would only waste time. "I've got Andrea outside, running interference with Rick Murphy. I didn't want to give him the chance to overhear us. We need to talk, Danielle."

Danielle brightened up considerably. "Then you're going to help me?"

"Of course I am, but I need to ask you some questions about Boyd. Can you forget how lousy you feel for a minute and concentrate?"

"I feel a whole lot better now that you're here." A little color came back to Danielle's cheeks, and she patted the side of her bed. "Sit down, Hannah, and I'll tell you everything I know. It's not much. Everything happened just like I said it did last night."

"You may know something without knowing you know it." Hannah realized that what she'd just said was confusing, and she tried another tact. "I'll ask the questions and you answer, okay?"

"Okay, but just tell me one thing first. Are they going to arrest me?"

"Not if I have anything to say about it. The last I heard, they were going to keep you in the hospital for at least five days."

"That's better than going to jail," Danielle said, but she didn't look convinced. "I didn't kill him, Hannah. You believe me, don't you?"

Hannah reached out and patted her hand. "I believe you. That's why Andrea and I are going to try to catch the real killer. Now think about this carefully, Danielle. It could be very important. Did you notice any change in Boyd's behavior lately? Say in the last week or so? Anything that made him unusually angry or upset?"

"Well . . ." Danielle hesitated, and Hannah knew she was thinking it over. "He was really mad about The Gulls. They missed nine free throws in their last game. But that wasn't unusual. He's always angry if they lose."

"How about his classes?"

"They were all okay. He was really proud of his fourth-period history class. They took some kind of an achievement test, and they all did really well."

"Was he having a problem with any of the faculty?"

"No." Danielle shook her head. "Everything was fine. The only thing I can think of that *really* upset him was that phone call he got on Tuesday."

Hannah felt a prickling of interest. Danielle hadn't mentioned a phone call before. "What phone call was that?"

"The one he got right after he came home for lunch. I was making him tomato soup in the microwave. He likes . . . liked that."

Danielle's lip started to quiver as she changed the verb to past tense, and Hannah knew she'd better distract her. "Let's get back to Boyd's phone call. Who called him?"

"I don't know. He didn't tell me."

"But you knew he got a phone call?"

"Yes. Boyd was in the living room, waiting for me to bring him his lunch, and I answered the phone in the kitchen. It was a woman, and she asked for Boyd, so I called out for him to pick up the extension."

"You didn't recognize her voice?"

"No. It wasn't anyone I ever talked to before. I'm sure of that. But I know it was a local call."

"How do you know that?" Hannah asked.

"It was noon, and I heard the town clock strike one."

"You heard the clock strike *one?*"

"Boyd was complaining about it the other day. It's still set for daylight saving's time because Freddy Sawyer was sick with the flu when it was time to turn it back. You know, spring forward, fall back?"

"I know."

"Well, nobody else wanted to climb up there on the ladder, and it was a week before Freddy got back to work. Nobody seemed to notice the clock was off, and they hadn't had any complaints, so they just decided to leave it until next spring."

"That figures." Hannah was amused. There were times when things were very laid-back in Lake Eden. "Let's get back to the phone call. Could you tell how old the woman was from her voice?"

Danielle thought about it for a moment. "She didn't sound as young as one of Boyd's students, but she wasn't old."

"Do you remember anything distinctive about her voice?"

"Well . . . she sort of slurred her words."

Hannah's ears perked up. "Did she sound drunk?"

"Not really. It was more like some kind of speech impediment. My grandmother used to call it a 'mouthful of mush.' Do you think that's important, Hannah?"

"It could be. Tell me everything she said. Repeat it word for word."

"Okay. The first thing she said was, *Is Boyd there?* Except it came out *iszh* instead of *is.* And when I said he was, she said, *Get him on the phone.* She slurred that, too, except I can't do it."

"Get him on the phone? Isn't that kind of rude?"

"I thought so. I mean, she didn't call me by name or say please, or anything like that. She sounded like she was in a big hurry. And I know that Boyd was really angry after he'd talked to her."

"How do you know that?"

"Right after he talked to her, he came storming into the

kitchen and his face was all red and kind of splotchy. It's always that way when he's mad. The first thing he did was accuse me of listening in on his private conversation, but I didn't, Hannah. I swear it."

"I believe you." Hannah thought she knew what had happened next. "Do you remember what he said?"

"Yes. He said his call was none of my business, and I deserved to be punished for eavesdropping. I swore I'd hung up right after he got on the line, but . . . but he said he couldn't trust me, and that's when he did this."

Danielle reached up to touch her black eye, and Hannah swallowed hard. Boyd Watson had been a real bully, but it wouldn't serve any purpose to point that out now. "You said you put down the phone right after Boyd picked up the extension. Did you hear either of them say anything before you hung up?"

"I heard Boyd say hello. I had to stay on the line until he picked up, or I would have cut off the call. And I heard the first thing the woman said to him. It was, *Boyd, we have to talk.*"

"And that's all you heard?"

"That's all. By that time I'd hung up. I even banged the phone down a little, so Boyd would know that I was off the line."

"So Boyd heard you hang up, but he still accused you of eavesdropping?"

"That's right. I know it sounds awful to say it now that Boyd is . . . is dead, but I think he was all riled up because of the phone call and was looking for a fight. You know how people get when they're frustrated. They have to take it out on somebody and I was . . . I was there."

That was good enough for Hannah. It was clear that the phone call was important. "What did Boyd do after he hit you?"

"He said he was sorry, and he hugged me." Danielle's lip started to tremble again. "He got me some ice for my eye, then he called Dr. Holland right away."

Hannah already knew that Dr. Holland was Boyd's therapist. Danielle had told her that before. "How long did Boyd talk to Dr. Holland?"

"Just long enough to make an emergency appointment. Then he called the school to get a substitute for his afternoon classes and drove to St. Paul to see Dr. Holland at his clinic."

Hannah made a mental note to check to make sure that Boyd had kept his appointment. That wouldn't be easy. Dr. Holland was a psychiatrist, and psychiatrists didn't like to give out any information about their patients. "What time did Boyd get back home?"

"It was a little after six. I know because I put the chili on at five-thirty and it said on the package that it had to cook for thirty minutes. It was all ready when Boyd got home, and he really liked it. He told me it was the best chili I ever made. And he was really sweet to me right up until the time he . . . he died."

Hannah couldn't think of anything to say. The wife beater had been sweet to his wife after he'd beaten her. It was faint praise in her book.

"This is a pretty room, isn't it, Hannah?" Danielle changed the subject, and Hannah let her. She was still sick and had been interrogated enough for one day. "I miss being at home, but this isn't so bad."

As Hannah glanced around, she realized that the chocolate she'd pressed on Danielle had done its work. The hospital room was perfectly ordinary and resembled a room in an unusually clean, low-budget motel.

"They told me the Lutheran Ladies made these quilts." Danielle reached out to stroke the patchwork quilt on the bed. "And some of the other church ladies donated the pictures. I really like that one next to the window. Boyd and I were always going to take a trip to see the ocean."

Hannah got up to look at the seascape that Danielle had mentioned. Then another picture caught her eye, the one that was hanging inside the open bathroom door. It was a cross-stitch sampler with hands folded in prayer, and it bore the legend, "Offer up your pain as a tribute to the Lord."

Hannah did a slow burn as she stared at the sampler. If the Lord was as merciful as all three local clergymen insisted, He certainly wouldn't want anyone to suffer. And the idea that pain could be a tribute was barbaric!

"What is it, Hannah?" Danielle asked. "Did you find another nice picture?"

"No. Does Doc Knight let you get up to use the bathroom, Danielle?"

"Not yet. He says I'm still too weak, and I might slip and fall. He promised me that I could get up tomorrow though."

"That's good." Hannah blocked the sampler with her body, lifted it off the wall, and slid it into the largest pocket of her parka. She salved her conscience by telling herself it wasn't stealing since she intended to bring the frame back tomorrow with something more appropriate inside. "I'd better go, Danielle."

"Are you going to look for the woman who made that phone call?"

"That's the plan." Hannah walked over to pat Danielle's shoulder. "I'll be back to see you tomorrow. And while I'm gone, I've got some homework for you."

Danielle actually smiled. "If I do my homework, will you bring me some more chocolate cookies?"

"Absolutely," Hannah promised. "I want you to make a list, Danielle. Write down the names of everyone who had some reason to be angry with Boyd."

"But Boyd didn't do anything wrong, Hannah. Why would anyone be angry at him?"

Hannah realized that Danielle was still in denial, and nothing she could say would convince her that Boyd hadn't been a good husband, a good neighbor, and a good man. "It doesn't matter whether Boyd did anything wrong or not. People still get angry at other people, and their reasons aren't always justified. Herb Beeseman gave my mother a speeding ticket three months ago. She admits that she was speeding, but she's still miffed at him."

"I see what you mean." Danielle pulled out the drawer on her nightstand and took out a Winnetka County Sheriff's Station notepad and a pen. "Mike Kingston gave this to me. It's funny, Hannah. He asked me to make the same kind of list."

"He did?" Hannah's eyebrows shot up. Perhaps she'd been hasty in her judgment of Mike. If he'd asked Danielle to make a list, he might not be knuckling under to Sheriff Grant after all. "Write down everyone you can think of and give us both a copy. List anyone who was irritated with Boyd, regardless of the reason."

Danielle flipped the notebook open and reached for another cookie. "I'm glad you asked me to do something, Hannah. It makes me feel like I'm helping. But are you sure you want me to write down *everyone?*"

"I'm sure."

"Even if it's over something silly?"

"Don't leave anyone out."

"Okay." Danielle wrote a name on the first line. "I'll start with Norman Rhodes."

"Norman?" Hannah was surprised. "Why was Norman angry with Boyd?"

"Because he canceled three appointments in a row and then his temporary filling fell out. Norman wasn't exactly happy when he had to go down to his office at midnight to glue it back in."

Hannah reconsidered her original instructions. "Maybe

you'd better make a note of *why* each person was angry with Boyd. That'll make it a lot easier for me."

"Okay, I'll do that. See you tomorrow, Hannah. I'll have the list all ready for you, I promise."

Hannah gave a little wave and headed for the door, leaving Danielle to her work. If the way Danielle's pen was practically flying over the paper was any indication, she'd have a list of suspects as long as the Lake Eden telephone directory.

"So?" Andrea asked, the moment Hannah had slid behind the wheel.

"So I left Danielle making a list of the people who were angry with Boyd." Hannah buckled her seat belt and turned the key in the ignition. "And she told me about a strange phone call that Boyd got on Tuesday when he came home for lunch."

Andrea listened as Hannah told her about the phone call and how Boyd had blackened Danielle's eye immediately after he'd hung up. When Hannah had told her the whole story, Andrea said, "Danielle's right. The phone call could be the key to Boyd's murder. Who do you know with a speech impediment?"

"There's Freddy Sawyer, but he's the wrong sex." Hannah named the mildly retarded man who did odd jobs around town. "And Lydia Gradin has a slight lisp, but she doesn't slur her words. How about you? Do you know anyone?"

Andrea thought about it as Hannah backed out of the parking spot. "There's Mrs. Knudson. She's been slurring her words since she had that stroke."

"Mrs. Knudson is eighty and Danielle said the woman sounded young," Hannah reminded her. "She also said that the woman was rude. Can you imagine Reverend Knudson's grandmother being rude?"

"No, she's always very polite. There's Loretta Richardson. She still has her Southern drawl, but Danielle would know her voice. And Helen Barthel stutters every once in a while when she gets nervous, but she doesn't slur her words."

"Anyone else?" Hannah drove around the hospital and down the snow-covered drive.

"I don't think so. It's got to be somebody we don't know. Is Danielle sure the call was local?"

"She's sure." Hannah braked at the stop sign, looked both ways, and pulled out onto Old Lake Road. "It could be someone who came to town for the bake-off. Most of them checked in on Tuesday morning. Do you have time to run out to the Lake Eden Inn?"

"I've got nothing *but* time. Tracey doesn't get out of preschool until four, and today's my day off. I'd still be in bed if it wasn't for Lucy Richards. That witch called at the crack of dawn this morning!"

"Witch?"

"Witch with a 'b.' Now that I'm a mother, I have to watch my language. It's like Tracey's teacher says, *Little pitchers have big ears.*"

"I'm not a little pitcher, I'm a big one. You won't corrupt me." Hannah grinned as she turned off on the road that led around the lake. "And I agree with you completely about Lucy Richards. She came in the shop this morning and tried to pump me for information about Boyd's murder."

Andrea looked surprised. "How did she find out that you were there?"

"She said one of her sources told her. I kept telling her that I didn't know anything and I couldn't tell her if I did, but it still took me ten minutes to get rid of her. And that's not the half of it. When she finally left, she skinned out without paying for her cookies and coffee."

"Lucy's the rudest person I've ever met." Andrea's voice was hard, and Hannah knew she was still angry about the early-morning phone call. "If she slurred her words, I'd suspect that she was the woman who called Boyd."

"But she doesn't slur her words."

"I know."

Hannah turned right at the reflective sign that said "Lake Eden Inn," and followed the gravel road that led through a large stand of oak. Their branches were black and stark against the leaden sky and they looked as dead as doornails. Of course they weren't. New green leaves would begin to pop out with the first breath of spring. They always did. She emerged from the oaks, drove around a curve, and the huge, rustic summer home that Sally and Dick Laughlin had converted to a lakeside hotel came into view.

"The inn's just gorgeous," Andrea commented. "Every time I drive out here, I'm impressed."

"Me too. Sally and Dick spent a lot of time and money renovating this place."

Hannah pulled into the parking lot and began to troll for a space. It was filled with the guests' cars, and the only one she recognized was Dick's old VW bus. It was parked at the end of the back row, and Hannah pulled in beside it, making her own space. That was one advantage to owning a four-wheel-drive vehicle in the winter. The Suburban could make its own space in the unplowed snow.

"Did you have to park here?" Andrea complained, opening the passenger door and staring down at the snow.

"Yes. All the regular spaces were full. Slide across and get out my side. There's less snow over here."

As Andrea slid over, Hannah thought about the lineage of the Lake Eden Inn. The original building had been in the Laughlin family for five generations. Built in the late nineteenth century, Dick's great-great-grandfather had spared no expense to build his summer retreat. Franklin Edward Laughlin, a lesser-known iron ore magnate, had packed up his family, his staff, and any friends who wished to spend a few months at the lakeshore, and they'd all traveled by carriage to the forty-room mansion he'd modestly called "Lake Eden Cottage."

"This place is practically a monument to Dick's great-great-grandfather, isn't it?" Andrea climbed out and led the way up the long winding path to the entrance of the inn.

"That's what I've always thought," Hannah agreed. F.E. Laughlin must have regarded his summer home as his personal edifice, because he'd established a fund to be used solely for upkeep on the property. The "cottage," in pristine condition but never modernized, had passed from oldest son to oldest son until Dick had inherited it four years ago. F.E.'s iron ore fortune had been passed along, too, as part of the legacy, but it hadn't fared as well. By the time Dick had inherited "Lake Eden Cottage," the family coffers were very nearly depleted.

Hannah gazed around her as they walked past Dick's topiary. His evergreen shrubs were growing nicely, and all of the animals were recognizable. The lion's mane still wasn't full enough, but a season's growth would take care of that. The squirrel, with its bushy tail was taking shape, and the bear looked great. It was standing on its hind legs and was already five feet tall.

Dick and Sally had been living in Minneapolis when he'd inherited the inn. They'd come out to look at the property, fallen in love with the place, and moved to Lake Eden the next week. They'd been forced to borrow heavily to install electricity, indoor plumbing, and a modern kitchen with restaurant-sized appliances, but that gamble was paying off. Last year, Dick and Sally had been fully booked for the entire season, and the Lake Eden Inn was finally showing a profit.

"Something sure smells good," Andrea said, as they climbed the wooden steps and pushed open the front door.

"Yes, it does." Hannah began to smile as she stepped into

the huge lobby with its massive wooden beams and gigantic rock fireplace. The scent in the air was mouth-watering. It was tantalizingly spicy, and under the spice she could detect a hint of chocolate. It had to be Sally's Chicken Mole, one of her favorite dishes.

"Come on, Andrea. Let's head for the bar." Hannah set off at a fast pace for the wood-paneled bar that also served as the dining room. "If the buffet is still out, I'll treat you to lunch."

Chapter Seven

The moment they entered the bar, Hannah spotted Sally Laughlin. She was hard to miss with her bright orange maternity top. The Laughlins' first child would be born in January, and Sally was sitting on a barstool with her feet elevated on a neighboring stool. The buffet table was still out, and Hannah turned to Andrea. "Just wait until you taste Sally's Chicken Mole. It's fantastic."

"I've never even heard of Chicken Mole before. What is it?"

"It's Mexican cuisine, chicken baked in a dark chocolate sauce with lots of spices."

"Chicken and chocolate?" Andrea shuddered. "That doesn't sound very appetizing."

"But it is. Just try it and see." Hannah bit back a grin. She should have remembered that Andrea wasn't very adventuresome when it came to food. Last Thanksgiving, Hannah had added red bell peppers and water chestnuts to the turkey stuffing, and Andrea had refused to try it.

"Come on, Andrea. Let's go say hello to Sally. I think Doc Knight is wrong about her due date. She looks like she's almost ready to pop."

Andrea looked as if she might object to that turn of phrase, but once she caught sight of Sally, she forgot to tell Hannah to be more tactful. "I hope having all these guests isn't too much for her. She doesn't look very comfortable."

"Hi there." Sally's face lit up in a smile as they approached her barstool. "I'm just taking a break. What are you girls doing way out here?"

"We came for the Chicken Mole," Hannah answered, before Andrea could say anything.

"Then go fill your plates and come back here. You can tell me all the local gossip."

"And you can tell us all the gossip about your guests." Andrea seized the opportunity and jumped into the conversation. "I love hearing about people from out of town."

Hannah waited until they'd walked over to the buffet table and then she turned to Andrea. "That was good, Andrea."

"What was good?" Andrea picked up a plate and dished out a helping of spinach salad.

"That bit about how you love to hear about people from out of town."

"Oh, that." Andrea dismissed it with a wave of the salad tongs. "I just thought Sally would be more likely to talk to us if we said we were interested. I just wish you hadn't said we came for the Chicken Mole."

"Why not?"

"Because now I'll have to take some, and since we'll be sitting at the bar with Sally, I'll have to eat it."

"Relax, you'll like it." Hannah patted her on the shoulder. "And think of how much fun you'll have telling Tracey about it."

"That's what you always used to say when you made supper and it didn't turn out right. *This is really exotic, Andrea. Try some so you can tell all your friends about it."*

Hannah winced. Andrea was wise to her, and whatever she said would only make matters worse. She watched her sister take a small helping of the mole and a large helping of macaroni and cheese in silence. She wasn't about to make the mistake of telling Andrea that Sally's macaroni and cheese didn't come out of a blue box.

Once their plates were filled, Hannah led the way back to the bar and they climbed up on stools next to Sally. Hannah was amused when Andrea tried her Chicken Mole first. When she'd been a kid, she'd done the same thing with her vegetables.

Andrea chewed thoughtfully and then she smiled at Sally. "This is wonderful, Sally. I wasn't sure I'd like chicken and chocolate, but I do."

"Thanks. The guests all raved about it, too. Buffet food is pretty standard, but I try to do one unusual dish every day to keep them interested."

"Are they a pretty good crowd?" Hannah asked, forging the way for a discussion about the guests.

"Super. Of course, some of the contestants are a little nervous. It's a pretty big deal, you know."

"How about the three ladies who were eliminated last night?" Hannah asked. "I know I probably shouldn't say it under the circumstances, but I bet they weren't exactly happy with what Boyd Watson said on television."

"That's an understatement!" Sally laughed. "They were hopping mad when they got back here, but the lady who won was so nice about it, they calmed down and had a good time at the party."

"Then all three ladies were at the party?" Andrea asked, catching Hannah's line of questioning perfectly.

"They were here and so were their families, so you can forget about them."

"Forget about them?" Hannah tried for a perfectly innocent look.

"Come on, Hannah." Sally reached out to squeeze her arm. "I know why you're asking, and I wondered how long it would take you. I figured you'd make small talk for at least five minutes, but I was wrong."

Hannah was impressed. Sally was quick. "I'm no good at small talk. I'm better off just jumping right in with both feet."

"How is Boyd's wife? It must have been an awful shock."

"It was." Hannah decided to confide in Sally. "And to make matters worse, she's the prime suspect."

Sally slid her feet off the barstool and sat up a little straighter. "She didn't do it, did she?"

"No, and Andrea and I are hoping to *prove* that she didn't. If I tell you something, will you promise not to repeat it?"

"You can count on me. I only met Danielle once, but I liked her. And she certainly didn't seem like the type to murder her husband. I've got to say that I didn't like him, though. They drove out here for dinner last summer, and all he could do was complain. After they left, Dick said he felt sorry for her. We only had to put up with him for a couple of hours, but she was stuck with him for a lifetime."

"A short lifetime," Hannah pointed out. "Danielle had good reason to kill Boyd and that's part of the problem. But we do have a possible lead."

"What is it?"

"Danielle told me that Boyd got a phone call from a woman on Tuesday around noon. It was a local call, and Danielle didn't recognize the woman's voice, but she said that Boyd was really angry after he'd talked to her. We thought it might have been one of your guests."

Sally thought about it for a minute, then she nodded. "That's certainly possible. Almost everyone checked in before noon, and there was nothing scheduled until the banquet at seven."

"This woman had some sort of speech impediment," Andrea told her. "Danielle said she slurred her words, but she didn't seem drunk."

Sally shook her head. "I haven't noticed anyone with a problem like that, but I'm not sure I've met all the guests. Why don't you do a little table-hopping after you finish your lunch? This crowd always sticks around for the dessert buffet."

"That's not surprising," Hannah remarked, "since most of them are entered in the bake-off. Maybe they're hoping to pick up a few pointers from you."

Sally seemed pleased as she slid from her stool. "I've got to run. Dick's in the kitchen filling the eclairs, and I have to put on the chocolate frosting. What are you baking on television tonight, Hannah?"

"Apricot Bread Pudding."

"Oh, good. Another recipe for my files. I had the station fax me your Pound Plus Cake recipe, and I baked four batches last night. Do you think I can serve it with canned peaches, since strawberries are so expensive?"

"Absolutely. You can use any canned or frozen fruit."

Sally gave her a little salute. "Thanks, Hannah. I'll be the first one to call the station after I watch you tonight."

When Hannah and Andrea were finished with their lunch, they headed off toward the tables. The room was huge, and they split up, each taking half. Hannah headed straight toward Mr. Rutlege. She wanted to see how he was feeling after his ordeal in Norman's dental chair.

"Hi, Mr. Rutlege." Hannah reached out to shake his hand. "I'm so sorry you had to bow out of the judging."

"I'm not." The pretty brown-haired woman sitting next to him smiled at Hannah. "I'm Belle Rutlege."

"Hannah Swensen."

"I know. I saw you on television last night. Jeremy and I were the only ones here. Everyone else went to the school."

"Are you sorry that your husband couldn't be a judge?"

"I'm sorry that his tooth acted up and he had such a rough time. But I'm glad he didn't have to speak on television last night!"

"Why?"

"All of our friends back home would have thought he'd fallen off the wagon. He was slurring his words, and he's the head of our local AA chapter!"

Hannah's senses went on full alert at this news. She turned to Jeremy Rutlege, and asked, "You sounded drunk?"

"As a hoot owl. I tried to explain to Belle that it was the packing. Norman said to leave it in for twelve hours. But every time I tried to talk, she laughed so hard she couldn't hear me."

Hannah spent another few minutes chatting with them, then she went over to get Andrea. She waited for Andrea to finish her conversation with the group she'd joined and pulled her out into the hall. "Mission accomplished."

"You found the woman who made the phone call?" Andrea was clearly excited.

"No, but I know where to look. Come on, Andrea. I'll explain it all on the way back to town. We have to go to see Norman Rhodes before his afternoon patients come in."

Hannah pressed the buzzer at the reception window and when Norman slid back the frosted glass panel, she was shocked. There were dark circles under his eyes, and he seemed nervous and ill at ease.

"What's wrong, Norman?" Hannah blurted out.

"Nothing. I guess I've just been working too late lately."

"Well, don't work so hard." Hannah said the first thing that came into her mind. Something was wrong, and it had nothing to do with Norman's dental practice, but this wasn't the time to ask about it. She'd wait until she had a moment alone with him.

"That's great advice, Hannah." Norman smiled, but it was a pale imitation of his normal grin. "Hello, Andrea. Do you have an emergency?"

"Yes, but it has nothing to do with our teeth," Hannah told him. "I need to look at your appointment book, Norman. It's really important."

"Why?"

"I can't tell you. It's confidential."

"And I can't let you look for the same reason."

"Come on, Norman." Hannah did her best wheedle, but she could tell that Norman wasn't buying it. "Okay, I'll tell you why I need it. It has to do with Boyd Watson's murder."

"You're investigating again?" Norman's eyebrows rose.

"Yes, but Bill doesn't know, and he'll kill me if he finds out," Andrea answered. "We can trust you to keep our secret, can't we?"

"Of course."

"Then we can look at your appointment book?" Hannah pressed her advantage.

Norman considered it for a moment and then he shook his head. "I can't let you do that, Hannah. It'd be different if you were actually working for the sheriff's department. Then I'd have to cooperate. But you're not. You do understand, don't you?"

Hannah stared at Norman. He looked very intense and as she watched, one of his eyelids closed in a wink. "Of course I understand. You can't give us permission. It would be a violation of your dental code of ethics."

"Right. Hold on a second. I'll let you in the back." Norman slid the glass panel shut. A moment later, he opened the door to the inner part of his clinic and motioned them in. "I'd better close this. It's my appointment book." Norman closed a red-covered spiral book on the counter. "Will you excuse me for a minute? I have some X-rays to check."

After Norman had gone off down the hallway, Andrea turned to Hannah. "What was all that about?"

"Norman treats his patient list like a state secret. He takes this whole confidentiality issue very seriously. He can't give us permission to look at his appointment book, but he's giving us the chance to sneak a peek while he's gone."

Andrea followed Hannah around the desk so that they could look at the appointment book. "That seems a little silly to me, but I'm not a dentist. I'm a real-estate agent."

"And real-estate agents don't have ethics?" Hannah couldn't resist teasing her a bit.

"Of course they do. They're just different, that's all. You want to check Tuesday, right?"

"Monday *and* Tuesday. Mr. Rutlege said he had to leave his packing in for twelve hours, and Norman handles after-hours emergencies. The woman who called Boyd could have been a late patient on Monday night."

Andrea flipped the appointment book open to Monday's date. "There's nothing after six, and his last two appointments were men."

"Okay. Try Tuesday morning."

Both sisters stared down at the page after Andrea had flipped it. Norman had been busy on Tuesday morning.

"Write down the names, Andrea. I'll read them off to you." Hannah waited until Andrea had grabbed a pad of notepaper and a pen. "Luanne Hanks at eight. Mr. Hodges had a nine o'clock appointment, but you don't have to write him down. Then Amalia Greerson came in at nine-thirty, and Norman saw Eleanor Cox at eleven."

"Luanne Hanks, Amalia Greerson, and Eleanor Cox. Is that it?"

"That's it." Hannah closed the book and stepped out from behind the desk.

"It can't be Amalia." Andrea followed her, staring down at the notes she made. "She called the office right before noon on Tuesday and asked for Al. I answered, and she wasn't slurring her words."

"Okay. Scratch her off. And scratch off Eleanor, too."

"Why?"

"Because Danielle knows her voice. They used to be neighbors before Otis and Eleanor moved out to the lake."

Andrea sighed. "That leaves Luanne. Do you think we should talk to her?"

"Of course. She works at the café until six. Let's drop by on our way back to the shop."

"I'm all through with the X-rays," Norman called out, ducking out of a treatment room and walking down the hallway toward them.

Hannah took one look at his worried face and wondered if what Delores had told her about Lucy Richards had anything to do with it. She'd promised her mother to make time for Norman, and she did want to talk to him alone. "Are you going to the bake-off tonight, Norman?"

"I wouldn't miss it. I should have said something before, Hannah, but I guess I'm just not very social."

"Huh?" Hannah was puzzled.

"The bake-off. I meant to tell you that you looked really good on television. And I thought you did a nice job making the contestants feel better after Boyd got through with them. He was pretty nasty, but I guess I probably shouldn't say that, now that he's dead."

"I don't know why you shouldn't say it. It's the truth." Hannah wondered what Norman's reaction would be if he knew exactly how nasty Boyd had really been.

"I know, but Mother's always saying that you're not supposed to speak ill of the dead."

"That's just an old superstition. In some parts of Medieval Europe, people believed that if you maligned someone who'd died, they'd come back to haunt you. You don't believe in ghosts, do you, Norman?"

Norman grinned and shook his head. "I've never been a big fan of the occult."

"It's the live people who can hurt you, not the dead ones." Andrea's voice was hard. "Nobody has to worry about Boyd Watson now."

Hannah nodded, knowing that Andrea was thinking about the abuse that Danielle had suffered. She shot her sister a warning glance; it wasn't their secret to tell, and hastily changed the subject. "If you're not busy, why don't you drop by my condo after the contest, Norman? We haven't had a chance to talk for a long time."

"That's true." Norman looked pleased as he nodded. "I'll be there, Hannah."

The buzzer at the window sounded and Norman slid back the glass panel. "Hi, Doc. I'll be with you in just a second." Then he turned to Andrea and Hannah. "I have to get back to work. My one-thirty's here."

"Doc Knight?" Hannah asked, hoping that it was. She might be able to ask him a few questions before Norman got out his drill.

"No, Doc Bennett. We worked out a deal. I do his dental work and he does mine."

Hannah was thoughtful as they walked out of the clinic. She'd never considered it before, but a dentist needed his own dentist, just like a doctor needed his own doctor. As they crossed the street and headed toward Hal and Rose's Café, Hannah wondered if a cookie baker needed another source of cookies, but she quickly rejected that idea. She liked her own cookies. She'd spent hours perfecting the recipes. Perhaps she was being a bit conceited, but she didn't see any reason to eat an inferior cookie when hers were the best in the state.

ples were pot roast, turkey dinner with all the trimmings,
and ham with homemade scalloped potatoes.

Chapter Eight

Hal and Rose's Café was across the street from the
Rhodes Dental Clinic, at the northwest corner of Main
Street and Second Avenue. The old yellow-brick building had
been erected in the forties, and Harold and Rose McDermott
were the second owners. There was a six-room apartment
over the café, and the McDermotts lived there. You could
count on Rose to start bragging every winter when the
weather turned cold because she could use the inside staircase and she never had to bundle up in her parka and boots to
go to work.

Hannah pushed open the door and they stepped into the
café. The air was fragrant with the scent of pot roast, and
Hannah was almost sorry she'd eaten. Flavored with a bou-
quet of bay leaf and rosemary, and surrounded with whole
onions, potatoes, and carrots, it was one of Hannah's favorite
dishes.

Rose was a good cook and served simple food. In addition to hamburgers, fried to perfection on the grill, her sta-

ples were pot roast, turkey dinner with all the trimmi
and ham with homemade scalloped potatoes. She also
served open-faced sandwiches, your choice of beef, turkey,
or ham. Each sandwich came with a scoop of mashed potatoes and gravy on top. The original owners had placed a sign
over the cash register. It read "Good Cheap Food," and Rose
lived up to that promise. Hannah couldn't think of any other
restaurant in Winnetka County where a customer could
order a hamburger, fries, and what Rose called her "bottom-
less cup of coffee," with as many refills as you wanted, for
two bucks.

The lunch crowd was long gone, and the wooden booths
that lined the sidewall were deserted, but there was the usual
crowd at the long wooden counter. Ed Barthel was sitting at
one end, his stool swiveled so that he could peer out the
plate-glass window and watch the ladies flocking into Trudi
Schuman's fabric shop for their quilting club meeting. It was
pretty obvious he'd driven his wife, Helen, to town for the
meeting, and he was passing the time with a cup of coffee,
waiting to drive her back home.

Lake Eden's mayor, Richard Bascomb, was holding court
at the other end of the counter. Richard was a good politi-
cian, a handsome silver-haired man in his fifties with a real
genius for small-town politics. Hannah had to admit that he
was a good administrator. Lake Eden had run smoothly
since he'd taken over the office. But there was something
about the mayor that she didn't like. She guessed it was his
insincerity. Mayor Bascomb pretended to be everyone's
good buddy, even if he'd never met them before, and he was
always on the lookout for a good political contact. He'd
come over to her serving table when she'd provided cookie
and coffee for his last fund-raiser, and while he had prais
her for doing such a good job, he'd been looking over
shoulder to spot the other, more important people ir
room.

As they walked toward the counter, Hannah heard several loud groans from the back room. Someone must have made a killing in the poker game that started when the café opened in the morning and didn't end until Rose doused the lights and told everyone that it was closing time. The room in back was Hal's domain. He loved to play poker, and he called the back room his "private banquet facility." As far as Hannah knew, there had never been a banquet served behind the curtained door, but there had been plenty of beer and coffee, and the cigar humidor was always well stocked. Any local poker player was welcome to join the game. The "private" designation was Hal's way around the law that prohibited smoking or gambling in a public restaurant.

Andrea nudged Hannah and gestured toward the large colored posters that were tacked to backs of the wooden booths. "Rose could use a good decorator. See the dates on those farm auction posters? Some of them are over twenty years old."

"Maybe she's hoping they'll turn into antiques?"

"They will, but not for another thirty years. And even then, I can't imagine who'd want to buy them."

Luanne Hanks came out of the back room, carrying a half-filled carafe of coffee. When she saw Hannah and Andrea, she set it down on the warmer plate and hurried over to them. "Hi. We've still got ham and turkey left if you want lunch."

"Just coffee," Hannah answered her. "Is it too much trouble if we sit in a booth?"

"Of course not. Go sit down, and I'll be right there."

Hannah and Andrea took a seat in the booth and waited for Luanne to bring their coffee. It didn't take long. Luanne rounded the corner carrying a tray in less than a minute. "Black for you." Luanne set a mug down in front of Hannah. "And you take cream, don't you, Andrea?"

"How did you remember that, Luanne? I'm hardly ever here."

"Tricks of the trade." Luanne smiled modestly. "Are you sure you don't want something to go with that coffee?"

Hannah shook her head. "We're sure. Do you have a second, Luanne? We really need to talk to you."

"Sure. Rose just skinned upstairs for a minute, but she's back now. What is it?"

"We need to ask you about your dental appointment. You saw Norman at eight on Tuesday?"

Luanne looked surprised. "Yes. I chipped a tooth on Monday night, and Dr. Rhodes filed it off for me. He's a really good dentist, and I was in and out in fifteen minutes. I didn't even need Novocain."

"So he just filed off your tooth?" Hannah asked, exchanging glances with Andrea. It didn't sound as if Luanne could be the woman who'd called Boyd.

"That's right. I was going to ignore it. I really hate to go to the dentist. But I kept catching my tongue on it, and Rose noticed. She made me go."

Hannah nodded. Another suspect eliminated. "Were you Norman's first appointment of the morning?"

"No. Another lady came in early, but she was already gone when I got there."

"He told you that?" Andrea asked.

"Not exactly. But there was a scarf on the back of the chair, and I handed it to him. He said his first patient must have left it, and he'd give it back when she came in for her next appointment."

"But you don't know who his first appointment was?"

"All I know is that she bought *my* scarf." Luanne sighed deeply.

"Your scarf?"

"The one I was going to buy for my mother. You must

have seen it, Hannah. Claire Rodgers had it in her window at Beau Monde. It was dark green cashmere and it had three beautiful pink roses embroidered on it. My mother really liked it, and I was saving up to get it for her Christmas present. I guess I should have put it on layaway, but it was so expensive, I didn't think anyone else would buy it."

"Thanks, Luanne." Hannah smiled. She had the information she needed. If the scarf was that expensive, Claire would be bound to remember who'd bought it. "How's Suzie?"

"Growing like a weed. She's walking really well now. Drop over and see us sometime. You two are always welcome."

"We will," Hannah promised. Luanne was doing a wonderful job of raising her daughter alone. It had to be difficult because she was supporting her widowed mother, too.

"Do you think she's ready for games yet, Luanne?" Andrea asked.

"What kind of games?"

"Tracey had a round plastic one with little animals on the buttons. If you pressed the picture, it made a sound. The cow went moo, and the pig went oink. I think there was a cat and a dog and a bunch of others."

"Suzie would love something like that for Christmas. Where did you buy it?"

"It was a gift. I still have it around somewhere. If I can find it, would you like it for Suzie?"

Luanne looked a bit uncomfortable. Hannah could tell that she wanted the game for Suzie, but she'd always been too proud to take charity. "Well . . . if you're sure Tracey doesn't want it . . ."

"She doesn't. Tracey hasn't played with it for years. I'll look around and see if I can dig it up. You might have to buy new batteries, though."

"I can do that," Luanne said quickly, and Hannah silently

complimented her sister for her tact. As long as Luanne had to buy something to make the game work, it wasn't exactly charity.

"If I find it, I'll bring it out. There's probably a couple of others, too. She had a lot of those battery games. Is it all right if I bring Tracey with me? She really liked Suzie."

"Sure. Suzie keeps asking about when she's coming out to play again." Luanne picked up the tray and stepped back. "I'd better get back to work. Mayor Bascomb drinks a lot of coffee, and he'll probably need a refill by now."

The moment Luanne had left, Andrea leaned across the table. "We're going to Claire's shop?"

"*I'm* going to Claire's shop," Hannah corrected her after glancing at her watch. "It's almost three. Will you have time to pass out some fliers or something in Danielle's neighborhood before you pick up Tracey?"

"Sure. I'll drop by Kiddie Corner first and take Tracey with me. She loves to go along when I pass out fliers. You want me to talk to Danielle's neighbors?"

"Yes. We need to find out if anyone saw or heard anything unusual between eight-thirty and ten last night."

"I'll do it, but Bill and Mike already canvassed the neighborhood. What good will it do for me to ask the same questions?"

Hannah realized that a little flattery was in order. "Danielle's neighbors might tell you something they wouldn't tell a cop. Besides, you're really good with people."

"Of course I am. I'm a real-estate agent." Andrea preened a bit. "Al's got a stack of calendars in the office, and I could deliver them personally. There's nothing like a freebie to get people talking. You can count on me, Hannah. If Danielle's neighbors know anything at all, I'll find out what it is and tell you at the bake-off tonight."

* * *

Hannah knew she'd been shirking her duties and felt guilty about asking Lisa to mind the shop for another few minutes. "Are you sure you don't mind, Lisa? It shouldn't take me more than five minutes. I just have to ask Claire a question."

"No problem," Lisa reassured her. "The baking's all done, and I like waiting on the customers." Lisa moved a little closer so the customers who were in the shop couldn't hear her. "Is it about Boyd Watson's murder?"

"Yes, but don't mention it. I'm not supposed to be nosing around."

"Mike's orders?" Lisa waited until Hannah had nodded, then she started to grin. "Mike's orders that you don't plan to follow?"

"You got it. And Bill doesn't know that Andrea's helping me, so it's a double secret."

"I wish I could help." Lisa sounded a bit forlorn. "Can you think of anything for me to do?"

Hannah thought about it for a moment. "Keep your ears open in here. Your mother probably told you not to eavesdrop, but in this case, it's for a good cause."

"I'll do it, but the customers probably won't say anything in front of me."

"Yes, they will. If you think someone's talking about the murder, just take the carafe of coffee and stand right next to them. People never pay any attention to the people who bring them coffee. It's like we're invisible."

"I can hardly wait to try it." Lisa looked amused. "I used to wish I could be invisible when I was in grade school. I just hated it when the teacher called on me. Anything else?"

Hannah knew she could trust Lisa and decided to take her into her confidence. "Listen for any young woman who slurs her words. Danielle said that Boyd got a call from someone like that and it made him really angry. It's our only lead at this point."

"I'll listen for her. You go talk to Claire and don't worry about anything here. I've got it covered."

Hannah slipped out the back way and hurried across the snow-covered asphalt to Claire's back entrance. The wind was kicking up, and even though Beau Monde was right next door, Hannah was shivering by the time she got there. She knocked loudly at the back door and waited, hugging her arms around her body to keep warm and wishing she'd grabbed her parka. The meteorologists were predicting that this would be the coldest winter on record. If they weren't exaggerating, Lake Eden residents would have to dress up in survival gear just to retrieve their morning papers.

"Hi, Hannah." Claire unlocked the back door and motioned her in. "Where's your coat?"

"Hanging up at the shop. Do you have a minute, Claire?"

"Sure. It's slow right now. The only one here is Marguerite Hollenbeck, and she's in the fitting room. Make yourself comfortable. I'll just go check on her and be right back."

Claire ducked through the flowered curtain that led to her shop and Hannah sat down on the stool in front of the sewing machine. Claire's back room was tiny and cramped. There were dress boxes stacked in the corner, an ironing board with an iron that was always set up against the back wall, and a small desk that Claire used for her invoices and bills. There was also a large counter stretching the length of the inside wall, and Claire used it for folding purchases, wrapping them in tissue paper, and placing them in lavender Beau Monde boxes. A long dress rack took up most of the remaining space, and it was filled with outfits waiting to be altered. Hannah noticed a vividly striped pantsuit in bright blue, lime green, and shocking pink, and she grinned as she saw the name on the tag. She should have guessed that Betty

Jackson had bought it. Betty always wore vertical stripes. Someone had once told her that they were slimming, but they'd neglected to mention that stripes couldn't fool anyone into thinking that a size twenty-six was petite.

"Marguerite's fine," Claire reported as she ducked back through the curtain. "She took in five dresses and she'll be busy for a while. Your outfit's all right for tonight, isn't it?"

"It's perfect," Hannah reassured her. Claire had provided all of her outfits for the contest, and both of them were grateful to Mr. Hart. Claire was grateful because he'd paid retail and given her an on-screen credit as a bonus. Hannah was grateful because Mr. Hart had told her to keep the clothes, and they were a welcome addition to her limited wardrobe.

"You're wearing the dark green sweater dress tonight?"

"Yes. It's really beautiful, Claire." Hannah knew she'd never have a better opportunity to ask Claire about the scarf. She'd decided not to let Claire know that she was investigating Boyd Watson's murder. She'd taken enough people into her confidence already. "I came about that scarf you had in the window, Claire. I thought it would look really good with tonight's dress, and I want to buy it."

"Which scarf was that?"

"The dark green cashmere with embroidered pink roses."

"Oh, *that* one." Claire's face turned a sickly shade of white and she leaned against her desk. "I'm sorry, Hannah, but that particular scarf is . . . gone."

"Somebody bought it?"

"Not exactly. It . . . uh . . . it faded in the window, and I had to return it to the manufacturer."

"Do you have another one like it?"

"No. The roses were hand-embroidered, and it was one of a kind. That's why it was so expensive."

Hannah watched as Claire picked up a dress box to assemble it. Her hands were shaking, and she couldn't seem to meet Hannah's eyes. There was only one conclusion Hannah could draw from Claire's sudden attack of nervousness. She was lying.

"You're sure no one bought it?" Hannah asked again. "I know you're rushed right before Christmas. You might have sold it to someone and forgotten."

"I didn't forget." Claire looked up and met Hannah's gaze squarely. "No one bought that scarf, Hannah. But you really don't need a scarf with your sweater dress. It's perfect just the way it is."

Hannah decided to give Claire an easy out and stood up to leave. "You're probably right. It was just a thought, that's all. I'd better get back to the shop. Lisa's holding down the fort alone, and we're really busy today."

"And I'd better get back to Marguerite before she thinks I've deserted her." Claire was clearly relieved that their discussion was over and walked over to open the back door. "I'll be watching you on television tonight."

As Hannah raced across the icy stretch of asphalt, she tried to make sense of what Claire had told her. When Claire had said that the scarf had faded in the window, she'd been lying. But when she'd insisted that no one had bought it, she'd been telling the truth. It was a puzzle and Hannah loved to solve puzzles, but this one had her stumped.

Hannah opened the oven door and popped the Apricot Bread Pudding inside. It seemed strange to put something into a cold oven, but she reminded herself that this was show business, and Julia Child had done the same thing on her show. Then, when the stage manager gave her the high sign, Hannah opened the lower oven and took out the dessert she'd baked before the news had begun. She'd spoon it out into dessert dishes while Rayne Phillips gave his weather report and pour on the heavy cream during Wingo Jones's sports news.

She walked over to the refrigerator, opened the door, and faced an array of gleaming shelves. They were perfectly bare. She'd been so busy sleuthing, she'd forgotten to bring the heavy cream!

Someone was waving at her in the wings and Hannah spotted Lisa holding up a quart of heavy cream. The stage manager also spotted her and motioned her forward, but Lisa shook her head. The gesturing went back and forth for a moment, the stage manager crooking his finger in a "come here" signal, and Lisa's head shaking back and forth in refusal.

Hannah bit back a grin as the stage manager ducked down beneath camera range and scuttled off to the place where Lisa was standing. There was a brief discussion, which Hannah could imagine. *"Come on, she needs that cream." "But I can't!" "Yes, you can. You don't want to let her down, do you?"* Finally, Lisa, blushing to the very roots of her light brown hair, walked onto the set and handed Hannah the cream.

Lisa turned her face slightly, so the audience couldn't see it. "He told me to help you deliver the desserts," she whispered.

"Good. I can use the help," Hannah whispered back. "I'll dish them up and you pour on the cream. Then I'll carry the tray and you can hand them to the newscasters, okay?"

Lisa nodded, and they dished up the desserts together. They'd just finished when the stage manager motioned them forward. Hannah stepped out with the tray and Lisa followed her up to the newscaster's long gleaming desk.

"It's a new face, folks," Chuck Wilson commented, and then he turned to Lisa. "Who are you?"

Lisa took a deep breath and Hannah guessed what was running through her mind. She had to answer. She'd look like an idiot if she didn't. "My name is Lisa Herman, and I'm Hannah's assistant at The Cookie Jar."

"Thanks, Lisa." Chuck smiled as he gazed down at the dessert dish. "This looks delicious. What is it, Hannah?"

"Apricot Bread Pudding," Hannah answered, hoping he wouldn't ask Lisa another question before she finished serving the other newscasters. Her hands were already shaking, and if she got any more nervous, Dee-Dee Hughes would end up with Apricot Bread Pudding all over her tight yellow sweater.

It seemed that Dee-Dee was on a mission to call attention to her perfect figure, because the moment after Lisa had served her, she said, "Christmas is coming and I know I have to watch my weight. This dessert isn't low-cal, is it?"

"It's not low-cal, but it has half the calories of a slice of apple pie," Lisa surprised Hannah by answering. "And it would be even less if you served it with milk instead of heavy cream."

Hannah silently applauded Lisa for figuring out the calories. She must have guessed that Dee-Dee Hughes would ask the same question she'd asked last night.

"I've never had bread pudding like this before," Wingo Jones put in his two-cents' worth. "Doesn't it usually have raisins?"

"Yes," Hannah answered this time. "But there's no reason why you can't use other dried fruit."

Wingo looked confused. "I didn't know raisins were dried fruit. I thought they were just . . . raisins. You know, in the box? For quick energy?"

"Raisins are dried grapes," Lisa explained. "Just like prunes are dried plums."

Rayne Phillips licked his lips, then gave the camera a blissful smile. "This is really good, folks! Aren't you going to tell us how to get the recipe so we can make it at home, Chuck?"

Chuck Wilson picked up on his cue and explained that

viewers could call the KCOW switchboard for a copy of Hannah's recipe. There was a final shot of the newscasters with Hannah and Lisa standing behind them, then the news was over.

Hannah waited until they'd gone back to the kitchen set to pack up the supplies. They worked in silence for a moment, then she turned to Lisa. "You were great tonight, Lisa. You said just the right things."

"I did?" Lisa sounded surprised. "I never could have done it if you hadn't asked me to help you dish up. Once I started working, I forgot to be so nervous."

"Was your dad watching at home?" Hannah picked up one of the boxes.

Lisa nodded, hefting the other and following Hannah toward the wings. "Mr. Drevlow came over to sit with him. I really hope he taped it for me. I didn't know that I was going to be on television!"

The stage manager was waiting for them, and he heard Lisa's comment. "Better tell him to stick in a tape for tomorrow night, too. I just got a call from the booth. Mason wants you to help Hannah on camera until the bake-off is over."

"Me?" Lisa's voice squeaked slightly, she was so excited. "Wait until I tell Dad! He's going to be so excited, I'll have to put on *The Sound of Music* to get him to sleep."

The stage manager looked puzzled, but Hannah knew exactly what Lisa meant. Lisa had told her that *The Sound of Music* was like a bedtime story to her dad. Julie Andrews's voice had such a calming effect that Jack Herman never got past the first few scenes before he dozed off for the night.

"It's her voice," Lisa did her best to explain. "It's very soothing. And he's seen it so many times, he already knows the story."

The stage manager looked a bit confused, so Hannah stepped in. "Everybody has a different trick to get to sleep.

My dad used to listen to Wagner. I prefer to read a bad cookbook myself."

"A *bad* cookbook?"

Hannah grinned as she nodded. "A good one makes my stomach growl, and then I *really* can't get to sleep."

Hannah said good-bye to Lisa, who was bubbling over with excitement, and set out to search for Andrea. Tracey was drawing the name of the replacement judge for tonight, and Hannah walked down the hall toward the classroom that Mr. Purvis had designated as the makeup room. She found Andrea standing next to Bill, watching a hairstylist comb and spray Tracey's hair.

Andrea spotted Hannah in the doorway and turned to Bill. "I need to talk to Hannah about the new listing I got this afternoon. Can you bring Tracey to the stage when she's ready?"

"Go ahead, honey," Bill agreed. "We'll join you just as soon as Tracey's finished here."

"What new listing?" Hannah asked, the moment they'd found a private spot in the wings. "I thought you were going to pass out calendars in Danielle's neighborhood."

"I did. That's where I got the listing. Mrs. Adamczak's cousin is selling his place. She got him on the phone, and I talked him into listing it with me. But that's not important, Hannah. I got some new information for us."

Hannah started to smile. She could always count on Andrea. "What is it?"

"You know Mrs. Kalick, don't you? She's the widow who lives at the end of Danielle's block."

"I know her. What did she tell you?"

"She said she was just getting ready for bed when she heard cars in the alley. She wasn't sure about the time, but she knows it was between eight-thirty and ten. Her bathroom window faces the alley, and when she glanced out, she saw Boyd's Grand Cherokee drive by. And there was another car following it."

"Good job, Andrea!" Hannah complimented her. "This could be really important. Did Mrs. Kalick recognize the second car?"

"No. The streetlight's at the other end of the block, and it was dark in the alley. But the moon was out and she noticed that the top of the car was light-colored. She said it was big, like a Cadillac or a Lincoln, but that's not the exciting part. There was a third car, Hannah."

"There was?"

"Yes. It drove up to the mouth of the alley, turned off its lights, and parked right there next to a big pine tree. All Mrs. Kalick could see was the bumper. There were just too many branches in the way."

"How long was it parked there?"

"About fifteen minutes, time enough for Mrs. Kalick to soak her teeth and put night cream on her face. She said that when she looked out again, it was gone."

"Did she tell Bill and Mike about it?"

Andrea shook her head. "She told them about the car that was following Boyd, but she didn't mention the third one."

"Why not?"

"She figured that it was Felicia Berger and her boyfriend. I guess this isn't the first time they've parked under the pine tree with the lights out. Mrs. Kalick likes Felicia, and she didn't want to get her in trouble with her parents. You know how strict the Bergers are, Hannah. They don't approve of makeup or dancing, and they'd skin Felicia up one side and down the other if they found out that she had a boyfriend."

Hannah knew the Bergers, and they were the strictest parents in town. "This could be really important, Andrea, especially if the car *didn't* belong to Felicia's boyfriend. Did Mrs. Kalick tell you anything else?"

"No, but Mr. Gessell did. He lives right next door to Danielle and thought he heard two men arguing in the alley. He was about to go out to see what was the matter when the voices stopped."

"What time was that?"

"He didn't know, but he said he'd just finished listening to the weather report on KCOW radio. I called the station and checked on it, Hannah. The weather report is on every night from eight fifty-five to nine."

"Good for you." Hannah was impressed.

"Your turn, Hannah."

"What?"

"I said, it's your turn. What did you find out about the scarf?"

"Nothing much, but Claire got really nervous when I mentioned it. I told her I wanted to buy it, and she said it was gone, that it faded in the window and she had to send it back."

"But we know that's not true," Andrea pointed out. "Luanne saw it in Norman's office. Do you suppose Claire had two scarves exactly the same?"

"No. She said it was hand-embroidered and was one of a kind. She was telling the truth about that. I could tell. I even gave her a chance to change her story. I said that I knew she'd been busy with the Christmas rush, and I could understand if she forgot who bought it. But she looked me straight in the eye and swore that she didn't sell it."

"So she lied when she said she returned it, but she told the truth when she said that no one bought it?"

"That's right. It just doesn't make sense, Andrea. The only thing that I can think of is that Claire *gave* the scarf to someone and didn't want me to know who it was."

"That's really strange." Andrea frowned slightly. "And it's

even stranger because Claire was so nervous about it. I think that scarf is important, Hannah. We have to find out who has it."

Hannah glanced around and saw Bill and Tracey coming toward them. "I know. We'll talk about this later, Andrea. Here come Bill and Tracey."

"Right." Andrea spotted them and gave a little wave. Then she turned back to Hannah. "You'd better dash over to makeup before the contest starts."

"I've already been there. They did my makeup before the news."

"Well, you need a touch-up," Andrea informed her. "Your lipstick's worn off, your face is shiny, and your hair's all frizzy again."

"Thanks for telling me, Andrea." Hannah tried to keep the sarcasm from her voice as she headed off to the makeup room. Andrea didn't mean to be critical; she just wanted Hannah to look her best. But with two gorgeous sisters like Andrea and Michelle, and a mother who still looked great in a bikini, only her sense of humor kept Hannah from walking down the sidewalks of Lake Eden with a brown paper bag pulled over her head.

Chapter Nine

After Mr. Hart had congratulated the winner, an elderly woman who had baked a delicious poppy seed cake, Hannah turned to Edna Ferguson, the new substitute judge. "You did a wonderful job, Edna."

"Do you really think so?"

"Yes." Hannah smiled at her warmly. "I thought you handled that gingerbread problem very well."

Edna made a face. "I really didn't like it."

"I know, but you complimented the contestant on her brandy sauce."

"It was a good brandy sauce. It just didn't taste right with the gingerbread, that's all."

"That's true." Hannah frowned slightly, remembering the combination of ginger and brandy. "All the same, I thought you were very kind."

"I tried to be. After what happened last night, I figured the last thing we needed was another tactless judge on the panel. They haven't arrested anyone yet, have they, Hannah?"

"I don't think so. I talked to Bill right before the contest, and I'm sure he would have said something."

"Well, I hope they catch him soon!" Edna shivered slightly. "Another murderer loose in Lake Eden! It just gives a body chills."

After she'd said good night to Edna, Hannah collected the boxes from her televised baking and stashed them in the back of her truck. As she drove toward her condo, where Norman had promised to meet her, she thought about what Edna had said. Perhaps Edna suspected that Boyd's murder had something to do with the bake-off. It would explain why she'd been so careful about criticizing the contestants' entries. But Hannah was convinced that the nasty comments Boyd had made as a judge had nothing to do with his violent demise. All of last night's contestants had airtight alibis, and that meant Boyd had been killed for another reason.

Hannah flicked her lights at a car that was weaving a little too close to the center line. It straightened out and she passed it. She was sure that the cars Mrs. Kalick had seen in the alley figured into the picture. So did the argument that Mr. Gessell had heard. The phone call Boyd had gotten on Tuesday was also an important part of the puzzle. Norman's first patient, the mysterious lady who'd left the scarf, could have made it. Hannah intended to ply Norman with cookies tonight and find out exactly who she was.

Hannah opened the door with a smile. For some strange reason, she was really glad to see Norman, and it wasn't only because she was planning to pump him for information about his mystery patient. Norman wasn't the kind of man to give a woman palpitations. To say his hairline was receding would be a kindness, and he was a little plump around the waist. But Hannah knew she could use a dose of his humor after the exhausting day she'd spent, and Norman was a very good friend. "Hi, Norman. I'm really glad you came over."

"You are?" Norman seemed both surprised and pleased at the warmth of her greeting. "Before I forget, you were great tonight, Hannah. And you were pretty, too. That dress made your hair look like copper."

"Thanks, Norman." Hannah decided not to make a crack about copper and how it turned green. It was obvious that Norman had paid her a sincere compliment, and she didn't want to spoil it. "Come on in. It's cold out there and I've got my fake fireplace on."

"Rrrrow!" Moishe also greeted Norman warmly, practically tripping him as he came in the door.

"Hi, big guy. Just a second." Norman slipped out of his coat, draped it over the chair by the door, and leaned down to pick up Moishe. "Have you terrorized any Chihuahuas lately?"

Moishe started to purr so loudly, Hannah could hear it all the way across the room. He didn't even object when Norman carried him belly-up in his arms, an action that would have earned anyone else several deep and painful scratches.

"Would you like some wine, Norman? I've got a bottle open." Hannah winced slightly as she remembered that all she had was the green gallon jug of Chateau Screwtop she'd bought at CostMart.

"No thanks. I'll just take a diet soft drink, if you've got it. Or water, if you don't."

Hannah grinned. Most Minnesotans didn't use the phrase, "soft drink." Although Norman had grown up in Minnesota, he'd lived in Seattle long enough to pick up that expression.

"What did I say to make you grin?" Norman asked.

"Soft drink. Everybody in Lake Eden calls it *pop*. You're in luck, Norman. I just stocked up for the holidays and I've got Coke, Diet Coke, root beer, red cream soda, or 7-Up."

"Red cream soda?" Norman started to smile. "I haven't had that since I was a kid. Where did you find it?"

"CostMart. I bought all they had left. The manager told me they got a partial shipment from some bottling plant in the South. It's not diet, though."

"That's okay. I'll take one anyway."

Hannah was smiling as she went into the kitchen to get Norman's drink. She'd wanted to buy him a small Christmas present, and a case of red cream soda would be perfect. She flipped the cap from the soft drink that looked like strawberry soda but wasn't and poured it out into one of her best glasses. After she'd filled her wineglass from the green jug that was labeled "White Table Wine," she carried both drinks out to the living room.

Norman was sitting on the couch holding Moishe. Hannah's pet was still purring and had a blissful expression on his face. Moishe liked Mike, but he adored Norman. As she settled herself on the other end of the couch, Hannah wondered if her pet knew something that she didn't know.

"Have an Oatmeal Raisin Crisp." Hannah gestured toward the napkin-lined basket she'd set out on the coffee table, filled with some of her "safe" cookies. Moishe didn't like raisins, and that made them cat-proof.

"Thanks." Norman reached for a cookie and took a bite. "These are my favorites."

Hannah laughed. "That's what you said about the Chocolate Chip Crunches. They can't *all* be your favorites."

"Yes, they can. Your cookies are so good that whatever I'm eating is my favorite at the time." Norman stopped and frowned. "Did that make sense?"

"It did to me," Hannah said with a grin. It always made her feel good when someone complimented her on her cookies.

"I like your fireplace," Norman commented. "It looks almost real."

"I like it, too. It provides a lot of heat, and I never have to lay in a supply of firewood. Andrea and Bill have a real one, and he always worries if the fire's still burning when they go up to bed."

"That's why I want a fireplace in the bedroom. You could put on a couple of logs before you went to bed and it would keep the room nice and warm. It'd be romantic, too."

Hannah had always thought a fireplace in the bedroom would be romantic, but she'd never heard anyone else say so before. "You're right, Norman. I don't know why more people don't have them."

"I guess it's because most people don't design their own houses. They buy a house that already exists, or they hire an architect who designs the whole thing. Maybe I should get one of those architectural programs for my computer and try my hand at designing the perfect house."

"That sounds like fun."

"If I get the program, would you like to help me? I don't know anything about kitchens and things like that. I'd probably forget to leave room for the dishwasher or the oven."

"Ovens," Hannah corrected him. "If you plan to do a lot of entertaining, you'll need two. A Thanksgiving turkey fills the whole oven. You need a second oven for the side dishes."

Norman laughed. "See what I mean? I never would have thought of that. It's pretty obvious I need you, Hannah. We'll work on it together and design our dream house."

Hannah began to feel uncomfortable. Designing a dream house with a man she'd only dated three times was pretty serious stuff.

"If it turns out all right, we can enter our plans in the dream house contest they're running at the Minneapolis paper. First prize is five thousand dollars, and we can split it. How about it, Hannah? Do you want to take a crack at it?"

"Sure." Hannah smiled in relief. Norman wasn't proposing anything more than entering a contest, and that would be fun. "You get the program, and I'll think about the perfect kitchen."

They were silent for a moment, watching the flames dance up from the holes in the gas log. It wasn't romantic, but it was cozy. Hannah was reluctant to break the mood by asking Norman about his patient, but she had to find out who'd left that scarf in his office.

"Norman?"

"Yes, Hannah?"

"I'd rather just sit here watching the fire with you, but I need to ask you a question."

"Okay. What is it?"

"It's about your first patient on Tuesday morning, not Luanne Hanks, but the one you didn't write down in your appointment book. Who was she?"

Norman sighed. "I was hoping you wouldn't find out about that. Do you really need to know, Hannah? Or are you just curious?"

"I really need to know. Maybe I don't need to know her name, but I have to find out if you pulled any of her teeth."

Norman looked puzzled. "Why do you have to know that?"

"Because a woman called Boyd Watson at noon on Tuesday and was slurring her words. It really upset him, and it might have something to do with why he was killed. Andrea and I think she might have come from your office with a mouthful of cotton wadding."

Norman sighed again, and Hannah could tell that he was reluctant to answer. It took him a minute, but then he said, "Okay, Hannah. I extracted two teeth in the upper right quadrant. When she left my office at seven forty-five, I told her to keep the packing in until one."

"Was she slurring her words?"

"Yes."

Hannah took a deep breath. "Then I really need to know

who she is, Norman. She's got to be the woman who called Boyd."

"It was Lucy Richards."

"Lucy? Why didn't you write down her name?"

"Because I'm doing her caps off the books. It's a favor for a favor."

Norman looked extremely ill at ease, and Hannah knew that there was a lot he wasn't telling her. Was Delores right about Lucy and Norman? Was he doing a favor for the woman he favored?

"There's nothing wrong with that, Norman." Hannah smiled in an attempt to put him at ease. "I know it's none of my business, but are you . . . uh . . . attracted to Lucy?"

Norman just stared at her for a moment, then he shook his head so hard, Hannah was afraid his brains would scramble. "No! Whatever gave you *that* idea?"

"Just a wild guess." Hannah wasn't about to mention either Norman's mother or hers. "So you're doing a favor for Lucy by giving her some free dental work. What favor is Lucy doing for you?"

For a long tense moment, Hannah didn't think Norman was going to answer. Then he sighed, and said, "She discovered something about me, Hannah, an incident that happened when I was living in Seattle. I do her caps and she agrees not to publish her story. It's simple, really."

"It's *blackmail,* really."

"Actually, it's extortion," Norman corrected her, "but I have to go along with it. She's got me over a barrel."

"Is what Lucy knows really that bad?" The question slipped out before Hannah had time to think about it, and she wished she hadn't asked. It was really none of her business.

"It's bad enough. It wouldn't completely destroy my life if it got out, but the people in Lake Eden would never look at me in the same way again. Mostly, I'm concerned about my mother. She'd be devastated."

Hannah's mind whirled. Norman had admitted that Lucy was blackmailing him. Could she have attempted the same thing with Boyd? And how about Claire? Lucy had waltzed into The Cookie Jar wearing a new coat from Beau Monde, and she owned the expensive scarf that Luanne had wanted to buy for her mother. The story Lucy had told about her book advance had been pure hogwash. Hannah had thought so at the time. And now she suspected that every penny of Lucy's newfound wealth had come from the people she'd threatened to expose.

"Hannah?"

"Yes?" Hannah put her thoughts on hold and turned to Norman.

"I asked you a question. Do you have to know what Lucy found out about me?"

Hannah made an instant decision. "No."

"Are you afraid you won't like me anymore if you find out what it is?"

"You should know better than that, Norman!" Hannah gave him a stern look. "Your secret is *your* secret. But if you ever choose to tell me about it, I absolutely guarantee that it won't change my feelings for you."

"Thanks, Hannah. Maybe I'll tell you later, but not right now."

"That's good enough for me." Hannah did her best to squelch her curiosity over what Norman had done. "Think carefully, Norman. Do you think that Lucy could be pulling this same thing with any other people in town?"

Norman shrugged. "That's certainly possible. As a reporter, she has access to all sorts of information. That's how she found out about me. Actually, I wouldn't put it past her. When she came into my office and demanded that I fix her teeth, I got the impression that she'd done this type of thing before."

"What made you think that?"

"She knew exactly what she was doing. She handed me her story, told me to read it, and said she had a deal for me. And she warned me that if I even thought about turning her in, I'd see it printed on the front page of the *Lake Eden Journal* the next day."

Hannah was surprised at Norman's naïveté. "And you believed her?"

"Of course not. I was sure that Rod would never print it, but she could still tell people, and you know how gossip spreads in a town the size of Lake Eden. Besides . . ." Norman hesitated, ". . . maybe I shouldn't tell you this part."

"Spill it, Norman," Hannah ordered. "I want to know."

"At that point, I was really angry. And I was looking forward to working on her teeth. I figured I could jab her with the dullest needle I've got."

Hannah laughed. She couldn't help it. And she was glad to see that Norman joined in. "Did you?"

"No. Once I started working, my professional side took over. I'm a good dentist, Hannah."

"I'm sure you are."

Norman took a sip of his red cream soda and sighed. "What do you think I should do about it, Hannah? Report it to Sheriff Grant?"

"Not yet. So far, you're the only victim we know about. I think we should try to find some of the others first."

"You're sure there are others?"

"I'm almost positive. Don't forget that Lucy called Boyd. She was probably pulling the same thing with him. And there have to be others. She's been spending money like it's going out of style."

"But how are you going to find her other victims? They're not going to come up and tell you about it. You're going to need proof."

"Proof." Hannah repeated the word and started to smile. "That's it, Norman. Did Lucy have proof that the story she wrote about you was true?"

"Yes. She had a letter from . . ."

"Never mind," Hannah interrupted him. "I don't need to know where it was from. But she did have proof?"

"Yes. The letter she showed me was a copy, but she said she had the original."

"Then all I have to do is find out where she keeps it. There's bound to be things from her other victims there. I can find out who they are and . . ." Hannah stopped speaking in mid-sentence, and a smile spread over her face. "Forget I said that. I must be tired. I don't have to track down Lucy's other victims. All I have to do is steal her proof."

"But how are you going to do that? You don't even know where she keeps it."

"It wouldn't be in the newspaper office. Rod might find it." Hannah began to eliminate the possibilities. "And she wouldn't keep it in a safe-deposit box because the bank's closed at night and she might need it. She wouldn't trust anyone else to keep it for her, it's just too important. And that means it's got to be in her apartment."

"That makes sense, but there's no way Lucy is going to give you permission to search her apartment."

"I wasn't planning to ask for her permission. When is her next appointment?"

"Tomorrow morning at seven. She's coming in early, and I'm doing impressions. But you can't break into her apartment, Hannah. That's illegal."

"So is extortion. How long can you keep her in the chair?"

"I don't know." Norman frowned, and Hannah could tell his morals were kicking up a fuss.

"You've got to cooperate with me, Norman. I'm going to need at least an hour."

Norman gave a sigh and caved in. "I can manage that. I'll mix in extra water with the impression powder and it'll take longer to set. But I can't keep her longer than an hour."

"That's okay. It's a small apartment, and I should be through by then. Call Lucy's number when she leaves your office so I'll know it's time to head out."

"Okay, but I don't like this, Hannah. What if you get caught?"

"I won't," Hannah reassured him, wishing that she had someone to reassure her.

Oatmeal Raisin Crisps

Preheat oven to 375° F.,
rack in the middle position.

1 cup melted butter *(2 sticks—¹/₂ pound)*
2 cups white sugar
2 teaspoons vanilla
¹/₂ teaspoon salt
2 teaspoons baking soda
2 large eggs, beaten *(just whip them up with a fork)*
2 ¹/₂ cups flour *(no need to sift)*
1 cup raisins *(either regular or golden, you choose)*
2 cups GROUND dry oatmeal *(measure before grind-
     ing)*

Melt the butter in a large microwave-safe bowl.
Add the sugar and mix. Then mix in the vanilla, salt,
and the baking soda.

When the mixture has cooled to room temperature,
stir in the eggs. Add the flour and stir it all up. Then
mix in the raisins.

Prepare your oatmeal. *(Use Quakers if you have
it—the cardboard canister is useful for all sorts of
things.)* Measure out 2 cups and dump it in the food
processor, chopping it with the steel blade until it's the
consistency of coarse sand. Dump it in your dough
and mix it all up. *(This dough will be fairly stiff.)*

Roll walnut-sized dough balls with your hands and place them on a greased cookie sheet, 12 to a standard sheet. *(If it's too sticky to roll, place the bowl in the refrigerator for 30 minutes and try again.)* Squish the dough balls down with a fork in a crisscross pattern *(like peanut butter cookies)*.

Bake at 375 degrees for 10 minutes. Cool on the cookie sheet for 2 minutes, then remove the cookies to a wire rack to cool completely.

Andrea likes these and she's never liked raisins— go figure.

Chapter
Ten

Andrea shivered as Hannah parked at the end of Vera Olsen's alley. "Are you absolutely sure we have to do this?"

"I'm sure." Hannah shut off the engine and checked her watch. It was seven o'clock and Lucy should be in Norman's dental chair by now. "Get a grip, Andrea. There's no way we can stand by and let Lucy get away with extortion!"

"I guess not." Andrea shivered again. It was a cold morning, and the wind was whipping up, but Hannah suspected that her sister was more scared than cold.

"Come on, Andrea. We don't have much time. Norman can't keep Lucy in his office forever."

"You're right. Let's get it over with." Andrea pulled her knit cap down over her ears, and opened the passenger door. "I'm glad Tracey spent the night with Grandma. I don't want her to find out that her mother's a criminal."

"You're not a criminal. I take full responsibility for any problems that might come up."

"What problems?" Andrea grabbed at Hannah's arm as they started to walk down the alley. "You didn't say anything about any problems when you called me last night."

Hannah winced. She should have kept her big mouth shut, but it was too late to swallow her words. "I really don't expect any problems."

"How about problems you don't expect? You'd better tell me, Hannah."

"Well." Hannah stopped speaking and sighed. She'd opened a real can of worms, and they were a long way from a fishing hole. "I guess it's possible that we could get caught. If that happens, I'm going to tell Bill that I dragged you here and you didn't know what I was planning to do."

"Oh, sure. And Bill will believe you. I'm beginning to regret this, Hannah."

"Would you rather stay in the truck and wait for me?"

"No. I said I'd help you, and I will." Andrea walked a little faster. "Hurry up, Hannah. We don't want anyone to spot us."

"Nobody will spot us. And if they do, they won't know who we are. That's why I told you to wear Bill's old parka and a cap."

The entrance to Lucy's apartment was off the alley, and Hannah knew the chance of anyone seeing them was slight. There was an outside staircase that was exposed to the elements, but a large evergreen with bushy branches would hide them from the neighbors' view.

When they reached the base of the staircase, Andrea hesitated. "What if she canceled her appointment, Hannah? What'll we do then?"

"We'll knock first. If Lucy answers, I'll say I just dropped by to give her some cookies for her birthday." Hannah held up the bag in her hand. "We'll stay for a while, then we'll leave."

"Lucy's birthday is today?"

"I don't know when it is, but it's a good excuse." Hannah led the way up the wooden stairs. "I can always claim that someone gave me the wrong date. But Lucy's *not* home. Norman told me she's never missed an appointment, and she's always on time."

"Then why did you bring the cookies?"

Hannah sighed, wishing her sister wasn't so alert in the morning. "Because it never hurts to be prepared."

When they reached the landing, Hannah knocked on the door. There was no answer, even when she knocked a second time. She turned to Andrea. "See? I told you Lucy wasn't here. Hold this bag. I need to use my credit card."

"Why?"

"To break in. You just slide it between the doorjamb and the lock and wiggle it around until the latch clicks back."

"That won't work. Lucy's got a dead bolt. See that second key hole?"

Hannah frowned. Andrea was right. There were two locks on Lucy's door. "I don't know how to pick a dead bolt."

"They're not pickable. Bill says a properly installed dead bolt is a homeowner's best defense against burglary." Andrea leaned out, over the rail, to examine the window that was to the right of the door. "Of course a dead bolt doesn't do much good if you forget to lock your combination windows."

Andrea pulled off her gloves and stuffed them into her pocket. She unlatched the storm window panel, slid it up next to the screen, and placed her palms flat against the inside pane. She pushed up, the window rose, and she turned to give Hannah a triumphant grin. "I'll wiggle through. I'm smaller than you are. You hold my parka, and I'll be inside in a second."

Hannah watched as Andrea straddled the rail and grasped the windowsill. She slid forward until her upper body was inside, then braced her feet against the rail and snaked the rest of her body inside. Hannah heard something fall with a crash and a few moments later, the door opened.

"I told you I could do it." Andrea smiled proudly. "But I sure wish Lucy hadn't stacked her dirty dishes in the sink. We owe her a plate and a coffee cup."

Lucy's attic apartment, under the sloping ceiling, consisted of a kitchen, a bathroom, and one large all-purpose room. Andrea and Hannah started with the tiny kitchen and made short work of that. After they'd opened all the cupboards and checked the stove, the refrigerator shelves, and even the inside of the freezer, they headed to the bathroom to search there.

The bathroom took even less time than the kitchen. There were only four drawers in the vanity to search, and they found nothing in the medicine cabinet except Lucy's makeup, a toothbrush, a half-used tube of toothpaste, and an outdated bottle of aspirin.

"Hold on a second." Hannah stopped Andrea as she was about to leave the room. "We didn't check the toilet."

"The toilet?"

"I saw it in a movie once. If you put things in a waterproof package, you can hide them in the tank."

Andrea watched while Hannah lifted the lid and peered inside the tank. "Did you find anything?" she asked.

"Nothing but water and the insides of the toilet," Hannah reported. "I guess Lucy didn't see that movie."

The large, all-purpose room was next. It served as Lucy's living room, office, and bedroom, and Hannah knew they had their work cut out for them.

"Where does that door lead?" Hannah asked, pointing to a door on the wall next to Lucy's bed.

"That's the original attic door," Andrea told her. "Vera brought me up here once when I was in high school."

"Why?"

"We were looking for props for the senior play. Vera had lots of things that belonged to her parents, and they were stored in this attic. Where do you want me to start, Hannah?"

"You take the closet, and I'll search Lucy's dresser."

Andrea had turned to head for the closet when they heard a tapping sound. Both sisters exchanged startled glances and Andrea whispered, "What's that?"

"Someone's knocking at the door," Hannah whispered back.

"What'll we do?"

Hannah could see that her sister was frightened and she reached out to pat her arm. "We won't answer. Relax, Andrea. If they had a key, they wouldn't have knocked."

The knocking went on for several more moments. Then there was silence. Both sisters held their breath, listening for footsteps going back down the stairs, but there was no sound at all. They waited, in an agony of suspense, but then the knocking began again.

"He's really persistent," Andrea whispered.

"I know. You'd think his knuckles would be sore by now." Hannah motioned Andrea down on the edge of Lucy's bed. "Lie low, Andrea. I think I can see the top of the landing from Lucy's kitchen window. I'm going to take a peek."

Hannah tiptoed into the kitchen and hugged the wall as she approached the window over the sink. If Lucy's visitor spotted her, she'd have a hard time explaining what they were doing in Lucy's apartment when Lucy wasn't home. The kitchen curtains were made of yellow cotton, held in place by white-plastic rings on a narrow rod at the top of the window. Andrea had closed them after she'd broken in, but there was a narrow gap between the two panels.

The gap between the panels was perfect. Hannah peeked out and craned her neck to the side. She could see the landing of the outside staircase, but it was empty. There was no one standing at the top of the stairs. Lucy's visitor was still knocking; she could hear the tap-tap-tapping, just like Poe's raven on the chamber door.

Poe's raven? Hannah seized that thought and started to grin. She reached out with both hands, pulled open the curtains, and met the beady gaze of a redheaded woodpecker, caught in the act of pecking away at the wooden frame around Lucy's door. The bird froze for an instant, then startled into flight, winging its way to the big pine tree that grew next to Lucy's staircase.

Hannah laughed as she retraced her steps to Lucy's large room and saw Andrea peeking out from the space behind Lucy's bed. "You can come out, Andrea. It was only a woodpecker."

"A woodpecker?" Andrea looked a little sheepish as she stood up and wiggled out of the tight space, dislodging a pillow in the process.

"There must be bugs in the wood on Lucy's doorframe. When he saw me, he took off."

Andrea gave a big sigh of relief. "All I could think of was Boyd's killer. I pictured him standing at the top of the stairs with a knife in his hand."

"I don't think the killer would be polite enough to knock." Hannah gave her sister a little push toward Lucy's closet. "Let's get going, Andrea. You check out the closet, and I'll handle the dresser and the bed."

Hannah examined every drawer in Lucy's dresser while Andrea tackled the long closet that was tucked in under the eaves on one wall. When she was through with the dresser, Hannah got down on her knees to peer under Lucy's bed.

"She's got a lot of new outfits in here," Andrea called out, her voice muffled by Lucy's clothing. "Most of them still have the tags on, and they're all from Beau Monde Fashions."

Hannah nodded as she stripped off Lucy's pillowcases

and shook them out. "That proves Claire is one of her victims. Lucy can't afford Beau Monde prices. She must have made Claire give them to her for free."

"There's nothing in her closet, Hannah." Andrea emerged from the long, narrow space. Her hair was tangled and she had several cobwebs on her sweater. "Lucy certainly wouldn't win the good housekeeping award. Her closet's a disaster. Where do you want me to look next?"

"Check under the furniture. She could have taped an envelope there. And don't forget the couch. Pat down the pillows and the cushions and feel for anything bulky inside. I'll take her desk."

Lucy had an antique rolltop, and Hannah eyed it with admiration. Delores had one that was very similar, and it was one of her prized possessions. Hannah had helped her haul it home from an antique auction, and Delores had shown her the hidden compartments. Luckily, Hannah remembered where they were.

After she'd searched the contents of all of the regular drawers, Hannah removed one of them and stuck her hand into the space to release the catch. The false back opened with a well-oiled click, and she reached in to pull out a gray envelope with two cardboard circles, one on the flap and the other right below it on the envelope. A length of red string joined them and acted as a seal. "I've got something, Andrea."

Andrea rushed over and watched as Hannah unwound the string. "Where did you find that?"

"In a hidden compartment."

"That envelope is really old-fashioned. I don't think they've made anything like that for years."

"You're right." Hannah began to frown. "It could belong to the original owner of the desk."

Once the string was unwound, Hannah lifted the flap and her eyes widened. There was a sheaf of hundred-dollar bills inside.

"How much is there?" Andrea asked, staring down at the money.

"I don't know. Let me count it." Hannah counted out the money and turned to Andrea. "Two thousand dollars. And it doesn't belong to the original owner of the desk. It's Lucy's, and she hid it in the secret compartment."

"How do you know that?"

"Some of the bills have the big-picture format. It's new money, not old money." Hannah replaced the bills in the envelope and rewound the string to close it.

"What are we going to do with it?"

"I don't know yet. It all depends on where it came from." Hannah reached back into the hidden compartment and pulled out another envelope. It was white, business-sized, and it had the insignia of the Seattle Police Department above the return address.

"What's that?"

"It's the reason Norman's being extorted." Hannah folded it and stuffed it into the back pocket of her jeans. "I'm going to return it to him."

"Aren't you going to open it first?"

"No."

"But don't you want to find out what Norman did?"

"Of course I do, but I'll wait for him to tell me about it." Hannah glanced at Andrea and noticed that her sister had a strange expression on her face. "What is it?"

"You'd open that letter in a heartbeat if it had the dirt on anyone else. You must like Norman a lot more than you say you do."

Hannah let that one pass and reached into the compartment again. It was clear that Andrea suspected romance, and Hannah didn't want to discuss her feelings for Norman. He was a friend, perhaps the best friend she had. That was enough for now.

"What else is in there?" Andrea asked.

"Photos and negatives. I think we found it, Andrea."

"The stash of ammunition for her dirty little schemes?"

"That's a mixed metaphor, but it doesn't really matter. The important thing is, we got the goods on Lucy. Just look at these pictures she took!"

"There's Claire and Mayor Bascomb going into the Blue Moon Motel." Andrea sounded slightly shocked as she glanced down at the first photo. "No wonder Claire gave her all those outfits!"

"Lucy probably put the bite on the mayor, too. He's married, and he wouldn't want his wife to see that picture." Hannah put down the photo and turned to another one. "Here's one that Lucy took at the Lake Eden Inn."

"You're right. That's the front desk in the lobby. Who are those two men?"

"One is Mr. Rutlege, the judge who had to be excused. And the other one is a contestant's husband. I can't remember his name, but he's holding the gray envelope we found."

"The one with the money?"

"It looks exactly the same."

"Did he bribe Mr. Rutlege so his wife would win the contest?"

"He *attempted* to bribe him. Mr. Rutlege must have turned it down, since Lucy ended up with the money."

Andrea thought about it for a moment, then she said, "That makes some kind of sense. Lucy must have seen what happened and confronted the contestant's husband. She probably threatened to make it public unless he gave her the envelope with the money."

"That sounds about right." Hannah pointed to another photo. "Look at this one. Lucy took it through Danielle's kitchen window."

Andrea winced as she stared at the photo. "That's Boyd, and he's hitting Danielle. She looks really scared. And Boyd looks so mean."

"He *was* mean." Hannah's voice was hard. "I can't work up much sympathy for him, Andrea. I know he didn't deserve to die the way he did, but I'm glad Danielle doesn't have to suffer anymore."

"Amen to that. It's a good thing you found this, Hannah. Now we know why Lucy called Boyd. She must have been trying to get hush money from him."

Hannah stared down at the photo for a long moment, her brow wrinkled in thought. "This picture's got to have something to do with Boyd's murder, but I'm not quite sure what."

"I don't know either, unless . . ." Andrea's voice trailed off, and her face turned pale. "Do you think that Lucy . . . I mean, if Boyd wouldn't pay her and she got mad at him, she . . . she wouldn't *kill* him, would she?"

"Not a chance," Hannah reassured her. "Lucy's short and Boyd was tall."

"So?"

"The blow that killed Boyd came from above. Lucy would have had to stand on a stepstool to hit him over the head with that much force."

"Okay. I can see that. But what if Boyd was kneeling and begging for mercy?"

"From Lucy? Boyd outweighed her by a hundred pounds, and we already know he wasn't squeamish about hitting women. If he'd thought that he was in any danger, he would have grabbed Lucy, hammer and all, and thrown her up against the wall."

"True. But maybe Lucy tricked him into kneeling. If she dropped something, and it rolled under the car, Boyd could have been trying to get it back for her."

"That doesn't play either," Hannah informed her. "There were oil spots on the garage floor and Boyd was wearing light gray pants. If he'd been down on the floor, he would have had oil stains on the knees of his pants."

Andrea breathed a big sigh of relief. "I'm glad you told

me that, Hannah. For a second there, I thought we might be searching the apartment of a murd . . ."

"Shh!" Hannah grabbed her arm to hush her. "I hear something!"

"Another woodpecker?"

"Not this time."

Both sisters held their breath, listening intently. They heard the sound of faint footsteps and Hannah turned to her sister. "It's Vera. She's coming up the inside staircase."

"She must have heard us walking around up here." Andrea looked panic-stricken. "We're going to get caught, Hannah!"

"No, we're not. Go hide in the closet. I'll be with you in a second." Hannah gave Andrea a little shove. "Hurry!"

Hannah gathered up the evidence they'd found, shoved it back in the hidden compartment, and replaced the drawer. Then she grabbed their coats, their caps, and the bag of cookies she'd brought and ran for the closet as fast as she could. If Vera Olsen caught them up here, she'd call Bill and Mike to report it. Andrea would get off with a slap on the wrist. Both Bill and Mike would believe that Hannah had been the instigator. But when Mike found out that Hannah had ignored his warning and was actively meddling in his case, he'd lock her up and melt down the key.

Chapter Eleven

"**S**he doesn't know we're here," Hannah whispered, pushing aside the long red skirt that was brushing up against her face.

"How do you know that?"

"If Vera thought we were burglars, she would have called the sheriff's station from downstairs."

Andrea was silent for a moment, then whispered back, "You're right. There's no way a woman Mother's age would confront a burglar herself."

Hannah grinned in the dim light that filtered in from the far end of Lucy's closet where a small window had been installed. Vera Olsen claimed to be fifty, but Hannah had seen her picture in the old 1957 Jordan High yearbook she'd paged through at the school library. Unless Vera had taken a decade to complete her senior year, she was a lot closer to sixty than fifty. But if Vera chose to lie about her age, Hannah wasn't about to bust her for it.

Lucy's closet door was made of knotty pine, and Hannah

poked Andrea and motioned toward a handy knothole. She found another for herself, and both sisters peered out to see what Vera would do. The door next to Lucy's bed opened and Vera stepped in with a smile on her face. She wouldn't be smiling if she thought that she was about to confront a burglar, and Hannah knew they were safe, at least for the present.

Vera crossed the floor and headed straight for Lucy's computer, which was sitting on a table just opposite the closet. She flicked on the switch, fired up the monitor, and sat down in Lucy's chair with her back toward them.

Andrea nudged Hannah. She was wearing a puzzled expression, and Hannah answered with a shrug. Then Hannah pointed to her eye and Andrea nodded her response. Their dialogue was complete without words.

What is she doing, Hannah?

I don't know. We'll have to watch and see.

Okay.

Vera hummed a little tune as the computer went through its warm-up. Since the room was narrow and Lucy's seventeen-inch monitor was sitting on top of the CPU, Hannah and Andrea could see the screen perfectly.

Once the warm-up was complete, Vera used Lucy's mouse to click on the Internet provider icon. There was the sound of a dial tone and the number was dialed automatically with a series of musical beeps. There was a burst of static and another few beeps as Vera was connected, and then a computer-generated voice said, "Welcome Hot Stuff. You've got mail."

Andrea slapped her hand over her mouth to stifle a giggle, and Hannah swallowed hard. The thought of Vera as "Hot Stuff" was enough to make both of them quake with silent laughter. Vera clicked on the mail icon and a message appeared on the screen. It was in large block letters and the two sisters could barely contain their mirth as they read it.

HELLO HOT STUFF—YOU ASKED FOR A PIC-
TURE. HERE IT IS. ALL YOU HAVE TO DO IS CLICK
DOWNLOAD. HOW ABOUT ONE FROM YOU? I'LL BE
CALLING YOU TONIGHT TO HEAR YOUR SWEET
VOICE OVER THE PHONE. LOVE YOU BABY, SILVER
WOLF.

As they watched, Vera downloaded the picture and a
photo of a man with silver hair appeared on the screen. He
was smiling at the camera and waving from the deck of an
expensive-looking sailboat. Vera turned on Lucy's color
printer and printed it out, snatching it from the tray with a
smile. Then she hit the button to reply and typed in a message.

I'LL SEND YOU MY PICTURE TOMORROW. I HAVE
TO FIND JUST THE RIGHT ONE. I PROMISE I'LL BE
WAITING BY THE PHONE FOR YOUR CALL. LOVE
YOU TOO, HOT STUFF.

Hannah didn't risk glancing at Andrea for fear she'd lose
it. Vera Olsen, a woman she hadn't even known was computer literate, was carrying on an online romance.

Once Vera had deleted her personal message and shut
down Lucy's system, she walked across the floor with a spring
in her step and Silver Wolf's picture in her hand. She opened
the door, stepped through, and closed it behind her with a
click.

Neither Hannah nor Andrea said a word as they listened
to Vera's receding footsteps. When they were certain that
she'd gone back downstairs, Hannah nudged Andrea. They
emerged from the closet, glanced at each other, and
promptly burst into a volley of laughter.

"Do you think Vera's really going to send Silver Wolf her
picture?" Andrea asked.

"Why not? She looks good for her age."

"She'd look even better if she got her roots touched up."

"Maybe she will." Hannah chuckled. Leave it to Andrea

to notice something like that. "Come on. It's only seven-thirty-five, but why take chances? Let's grab the evidence and get out of here."

"I've been thinking about that. Won't Lucy notice that it's missing?"

"Of course she will, but she won't know who took it. And she can't very well complain that it's been stolen."

Andrea started to grin. "I guess not. She'd have to explain how she got it in the first place. How about the money? Are you taking that, too?"

"Absolutely. It doesn't belong to Lucy. I'm going to return it to the contestant's husband and give him a lecture about trying to bribe a judge."

Andrea found a stack of large manila envelopes next to Lucy's computer and handed one to Hannah. "Put everything in here, and I'll stuff it under my parka."

"Good idea." Hannah pulled out the drawer, released the catch on the false back, and retrieved the evidence. She dropped it into the envelope and stuck her hand back into the compartment to make certain she hadn't missed anything. "Here's a roll of exposed film. I'd better take that, too. Norman can develop it for us."

Andrea pointed toward several other rolls of film that were scattered on Lucy's desktop. "There's more film here. Do you want to take it?"

"No. If it were important, Lucy wouldn't have left it out. The roll she hid in her secret compartment is different. It could be evidence that she didn't have time to develop."

"Do you want me to check around to make sure we didn't leave anything?" Andrea offered.

"Yes. Check the kitchen and the bathroom, and I'll look around in here."

Hannah had just concluded that they'd left no telltale traces when Lucy's phone rang. Hannah glanced at her watch and frowned. It was only seven-forty, and Norman was supposed to keep Lucy in his dental chair until eight.

"Is it Norman?" Andrea appeared in the doorway looking concerned.

"I don't know yet. We'll have to wait for her answering machine to pick up."

The phone rang a second time, and then a third. Lucy's machine kicked in before the fourth ring and they listened to her outgoing message. *This is Lucy Richards, feature journalist. Leave a number and I'll get back to you.*

Hannah rolled her eyes at the ceiling. The closest Lucy ever got to journalism was writing a description of a wedding dress.

Lucy? Where are you, Lucy? Hannah's eyes widened as she recognized the voice on the speaker. It was Norman, and he sounded nervous. *I came in at seven to do the impression for your caps, and you're over thirty minutes late. I can't hold any more time for you. You'll have to call me to reschedule.*

The answering machine clicked off, and Hannah met Andrea's startled gaze. "Come on, Andrea. It's time to run for the hills."

Hannah's heart was still thudding as they walked into the Rhodes Dental Clinic. They'd left Lucy's apartment on the fly, and only luck had kept them from running into her.

Norman slid back the panel just as soon as he heard the front door open, and he looked very relieved to see them. "It's a good thing you didn't go over to Lucy's! She never showed up for her appointment, and she didn't call to cancel."

"We did go." Hannah was still a little miffed that Norman hadn't called to warn them. "We were just leaving when you called. Why didn't you let us know earlier?"

"I tried to. At first, I thought she was just running late, but at ten after seven, I called Andrea's cell phone." Norman turned to Andrea. "You didn't answer, and I called at least a dozen times."

Andrea sighed. "I left it in Hannah's truck. I didn't want it to ring while we were breaking in. I thought maybe Vera might hear it."

"All's well that ends well," Hannah reassured her. And then she reached into her back pocket and handed Norman the envelope from the Seattle Police Department. "I think this belongs to you?"

Norman's mouth dropped open as he stared down at the envelope. "You found it!"

"That and a lot of other stuff." Andrea reached inside her parka and pulled out the manila envelope. "Lucy had five victims that we know about, and there may be more."

"More?"

"That's right." Hannah opened the envelope and drew out the canister of film. "We found everything in a secret compartment in her rolltop desk, and this roll of film was there, too. It's got to be more evidence, or she wouldn't have hidden it. Can you develop it for us right away?"

Norman glanced down at his appointment book and shook his head. "I'd like to help, but Mrs. Haversham is coming in at eight-thirty. There's no way I can run back home and develop it in less than forty-five minutes."

"I'll take care of Jill Haversham for you," Andrea offered. "I'll just tell her that you had an emergency and ask her to reschedule. And then I'll take her over to the café and treat her to breakfast for being so cooperative. She doesn't get out that much, and she'll love it."

Hannah turned to her sister in surprise. Andrea wasn't usually this generous with her time. "Does this have anything to do with that rental duplex she owns over on Maple Street?"

"Well . . . actually it does." Andrea's face turned slightly pink. "I've been meaning to talk to her about it anyway. I've got a buyer that's interested, and she could make a nice profit."

Hannah grinned. Her sister was as tenacious as a pup with a bone when it came to selling real estate. Andrea had been trying to get Jill Haversham to sell her duplex for at least a year, and she wouldn't quit until she got the listing.

"If you want to take care of Mrs. Haversham, that's fine with me," Norman agreed. "I don't have another appointment until ten, and that'll give us plenty of time. Come on, Hannah. Bring that film, and let's go over to my darkroom to see what you've got."

"Your mother acted really surprised to see me." Hannah stepped into the large walk-in closet that Norman had turned into a darkroom. "And I'm not sure she approved when you told her that we were going upstairs to your room."

Norman laughed. "That was a mistake on my part. I should have said that we were going upstairs to develop a roll of film. It wouldn't have been so bad if Mrs. Beeseman hadn't been visiting. Mother would never gossip about you, but I'm not so sure about Mrs. Beeseman."

"I am. Mrs. Beeseman will tell everyone within a five-mile radius and then some."

Norman gazed at her curiously as Hannah handed him the roll of film. "You don't seem too upset about that."

"I'm not. Anyone who knows me won't believe it. And anyone who doesn't know me doesn't matter."

"That's a good attitude." Norman held the film canister up to the light. "It's black-and-white. It's a good thing I've got a complete setup. I started out in black-and-white because I liked the contrast. It was at least ten years before I added color. Almost everyone uses it now."

"Then it's unusual that Lucy used black-and-white?"

"Not really. She works for Rod, and he doesn't print color very often. It's just too expensive. Lucy probably loaded her camera with black-and-white so that she could develop it in Rod's darkroom. He does his own black-and-white at the office, but he sends all his color work out."

"That makes a lot of sense. Lucy wouldn't want to send any incriminating film out to be developed."

"Sit over there, Hannah." Norman pointed to a stool in the corner. "I'll have to go to total darkness until I have this film in the tank."

Hannah headed for the stool and sat down. She was interested because she'd never been in a darkroom before. "How can you see what you're doing if it's totally dark?"

"I can't. But I've done it so many times before, my fingers know the moves. A lot of photographers use a pouch, but I don't like them. They make my hands sweat. Are you ready for me to turn out the light?"

"I'm ready." Hannah reached out and grasped the edge of the long troughlike sink. She didn't want to lose her balance and fall off the stool when the lights went out.

Norman clicked off the lights, and Hannah glanced around. She knew it was broad daylight, but not even one tiny crack of light penetrated Norman's darkroom. The complete darkness made her feel a bit off-balance, and she was glad that she'd thought to grip the edge of the sink.

Sounds seemed to be magnified in the darkness. Hannah heard a pop and figured that Norman must have taken the cap off the film canister. There was a crinkling noise that was followed by a shushing sound, as if he were unwinding something. She felt a bit disoriented, now that she could no longer judge the dimensions of the room by sight. She reminded herself that this must be how blind people felt and gave thanks that she wasn't sightless.

Hannah heard something clink against metal, perhaps the side of the developing tank. That was followed by a clank that reminded her of a solid metal lid being placed on a saucepot, and then a white light filled the room.

"It's only a hundred watts, but it seems bright, doesn't it?"

"That must be because our pupils are dilated. What do you have to do next?"

"Pour in the developer and agitate it gently for two to three minutes. Then I'll pour out the developer and put in the stop bath."

"Do you have to turn the lights out again?"

"No, the can has a light trap so I can pour liquids in and out."

Hannah watched as Norman poured in the developer. She could smell it, and it had a very pungent odor. He swished it around in the metal canister very gently until his timer went off. Then he poured out the liquid and added some from a different bottle.

"Is that the stop bath?" Hannah asked.

"That's right." Norman swished it around in the tank for a few seconds, then dumped out the stop bath. "Now I have to add the fixer."

Hannah listened as the timer ticked down. She couldn't see the dial from where she was sitting, but when it dinged, she judged that it had taken three or four minutes. "What next?"

"I'm going to open the tank and wash the negatives for five to ten minutes. Then I'll photo flo them and put them in the dryer."

"The dryer?" Hannah asked. "That's not what I'm thinking, is it?"

"No, it's a negative dryer."

"And then we'll have pictures?"

"Not yet. We'll have dry strips of negatives to put under the enlarger to make prints. You'll like that part, Hannah. When the prints come up, it's almost magical."

"But how can you see them if it's dark?"

"It won't be dark. We'll use the safe light for printing. It's kind of orange, and it's dim, but you'll be able to see."

"This is really interesting, Norman. I kind of wish I'd gotten interested in photography. Can you turn on the safe light so I can see what it looks like?"

"Sure."

Norman hit a switch, and the bright light in the room clicked off. It took a moment for her eyes to adjust, but then Hannah became aware of a dim orange glow. It reminded her of sitting in front of a campfire, the one summer she'd gone to camp. She'd hated the cots, the food, and the counselors. She'd never been fond of organized activities, where everyone had to take part and pretend that they were having fun. But the campfires had been wonderful, a glowing circle of light with the dark woods beyond.

"Do you want to learn?"

Norman's question jolted Hannah from memories of ice-cold lakes, mosquito bites, and hot dogs that were both raw and incinerated, a combination that could only be achieved over a campfire. "Learn what?"

"Photography. I could teach you."

Hannah considered it for a minute. "Yes, I'd like that. But don't forget that we have to design our dream house, too."

"It's a good thing I didn't mention *that* to Mother this morning," Norman said with a teasing grin, "or Mrs. Beeseman would probably wear out her phone."

Chapter Twelve

Norman stepped into the kitchen. "Hannah? Your prints are ready."

"Oh, good. I can hardly wait to see how they turned out." Hannah gave Mrs. Beeseman the most innocent smile she could muster. Norman had suggested that she go down and have coffee with his mother and Mrs. Beeseman to practice a little damage control. "It's been nice talking to you, Mrs. Beeseman. And you too, Mrs. Rhodes."

Hannah got up from her chair to follow Norman out of the room and up the stairs. When she was sure they were out of earshot, she asked, "What did we get?"

"Four prints. One of them is good, but I couldn't do much with the other three."

"Only four? What about the rest of the roll?"

"It was blank. Lucy must have rewound the film once she got what she wanted."

Norman opened the door to the darkroom and Hannah

stepped in. The prints were arranged on the counter opposite the sink.

"I put them in order," Norman explained. "The one of Sally Laughlin at the Lake Eden Inn was taken first."

Hannah stared down at the picture of Sally. She was removing a tray of stuffed mushrooms from one of her ovens at the inn. Then she moved on to the second print and started to frown. The lighting was poor, and she couldn't make out much in the background. "What is it?"

"I'm not sure. It looks like some kind of a building. There's a car," Norman pointed it out, "and two men. I tried to lighten it up a little, but I didn't have much success. Lucy used existing light instead of her flash."

Hannah examined the third print. The two men were a bit more visible. While they'd appeared to be standing and talking in the earlier picture, in this one they had assumed a more adversarial stance. She peered down in silence for a moment, then asked, "Do you think the one facing the camera could be Boyd Watson?"

"It's difficult to tell. There just isn't enough light."

Hannah moved on to the final print. The man whose back was to the camera was raising his right arm. There was something in his hand, but Hannah couldn't quite make it out. She stared at it for a moment, then she gasped.

"What is it?" Norman looked anxious.

"This is a picture of Boyd Watson's murder!"

"Are you sure?"

"No, but it makes sense if you think about it." Hannah took a deep breath and let it out slowly. Her heart was pounding so fast, she felt slightly woozy. "I told you about the third car that Mrs. Kalick saw. She thought it was Felicia Berger and her boyfriend, but this changes everything."

"You think it was Lucy?"

"Yes. She must have parked her car and followed Boyd

and his killer down the alley on foot. That's the only way she could have taken these pictures."

Norman moved closer to examine the print again. "You could be on to something, Hannah. It would explain why Lucy didn't use her flash. She didn't want Boyd and his killer to know she was there. Unfortunately, it's all speculation."

"What do you mean?"

"These photos don't really *prove* anything. No one can identify the two men. It's just too dark. They could be anyone in town, or out of town, for that matter. And the background doesn't help us pin down the location. All we can see are two men and a car, and we can't even tell what kind of car it is."

Hannah frowned. "But I'm sure it's Boyd's garage."

"I think you're right, but we can't prove it. These prints could have been taken anywhere. We don't even know *when* they were taken."

"There's no date on the film?"

"No. If Lucy had a date-stamp feature on her camera, she didn't use it. We can't even prove she took them the night of Boyd's murder. We can ask her, but I don't think she's dumb enough to admit that she witnessed a murder and didn't report it."

Hannah thought about it for a minute. "You're right, Norman. Lucy won't tell us anything. And I can't run out to the sheriff's station with these prints. Even if I tell them I found that film in Lucy's desk, it'll be my word against hers, and that's a wash."

"But Andrea was there. She can swear that the film was in Lucy's desk."

Hannah sighed deeply. "That won't work, either. I can't involve her, and it's not just Bill's reaction I'm worried about. Even if Mike and Bill manage to identify Boyd's killer from the evidence we found, the whole thing could be thrown out of court."

"You're right, Hannah. Some smart lawyer for the defense could argue that since the illegal search of Lucy's apartment was performed by the wife and sister-in-law of a detective assigned to the case, it's tainted."

"Fruit of the poisoned tree." Hannah repeated a phrase she'd learned from an episode of *Law & Order*. "I'm stuck between a rock and a hard place, Norman."

"Maybe not." Norman looked thoughtful. "If we can identify the killer without involving Lucy, you might be able to find new evidence. And if Bill and Mike would have discovered it eventually, without the help of Lucy's photos, it'll stand up in court."

Hannah was impressed. "That's brilliant, Norman."

"I watch *Law & Order*, too. So all we have to do is identify the killer and go on from there."

"Right." Hannah sighed deeply. "The killer's back is to the camera, and the prints are so dark, we can't recognize anything about him. We can't prove where the pictures were taken because there's not enough light to see the background. And we don't even know, for sure, *when* the photos were taken. This should be a snap, Norman."

"That's what I like about you, Hannah. You always have such a positive attitude."

Norman laughed, and Hannah glanced at him in surprise before she joined in. Usually people hated it when she was sarcastic, but Norman just gave it right back to her in kind. She glanced down at the counter again, examining each of the pictures in turn. And then she got an idea. "Wait a second. Can we prove that the picture of Sally came first?"

"Of course. The negatives are numbered."

"Then we know that Lucy took the pictures of the murder *after* that shot of Sally. That gives us one end of a time frame. All I have to do is ask Sally when she made stuffed mushrooms, and we'll know when Lucy took her picture."

"That could narrow it down," Norman agreed. "Let's just hope that stuffed mushrooms aren't a regular item on Sally's menu."

Hannah groaned. "Thanks for raining on my parade, Norman. I didn't even think of that."

"I aim to please." Norman picked up the last print, the one they assumed was the murder picture. "I just noticed something."

"What?"

"When the killer raised his arm, his coat sleeve pulled back. See this little spot of light here?"

Hannah nodded. "What is it?"

"I think it's his cuff link. It must have caught the light from the moon, and it's clearer than the rest of the print. Some-times cuff links have initials. Do you want me to try to blow it up?"

"You're a genius, Norman!" Hannah was so excited, she threw her arms around Norman and kissed him on the cheek. Norman looked slightly startled, but he hugged her back.

Hannah sat on her stool while Norman enlarged that section of the negative. He was right. When the print came up, it *was* like magic.

"Let me dry it. It'll only take a minute." Norman flicked on the bright light and led the way to something he said was his print dryer, a huge metal drum with a shiny surface.

"How long will it take?"

"Just a couple of minutes. This is a commercial drum dryer, and it's fast. I picked it up from a studio in Seattle when the owner retired." Norman stuck the wet print face-down against the metal drum. "When the print slides off, it's dry."

The shiny drum started to revolve like a Ferris wheel, and

Hannah watched until the print fell off and landed in the canvas sling below the dryer. "Can I pick it up now?"

"Yes. Bring it over to the counter, and let's take a good look at it. I think we may have something, Hannah."

Hannah carried the print to the counter, and her heart raced as she examined it. The killer's cuff link was distinctive, a side view of a horse's head with something that looked like a diamond for the eye. "That's an antique design."

"How do you know that?"

"Mother collects antique jewelry, and she's got all sorts of reference books. Let's get back to the clinic, Norman. I'm going to hop in the truck and drive out to Sally's to find out about those stuffed mushrooms. And then I'm going to track down Lucy and have a little talk with her."

"Careful, Hannah," Norman warned her. "You can't ask her about the photos."

"I know, but we can talk about antique jewelry. And I can mention that Mother's interested in buying a pair of antique cuff links with horse heads on them."

"Won't that tip her off?"

"How could it? If I catch her before she goes back to her apartment, she won't know that her film is missing. She never got a chance to develop it, and she doesn't know that she got a clear picture of the killer's cuff link. Don't forget that we had to blow it up to see it."

Norman thought about it for a minute. "You're right. It would have been just a speck of light through the viewfinder."

"I figure that if Lucy tailed him all the way to Boyd's house, she could have noticed his cuff links. If she did, she might tell me his name."

"You think Lucy would actually tell you the name of the killer?"

"Why not?" Hannah shrugged. "She always brags about

being so observant, and that'll give her a chance to show off. She'll never suspect that I know the man with the antique cuff links is Boyd's killer."

"It *could* work, I guess." Norman sounded doubtful.

"It's worth a shot." Hannah cleared her throat and looked Norman straight in the eye. "About that envelope I gave you . . . I just want you to know that I put it in my pocket the moment I found it. And I didn't take it out until I handed it to you."

"I'm surprised you're still alive, Hannah."

"Of course I'm alive." Hannah was puzzled by his abrupt change of subject. "Why wouldn't I be?"

"I thought your curiosity would have killed you by now." Norman laughed. And then he put his arms around her and gave her a big hug.

Hannah whizzed past the park and approached Jordan High at thirty miles an hour. The streets were deserted, she wasn't driving recklessly, and it was a real treat to speed through town.

"You'd better slow down, Hannah. You're five miles over the limit."

"I know." Hannah flashed her sister a saucy grin. "But Herb Beeseman's guarding the door to the auditorium, and he can't give me a speeding ticket."

"Knowing Herb, he's probably set up a speed trap. I heard that the city council voted to use the proceeds from this month's traffic violations for the children's Christmas party."

Hannah considered it for a split second, then lifted her foot from the accelerator. "You could be right. And Mother will never let me live it down if I get a ticket, especially when I gave her such a rough time about hers."

"Are you sure Lucy's at the school?"

"No, but Rod told me she was working on a story about

today's bake-off contestants. The way I see it, there are only two places she could be."

"The school, or the inn?"

"That's right. If Lucy's not at the school, she'll be out at Sally's. And we have to go there anyway to find out when she served those stuffed mushrooms."

They rode in silence for another few blocks, then Hannah noticed that Andrea was shivering. "Sorry about the heater. I've got it cranked up all the way, but this is all the heat it puts out."

"It's okay. I'm not that cold."

"Then why did you shiver?"

"Because I've been thinking about those murder pictures. This might be completely off the wall, Hannah, but something just occurred to me."

"What?" Hannah turned into the teachers' parking lot and found a space near the kitchen door. She'd shown the prints to Andrea, and Andrea had agreed that they looked like pictures of Boyd's murder.

"Why didn't Lucy turn her film over to Bill and Mike? If I got close enough to a murderer to take his picture, I'd head for the sheriff's station as fast as I could."

"So would I. But Lucy didn't do that. What's your point?"

"That roll of film was with her other blackmail stuff, right?"

"Extortion stuff," Hannah corrected her.

"Okay, extortion stuff. But it was there in the secret drawer."

"Right." Hannah shut off the engine and turned to stare at Andrea. "What are you thinking?"

"I'm thinking that maybe Lucy is planning to blackmail Boyd's killer."

Hannah's mouth dropped open. That possibility had never even crossed her mind. She didn't think it had occurred to Norman either. He would have said something.

"It was just a thought." Andrea sounded very defensive. "I'm just throwing things out for you to consider."

Hannah was silent for a long moment and then she let her breath out in a whoosh. "That's not as weird as it sounds, Andrea. I think you could be on to something."

"You do?" Andrea looked very surprised. "But Lucy ought to know that blackmailing a murderer is too dangerous."

"Maybe, but her confidence level has got to be high right about now. She's got a new car, a new wardrobe, a bunch of money, and Norman is doing her caps for free. Lucy may figure it's time to move on to something bigger that'll net her a lot more profit."

"But that's . . . crazy!"

Hannah just nodded and left it at that.

Andrea stared at her for a moment, then she sighed. "You're right. We both know Lucy's crazy for sneaking around and taking those pictures in the first place. But do you really think she's *that* crazy?"

"I don't know." Hannah opened her door and motioned for Andrea to get out of the truck. "But I think we'd better find Lucy. I don't know how we're going to warn her off without mentioning that stash of evidence we confiscated, but we've got to try. If she puts the bite on Boyd's killer, she'll be in more trouble than a long-tailed cat in a room full of rocking chairs."

 **Chapter Thirteen**

"Sorry, Hannah. I haven't seen Lucy since last night. If she shows up, I'll tell her you're looking for her."

"And you've been here all day?" Andrea asked.

"Right here." Herb patted his chair. "I took a break a couple of minutes ago, but I locked the door before I left. Do you want me to take those boxes in for you, Hannah?"

"That would be great. Thanks, Herb." They set down the boxes they were carrying, and Hannah handed Herb the bag of cookies she'd brought for him. "This is Lisa's new recipe. She calls them Cherry Winks."

Herb opened the bag and peered inside. "It's a good name. The cherries on top look like they're winking. What are you baking tonight, Hannah?"

"Hawaiian Flan."

"What's that?"

"Baked custard with pineapple," Andrea explained. "Hannah learned to make it when we were in high school, and it's my favorite dessert."

"Sounds good. I like pineapple. Say . . . why don't you ever use it in your cookies?"

"I don't know." Hannah thought about it. She'd made cookies with raisins, dates, and bananas, but she'd never considered using pineapple. Actually, it wasn't a bad idea. "Thanks for the suggestion, Herb. I'll have to see what I can come up with."

"I think pineapple cookies would be really popular, especially if they tasted like pineapple upside-down cake. Do you think I should mention it to Lisa? Her pineapple upside-down cake is even better than Mother's."

"Good idea." Hannah stifled a grin. If Marge Beeseman ever found out that her youngest son liked Lisa's cake better than hers, there'd be a full-scale war in Lake Eden. "We've got to run, Herb. It's turning out to be a full day. I promised to go out to the hospital to see Danielle. Then we have to make a flying stop at the Lake Eden Inn and get back to the shop in time to bake for the Regency Romance Club meeting this afternoon."

"Mother told me they're doing a reading in costume, and Lucy's supposed to be there to take pictures for the paper. I just hope she shows up."

"Why wouldn't she?"

"When I saw her at the bake-off last night, she said she was working on a big assignment."

Hannah was almost afraid to ask, but she did. "Did Lucy tell you anything about it?"

"Not really"—Herb shook his head—"but she did say that if it worked out the way she thought it would, she'd earn enough money to pay off that new car she's leasing."

They said their good-byes and walked back out to Hannah's truck in silence. Hannah was hoping that Lucy's big assignment didn't have anything to do with confronting Boyd's killer, and she suspected that Andrea was hoping the same.

* * *

After a brief stop at the hospital, they got back on the road again. Hannah had replaced the offensive cross-stitch sampler with a picture she'd cut out of a magazine. Cows grazing in a field might not be fine art, but they were innocuous.

The Lake Eden Inn was only two miles from the hospital, and they made good time. When they walked into the rustic bar, the second day in a row, Hannah felt a sense of déjà vu. The lunch buffet was out, the guests were at the same tables, and Sally was sitting on the same barstool, with her feet propped up in exactly the same position. The only difference was the color of her maternity top. Sally's choice today was electric blue with white block letters proclaiming, "MOTHER AT WORK."

"Hi, Sally." Hannah walked over to her with Andrea in tow. "We didn't come to free-load again, I promise."

Sally laughed. "Help yourselves. I always make a ton of food, and that beef Stroganoff won't stand up to reheating. It's got too much sour cream."

"Does your beef Stroganoff have mushrooms?" Andrea asked, tearing her glance away from the buffet table.

"Four different kinds." Sally ticked them off on her fingers. "Champignon, shiitake, oyster, and kikurage."

Hannah noticed that Andrea was listing in the direction of the beef Stroganoff. Andrea never ate breakfast, and she was probably starving by now. "Speaking of mushrooms, when is the last time you made your stuffed mushrooms with bread crumbs and sausage?"

"I served them on Wednesday for the five o'clock happy hour," Sally told her, "but I don't think I'll do it again. They're just too much work at the last minute."

Hannah filed that away for future reference. "Stuffed mushrooms aren't a regular item on your menu?"

"No, I only make them for special occasions. They don't

hold up very well on the warming table, and they have to be served while they're hot. I probably won't make them again until my annual Christmas cocktail party. You're coming, aren't you?"

"I wouldn't miss it," Hannah said.

"Me, neither." Andrea started to smile. "You always throw such a great party, and your food is just incredible."

"You sound hungry. Why don't you hit the buffet table?" Sally suggested.

Hannah glanced at Andrea. Her list toward the food table had grown more pronounced. "Okay, but are you sure you have enough?"

"I'm sure. Go fill your plates and come back here, just like yesterday."

"With one difference." Hannah was insistent. "You have to let us pay."

Sally shook her head. "Don't be silly. You'll be doing me a favor by taking my mind off Dick Junior. He's kicking up a fuss today. Dick says he thinks I'm going to give birth to a black-belt karate expert."

It didn't take Hannah or Andrea long to load up on food. Once they'd returned to the bar with their overfilled plates, Hannah got down to the business at hand. "I'm trying to find Lucy Richards. Have you seen her today?"

"No." Sally shook her head. "She was here for the wrap party after last night's show, but I haven't seen her since."

Andrea swallowed her bite of beef Stroganoff, then asked, "Do you know what time she left?"

"She was still here when I crashed around eleven. I just couldn't keep my eyes open. You should ask Dick. He didn't close until one."

"That late?" Hannah was surprised. "I thought you usually closed at midnight."

"We do, but there were a lot of people here, and we make a good profit on the drinks. Dick said that everyone was having such a good time, he didn't have the heart to flick the lights."

"Were there many people who drove out from town?" Andrea asked, spearing another forkful of Stroganoff.

"Yes, but they didn't stay late because they had to go to work in the morning. The only townspeople who were here when I left were Mayor Bascomb and his wife, Mason Kimball, Cyril Murphy, and your mother and Mrs. Rhodes."

Andrea almost choked on a shiitake mushroom. When she'd managed to swallow she asked, "Mother was here that late?"

"That's right. She was dancing with that handsome KCOW anchorman. I can't remember his name. And Mrs. Rhodes was sitting at the table with that cute guy who does the weather."

"Chuck Wilson and Rayne Phillips?"

Sally nodded, and Hannah's eyes widened. She wondered what Norman would say if he knew that their mothers had been out bar-hopping with two handsome men who had to be almost thirty years younger than they were.

"Dick said the real diehards were the contestants and some of the KCOW television people. They're all staying here, and they don't have to worry about driving home." Sally slid off her stool. "Time to put out the dessert buffet. Do you want me to send Dick out so you can ask him about Lucy?"

"Yes, if you can spare him."

"No problem. We took the easy way out today. Of course, you already know that."

"I do?"

"I guess you don't." Sally gave her a big grin. "Well, you're going to be in for a big surprise when you see what we're serving."

After Sally had left, Hannah turned to her sister with a puzzled look. "What was she talking about?"

"I don't know, but that's not important. What are we going to do about Mother and Chuck Wilson?"

"Nothing."

"But this is a crisis!" Andrea took a sip of water and fanned her face with her napkin. "Think about it, Hannah. What are people going to say when they find out that Mother is dating Chuck Wilson? He's young enough to be our brother!"

Hannah was amused at the role reversal. Andrea was acting like a mother who'd just discovered that her child had done something perfectly dreadful.

"We'd better have a mother-daughter talk with her, Hannah. This just isn't . . ." Andrea struggled to find the right word, ". . . appropriate for a woman of her age!"

"Relax, Andrea. Sally didn't say that Mother was *dating* Chuck Wilson. She just said that they were dancing."

Andrea thought about it for a moment. "You're right. I guess dancing is okay, as long as it wasn't a slow dance. Do you think we should ask Sally what kind of dance it was?"

"I think we should butt out. Mother's old enough to know what she's doing." Hannah saw Dick heading their way. "Forget about it, Andrea. It's probably nothing anyway. Here comes Dick, and we've got questions to ask."

Five minutes later they had some of their answers. Lucy had arrived with the rest of the crowd who'd come from the Jordan High auditorium after the show. As far as Dick could tell, she hadn't been with anyone in particular and had spent a couple of hours table-hopping, talking to the contestants and members of the KCOW television crew. He'd served her one drink, a glass of white wine, and she'd refused a refill. Lucy had told him that she was working on a big story and wanted to keep her head clear. Dick didn't know if she'd gotten her story, but he said that she'd been smiling when she left.

"When was that?" Andrea asked.

"Around midnight. I saw her go out the door."

"Was she alone?" Hannah stepped in to ask the question.

"She was when she went out the door."

Hannah started to frown. "Could someone have followed her?"

"Sure, but I wouldn't have noticed. It got busy right then, and I had my hands full."

"Do you know if she drove out of here in her own car?"

"She did. Right after she got here, someone came in and told her she'd left on her lights. Lucy handed me the keys and ordered me to run out to the parking lot to turn them off. I almost told her to stuff it, but I wanted to see her new car."

"Is it possible she rode home with someone else and picked up her car this morning?" Hannah asked her final question.

"No. Mayor Bascomb's battery was low, and I went out to give him a jump start at twelve-thirty. I know Lucy's car was gone by then. She was parked right next to him, and I backed into her space to connect the cables."

"Thanks, Dick. That's all I need to know." Hannah dismissed him with a smile.

"Okay, but I've got a question. Why are you so interested in Lucy?"

"I need to track her down," Hannah answered truthfully. Then she crossed her fingers. "Nobody's seen her since last night, and I've got to check that story she's doing about the bake-off. She misquoted me last week, and I don't want it to happen again."

"Well, good luck finding her. I've got to go. The dessert cart's heavy, and I don't want Sally to push it out here by herself."

"Bill was the same way when I was pregnant with

Tracey," Andrea said when Dick had left. "He even came out to the car to bring in the groceries for me."

Hannah smiled. "That's nice. Does he still do it?"

"Are you kidding? Now he's glued to the television, and I have to lug in the sacks all by myself. He'll help if I ask, but he sure doesn't volunteer anymore." Andrea looked thoughtful. "He really was a lot more considerate when I was carrying Tracey. Maybe there's something to that barefoot and pregnant thing."

Hannah laughed and slid off her stool. "Only if you live on a tropical beach and have an unlimited supply of disposable diapers. Come on, Andrea. Let's check out that dessert buffet and see why Sally is standing there grinning like the Cheshire cat."

There was a crowd milling around the dessert buffet, and it took them a while to get close enough to see what was there. Once Hannah, who was five inches taller than her petite sister, managed to sneak a peek over someone's shoulder, she gave a soft chuckle.

"What is it?" Andrea tapped her on the arm. "This isn't fair, Hannah. You can see and I can't."

"That's just one of the advantages of being tall."

"What is it? Tell me."

"It's my cookies. Sally's got six different kinds, arranged in baskets, and there's ice cream and all sorts of toppings to make your own sundaes."

"And you didn't know?"

"No, I didn't go in this morning. I just called Lisa and asked her if she could handle the shop alone until this afternoon. When I left my condo, I drove straight out to pick you up so we could get to . . ." Hannah stopped and glanced around her. No one appeared to be listening to them, but it paid to be careful. ". . . to that *apartment* in time."

Andrea looked puzzled for a moment. "Oh, yes. *That* apartment."

"Do you want to stand in line for some cookies and ice cream?"

Andrea shook her head. "No thanks. Besides, you've got cookies in the car. Let's go find Mr. Rutlege. We've got to talk to him about . . ." Andrea stopped and cleared her throat, ". . . uh . . . that *thing* we wanted to ask him about."

By one o'clock, they were ready to leave. They'd learned everything they could at the Lake Eden Inn. Hannah stopped at the front desk and turned to Andrea. "Try calling Lucy's number once more. Maybe she's home by now."

"What am I going to say if she answers?"

"Ask her if we can come over."

"But she'll want to know why." Andrea started to frown. "What do you want me to tell her?"

"Say that we're looking for a piece to round out Mother's collection of antique jewelry. Flatter her a little and tell her that she's the only person in town who might be able to help us. That should do the trick."

"Okay."

As Andrea picked up the phone and punched out Lucy's number, Hannah thought about the information they'd learned from Jeremy Rutlege. He'd admitted that Mrs. Avery's husband had tried to bribe him, but that he'd turned down the money. Hannah knew that was the truth. Lucy had hidden the bribery money in her desk, and it was now in the bottom of Andrea's leather purse. Mr. Rutlege had also told them that he'd talked to Mrs. Avery about it and she'd convinced him that she hadn't known anything about the bribe. And then, when his tooth had acted up and he'd had to excuse himself from the judging, Mr. Rutlege had decided not to report it. As it turned out, Mrs. Avery, the contestant who'd baked the nut-filled pastry, had been eliminated anyway.

"She's not home." Andrea interrupted Hannah's thoughts.

"I don't think she's been home all day. There were fifteen messages on her answering machine."

"How do you know that?"

"I counted. Lucy's got one of those machines that beeps for each message and there were fifteen beeps. I didn't leave a message from us. I just counted the beeps and hung up."

"Good work, Andrea." Hannah patted her on the back, and they went out the door and started to walk to the parking lot. "If Lucy hasn't been home, she doesn't know that her evidence is missing. That means she'll be less suspicious when I run into her at Mother's Regency Romance Club meeting."

"What time is that?"

Hannah glanced at her watch. "They start at three, but I don't have to be there until three-fifteen, and I have to bake six dozen Cocoa Snaps first. It's ten after one now, and that should give me plenty of time. Do you want to come down to the shop and help me?"

"Me?" Andrea looked shocked at the suggestion. "You know I don't bake."

"Then just sit at the workstation and talk to me while I do it. We can work out a game plan for me to use with Lucy."

By this time, they'd arrived at Hannah's truck. Hannah unlocked it, and Andrea slid in. Hannah noticed that she was smiling as she wiggled past the gearshift and buckled herself into the passenger's seat. "What's so funny?"

"Nothing. I'm just glad that you invited me down to your shop." Andrea's smile grew bigger. "You're trying to tell me that you need me, aren't you, Hannah?"

"Of course I need you." Hannah slid behind the wheel. Andrea seemed so grateful to be needed that she felt a pang of regret for all the harsh things she'd said to her when they were growing up. Andrea had deserved every one of them, but Hannah wished she'd been more tactful. Instead of calling Andrea an idiot for flunking her math test, she could have offered to help her study. And instead of yelling at

Andrea for taking too long in the bathroom, she could have helped her rig up a makeup table in Andrea's room. Tact had never been one of Hannah's strong suits. She knew that. It still wasn't, but she was learning, and she turned to her sister with a smile. "As far as sisters go, you're not half-bad."

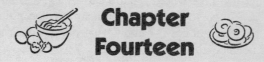

Chapter
Fourteen

Once Hannah had checked in with Lisa and thanked her for the extra work she'd done to fill Sally's order for the dessert buffet, she conducted a poll of the customers in her coffee shop. None of them, including Rod, who'd come in on a late lunch break, had seen Lucy all day.

"Nothing?" Andrea asked, as Hannah came back to the counter.

"No sightings. Come on, Andrea. I've got to bake." Hannah took Andrea back to the bakery and got her settled on a stool with a mug of coffee and a plate of Pecan Chews.

"I can help you if you tell me what to do," Andrea offered.

"I'll let you know." Hannah headed off to the cooler to retrieve the chilled bowls of Cocoa Snap dough that Lisa had mixed up. She plunked them down on the surface of the stainless-steel work counter and watched as Andrea finished her third Pecan Chew. "Hand me that cookie scoop, will you? The medium-sized one."

Andrea found the right scoop and handed it over. "Anything else? I really want to help you, Hannah."

"You can . . . wait . . . let me think." Hannah caught herself just in time. She'd been about to ask Andrea to help her scoop out dough, roll it into balls, and dip the balls in white sugar, but that task would require explaining, and Hannah didn't have time to instruct Andrea in the fine points of cookie baking right now. "I know what you can do. You can get that notebook by the sink and write down all the facts we learned today. We need some kind of record."

Andrea jumped up to retrieve the notepad. "Okay. I'm good at taking notes. What shall I write down first?"

"Make a list of Lucy's victims. We'll have to talk to them all eventually to find out exactly what she extorted from them. Start with Norman."

"Okay." Andrea wrote down Norman's name. "He was just doing her caps, right?"

Hannah nodded as she rolled cookie balls and placed them in the bowl of sugar. "Then there's Claire. We know she gave Lucy clothing."

"And Mayor Bascomb, but we don't know what he gave her."

"It's probably money, but I'll have to check. Just put down a question mark for now." Hannah placed twelve sugar-coated dough balls on a cookie sheet and flattened them with a spatula. "Write down the contestant's husband next."

"Mr. Avery?"

"That's right. Put down cash after his name, but don't specify the amount."

Andrea looked up with a puzzled expression. "But you counted the money. You said it was two thousand dollars."

"It was, but there could have been more. Lucy may have spent some of it. I'll have to talk to Mr. Avery to find out how much was in the envelope when he gave it to her."

"Okay." Andrea put a dollar sign next to Mr. Avery's name and added a question mark. "Who's next?"

Hannah carried two cookie sheets to the oven and slid them inside. She set the timer and came back to the work-station to roll more dough balls. "Put down Boyd's name. We're not sure if Lucy actually succeeded with him, but I'll have Danielle check her bank records to see if there's any money missing."

"She should check her credit-card bills, too. Boyd might have charged something for Lucy or taken a cash advance."

"Good point. Jot down a note so I don't forget to tell her." Hannah filled two more cookie sheets and carried them over to her second oven. When she came back to the workstation, she saw that Andrea was frowning. "What is it?"

"I was just thinking about Lucy's evidence. I know you gave back Norman's letter, but are you going to turn the rest of it over to Mike and Bill?"

"I don't know yet. I guess I'll have to, if it has anything to do with Boyd's murder."

"But what if it doesn't?"

Hannah thought about it for a moment. "I guess that'll be up to Lucy's victims. When I return the photos to them, I'll ask if they want to prosecute."

"They won't."

Andrea sounded very definite, and Hannah glanced at her. "They might. What Lucy did is illegal."

"And what *they* did is embarrassing. Claire and Mayor Bascomb won't want his wife to find out about their affair. That's why they gave Lucy what she wanted in the first place."

"That's true." Hannah started to roll more dough balls.

"And Norman won't prosecute. You said he told you that his mother would be devastated if she found out what was in that letter."

Hannah picked up the bowl with the dough balls and sugar and shook it to coat them. "You've got a point. Mr. Avery won't want to prosecute either. And Boyd's dead, so he can't."

"Then Lucy's going to get away with it?"

Hannah shrugged. "Maybe. If her victims choose not to file charges, there's nothing we can do about it."

"But that's not fair!" Andrea assumed an expression very similar to the one that Hannah had seen on Moishe's face the only time she'd tried to give him a bath. Her sister was spitting mad and outraged. "We've got to do something, Hannah. We can't let Lucy get off scot-free!"

Hannah certainly agreed with her sister's sentiments. It wasn't fair to let Lucy get away with extortion. "Maybe we've already done something. Lucy won't know who broke into her apartment and took her stash of evidence. She'll wake up every morning, wondering when the other shoe is going to drop. And when her victims stop paying her off, she'll really start to sweat."

"I get it." Andrea started to smile. "Lucy won't know if they're planning to prosecute her. Being locked up in jail must be awful, but at least you know when you're going to get out. Lucy'll have this sword hanging over her head."

The timer beeped, and Hannah got up to take the first two pans of cookies from the oven. She set them on the bakers' rack to cool for a moment and slid in two more.

"That must be exactly how her victims felt," Andrea went on. "Even if they gave Lucy what she asked, they could never be sure that she wouldn't turn around and expose their secrets anyway. I know they shouldn't have done what they did, but it's minor compared to what Lucy pulled."

Hannah stared at Andrea in surprise. Her sister looked as grim as a judge preparing to hand down a death sentence. Andrea really had it in for Lucy, and it wasn't like her to be this vindictive. "Does this have anything to do with the phone call you got yesterday morning?"

"That's part of it." Andrea's grim look got a lot grimmer. "Lucy should have known better than to call me that early on my day off!"

Hannah stood behind the refreshment table and watched as Gail Hanson, Bonnie Surma, and Irma York headed off to the ladies' room with bulging garment bags containing their costumes. She'd dropped Andrea off at home after they'd finished baking the cookies. They planned to meet at Hannah's bakery later, just as soon as Hannah was through with her catering and Andrea had finished showing the farmhouse she'd scheduled for three.

The Cocoa Snaps had turned out just fine, despite Andrea's "help." When Hannah had run out of things for Andrea to write in the notebook, her sister had insisted on rolling dough balls for her. Most of Andrea's had been lopsided, but Hannah hadn't wanted to embarrass her by rerolling them, and she'd baked them without saying a word. Now, she stashed them on the bottom layer of the platter and piled three layers of perfectly round cookies on top. If the members of the Lake Eden Regency Romance Club were hungry enough to eat their way to the bottom layer, they'd just have to put up with Andrea's misshapen efforts.

When the coffee was perking, both caf and decaf, and the water for tea was simmering, Hannah set out cups next to the urns and stood back to assess her work. She had cream, sugar, and artificial sweetener, as well as a small cut-glass bowl filled with lemon wedges for the ladies who took lemon with their tea. Everything was ready. Once the reading was over and the brief meeting had concluded, she could serve.

Hannah looked up and the sight that greeted her was almost enough to make her break out in laughter. Bonnie, Gail, and Irma had come back in costume, and they were a sight to behold.

Delores had told her a bit about the reading while Hannah had lugged in her supplies. There were only two main characters, a young miss who'd lost her memory in a carriage accident, and a captain on Wellington's staff who claimed to be her fiancé. Bonnie, who had short dark hair and a slim figure, was playing the young miss. Gail, a full-figured woman with curves to spare, was playing her intended husband. Somehow, Hannah managed to keep a straight face as she stared at the odd pairing. If she'd been consulted about the casting, she would have reversed their roles. Gail was practically popping the buttons on the front of her red regimental jacket, and her white pants were straining at the seams. She'd stuffed her long blond hair up under a military-style cap that Hannah suspected was far from authentic for the period, but she'd forgotten to take off her diamond earrings.

Bonnie looked equally ridiculous in a sprigged muslin traveling gown with a high neck and bustle. The bodice of the dress had been cut for a bustier woman and drooped down in folds to her waist. She'd attempted to look more feminine by adding a straw hat decorated with streamers and a red-plastic bird, but the hat was too large and kept slipping down over one eye.

The scene was set in a carriage, and Hannah had to admit that they'd done that well. Two piano benches draped with green velvet served as the carriage seats, and a canopy of black material had been draped in an arch that rose around and above them to simulate the sides and top of the coach.

Irma York was in costume as well, and Delores had explained that she was their "tiger," the boy who hung on to the back of the carriage and rode on the outside. Irma was dressed in a suit of livery. It was actually her son's Jordan High band uniform, but the illusion wasn't bad. Delores had told her that Bonnie and Gail would speak the lines of dialogue and Irma would read the descriptive passages.

They were almost ready to begin, and Hannah glanced around for Lucy. She failed to spot her in the rows of chairs that had been arranged for the audience, but perhaps she was coming later.

Irma climbed up on a ladder so that her head appeared above the top of the black canopy. She looked a little nervous, and Hannah could understand why. The canopy was high, and Delores had once mentioned that Irma wasn't comfortable with heights. Irma cleared her throat, then began.

"We're doing a reading from *A Secret Scandal* by Kathryn Kirkwood." Irma's voice squeaked slightly. She was holding the book open with her left hand and clutching at the rail of the ladder with the other. "Captain Hargrove, played by Gail Hanson, has managed to locate his long-lost bride-to-be. She's Lady Sarah Atherton, played by Bonnie Surma. Lady Sarah is the victim of a carriage accident, and she's lost her memory. Is she really Sarah Atherton? And is Captain Hargrove really her intended husband?"

Irma cleared her throat again and looked down at the book. She squinted slightly and began to read. *"Sarah was silent as the carriage began to move. She raised her eyes to look at the captain, and his expression did not reassure her. He was gazing at her intently, almost as if he were searching for something. Why was he staring at her so?"*

Bonnie took her cue and looked up at Gail. When she did, her hat slipped all the way to the back of her head. "Please do not stare at me so, Captain Hargrove."

"My apologies," Gail said, her voice as deep as she could make it.

Bonnie looked up again, taking the precaution of holding her hat. "You said you were taking me home, Captain. Where *is* home?"

"I had forgotten that you would not remember," Gail responded, still trying for the deep voice. "I am carrying you to Hargrove Manor."

Bonnie frowned, turning toward the audience so that they could see it. "But Hargrove Manor would be *your* home, not mine."

"It is not my home either. Hargrove Manor belongs to my brother, the Duke of Ashford. Our wedding shall take place there."

"And when will that be, Captain?"

Gail paused for dramatic effect, then she said, "We shall exchange our vows in less than a fortnight. The invitations have already been issued."

"You would wed me when I cannot remember you?" Bonnie opened her mouth and put her hand to the side of her face in a gesture that Hannah assumed was designed to portray shock.

"Of course. I fail to see what difference it will make, so long as I remember you."

"It makes a great difference to me! I shall *not* wed a stranger!"

Gail reared back to convey surprise, but she carried it a bit too far. The black cloth quivered as she poked it with her elbow, and she came close to overbalancing on the piano bench. "You would choose to disappoint our wedding guests?"

"Better them than me, Captain." Bonnie turned to face the audience and gave a brave little smile. "Better them than me."

Irma York brought her hands together in a signal for the audience to applaud. The audience took their cue, and there was a rousing ovation. As Hannah checked to make sure she had everything ready at the refreshment table, she wondered if people in Regency England had actually spoken in such a formal and stilted way. Perhaps it was all a hoax that had been initiated by her mother's all-time favorite Regency Romance author, Georgette Heyer, and been perpetuated by every other author who had followed in her footsteps.

Bonnie rushed up to the refreshment table, still holding her hat. The bird had slipped. It was hanging by one foot, and its painted eyes looked startled. "Have you seen Lucy Richards?"

"No. You're losing your bird, Bonnie."

"That dumb bird! I glued it on three times." Bonnie reached up and yanked it off. "She promised to be here to take pictures for the paper."

"If you have a camera, I'll take them."

"You will? That's nice of you, Hannah." Bonnie looked very relieved. "Come up to the stage and we'll do it right now. Did you like the reading?"

"It was very entertaining," Hannah said the first thing that popped into her head, then realized that it was true. The reading had been so entertaining, she'd be chuckling about it for weeks.

COCOA SNAPS

DO NOT preheat oven yet—
dough must chill before baking.

1 ½ cups melted butter *(3 sticks)*
2 cups cocoa powder *(unsweetened)*
2 cups brown sugar
3 large eggs beaten *(just whip them up in a
    glass with a fork)*
4 teaspoons baking soda
1 teaspoon salt
2 teaspoons vanilla
3 cups flour *(not sifted)*
½ cup white sugar in a small bowl (for later)

Melt butter and mix in cocoa until it's thoroughly
blended. Add brown sugar. Let it cool slightly, then
mix in beaten eggs. Add soda, salt, and vanilla and stir.
Add flour and mix thoroughly. Chill dough in the refrigerator for at least 1 hour. *(Overnight is fine, too.)*

Preheat the oven to 350 degrees F., rack in the middle position.

Roll dough into walnut-sized balls with your hands. This dough may be sticky, so roll only enough for the cookies you plan to bake immediately, then return the bowl to the refrigerator. Roll the dough balls in the bowl of white sugar and place them on greased cookie sheets, 12 to a standard sheet. Flatten them with a spatula *(or the heel of your hand if the health board's not around).*

Bake at 350 degrees for 10 minutes. Cool on cookie sheets for a minute or two and then remove the cookies to a wire rack to finish cooling. *(If you leave them on the cookie sheets for too long, they'll stick.)*

Tracey says these taste like her favorite chocolate animal crackers, except better because she doesn't have to pick them out from all the vanilla ones in the box.

Chapter Fifteen

When Hannah got back to the shop at four o'clock, she found Andrea waiting for her. "I thought you had a showing."

"I did." Andrea started to smile. "I sold it, Hannah. John and Wendy Rahn made an offer, and Mrs. Ehrenberg accepted it. John's older brother owns the land next to it, and they're going to farm the whole parcel together."

Hannah patted Andrea on the shoulder. "Good for you!"

"Al said I was a genius for showing it to John and Wendy. And he told me that from now on, I can work my own hours. That means I'll have even more time to help you. Do you have to bake more cookies, Hannah? I think I've got the hang of rolling those dough balls now."

"Thanks, but the baking's all done for today." Hannah draped a towel over the box she'd carried in from her truck, so her sister wouldn't notice that the only cookies left were the lopsided ones she'd made.

"How about Lucy? Did you get a chance to talk to her at the meeting?"

"She never showed up. Gail Hanson brought her camera, and I ended up taking the pictures."

Andrea frowned. "I wonder where she is. Nobody's seen her all day."

"Bonnie Surma said this isn't the first time that she's flaked out on an assignment. Lucy was supposed to cover the Brownie Scout award ceremony last month. She never showed, and Bonnie had to ask one of the mothers to take pictures."

"Then you think she's just out chasing down a bigger story?"

"I don't know what to think, but I don't have the time to drive around town looking for her. We'll just have to catch up with her at the bake-off tonight. If she's alive and kicking, she'll be there."

Andrea shivered at Hannah's choice of words. "I wish you hadn't said that. I've got a real bad feeling about this."

"Don't borrow trouble," Hannah advised. "We've spent the whole day chasing after Lucy and we should have been trying to help Danielle. Are you any good at talking to shrinks?"

Andrea's eyebrows shot up. "You mean, like in counseling sessions?"

"No, on the phone. Danielle said that Boyd made an appointment with his shrink on Tuesday, right after he gave her that black eye. I need to find out if he kept it."

"I can do that." Andrea reached for the phone. "That's Dr. Holland at the Holland Clinic in St. Paul?"

"Right. I'd like to find out what they talked about, but I don't think Dr. Holland will tell us that. Shrinks don't like to discuss their patients, even if they're dead."

"Leave it to me." Andrea looked very confident as she

punched out the number for directory assistance and asked for the number of the Holland Clinic.

Hannah listened as her sister got Dr. Holland on the phone. That took some doing because he was with a patient, but Andrea managed to convince the receptionist that her call was an emergency. She couldn't tell much from Andrea's side of the conversation. "I see," and "Of course I understand," weren't very revealing.

"What did he say?" Hannah asked, after Andrea had hung up the phone.

"Not a whole lot. Boyd kept his appointment, but Dr. Holland said he couldn't tell me what they discussed. He told me that Boyd arrived at two o'clock and he left the clinic at two-thirty."

"That's only thirty minutes." Hannah was surprised. "Don't most counseling sessions last an hour?"

"Fifty minutes. I asked Dr. Holland about that. He said that Boyd cut his session short because he had to drive back to Lake Eden for a parent-teacher conference after school."

"Danielle didn't mention that." Hannah pushed the steno pad over to Andrea. "Check out our notes."

Andrea paged through it to find the notes she'd taken. "Here it is. Danielle said Boyd drove to St. Paul to see Dr. Holland, and he didn't get home until after six that night."

"Danielle didn't know he'd gone back to the school." Hannah thought about that for a moment, then reached for the phone. "I'd better call Charlotte Roscoe before she leaves for the day. She probably keeps a record of parent-teacher conferences, and she can tell us who was at the meeting."

Hannah gave a little toot on her horn as she parted company with her sister. Andrea was going to collect Tracey at Kiddie Korner, and they'd meet later, at the bake-off.

As she drove past the park, Hannah flicked on her lights. This was the most dangerous driving time of the day. Night was falling fast, and while she could still see, everything outside the range of her headlights had lost its color and faded to shades of gray.

There weren't many cars in the school parking lot. The teachers had gone home, and the audience for tonight's bake-off wouldn't arrive for another hour and a half. Hannah had brought her outfit with her and was planning to dress in the girls' locker room. She'd have a miffed feline to contend with when she arrived at her condo after the show, but Moishe could get along on his own for another few hours.

Charlotte Roscoe, Jordan High's secretary, had been very helpful on the phone. She'd checked Boyd's schedule but hadn't found a record of the meeting. She'd told Hannah that Jordan High teachers only kept records of their academic conferences. She'd suggested that the conference could have involved one of Coach Watson's team members and advised Hannah to check with Gil Surma, Jordan High's counselor, to see if he'd been involved. Gil was still at the school, meeting with his Cub Scouts. Since it was winter outside and the auditorium was off-limits during the bake-off, Gil was teaching them to pitch a canvas teepee in the hallway outside the principal's office.

Once she'd parked and climbed out of her truck, Hannah walked around to the back to grab a large bag of yesterday's cookies. Cub Scouts were always hungry, and they could eat them on their way home. She hurried across the parking lot, darted around the side of the building, and entered through the main door.

Hannah started to grin as she came around the corner and encountered an unusual sight. A khaki-colored teepee was collapsed in a heap near the principal's door. There were several squirming lumps inside, making it seem as if it had developed a life of its own, and she could hear Gil's voice as he attempted to take command.

"Come on, boys. Stop wiggling and let me find the opening. You don't want to stay here all night, do you?"

This was followed by a volley of childish laughter, and Hannah decided to lend a hand. She walked up to the jiggling teepee, lifted the front peak of the canvas, and held it up until a head emerged.

"Thanks, whoever you are." Gil crawled out of the opening on his hands and knees. Then he looked up and smiled. "You saved us, Hannah. I was just showing my troop how easy it was to set up a teepee."

Gil got to his feet and took her place, holding up the peak of the teepee. Five young Cub Scouts crawled out, one after the other, and all of them looked delighted to see Hannah. Hannah knew it wasn't her winning personality or the fact she'd helped to extricate them from the tent; they'd spotted the bag of cookies she'd brought.

"Is your meeting over, Gil?" Hannah asked.

"Yes. It should have been over fifteen minutes ago, but the teepee wasn't very cooperative."

Hannah passed out the cookies, four to each boy, and they left crunching happily. When the last one was out of earshot, she said, "I need to talk to you, Gil. It's about Boyd Watson."

"A terrible thing." Gil shook his head. "Mr. Purvis told us that the authorities were investigating the possibility of foul play, but one of the other teachers mentioned that Boyd had seemed depressed lately. Do you think that it was suicide?"

"No way. Nobody commits suicide by cracking his own skull open with a hammer." Gil looked a little sick, and Hannah wished she hadn't been quite so descriptive. "Are you all right, Gil?"

"I'm okay. They didn't describe exactly *how* Boyd died on the news. And Danielle was the one to find him like that?"

"Yes."

"Poor Danielle. She must really be hurting. I'd better drop by the house and see if there's any way I can help."

"She's not at home, Gil. Doc Knight put her in the hospital."

"She's that sick?"

Hannah decided that stretching the truth wouldn't hurt. She certainly didn't want Gil to know that Danielle was a suspect in Boyd's murder. "She's had a bad cold for a week or so. The shock made it worse, and Doc decided to keep her at Lake Eden Memorial until she recovers."

Gil looked very sympathetic. "We'll send flowers. I'll set up a donation can in the faculty lounge. And the players on The Gulls can chip in. Danielle should know that she's not alone at a time like this."

"That's what I wanted to talk to you about." Hannah jumped in before Gil could do any more planning.

"The flowers?"

"No, The Gulls. I just found out that Boyd had a conference with one of his team members on Tuesday after school. Were you there?"

Gil shook his head. "I have chess club on Tuesdays. Of course, I would have canceled if Boyd had asked me to sit in, but he didn't."

"But you were here, at the school?"

"No. I took the whole club to my house. It's only three members, two seniors and a junior. We watched a tape of Bobby Fischer's last match."

Hannah sighed. This wasn't working out the way she'd hoped it would. "Then you didn't see who Boyd met with?"

"I'm afraid not. We left right after the bell rang. Why do you want to know?"

Hannah sighed. She really didn't want to lie, and perhaps she didn't have to make up another story to disguise her true motive. Gil was the Jordan High counselor and obligated to obey the same set of shrink confidentiality rules that Dr. Holland did. "If I tell you something in confidence, you can't repeat it, right?"

"Yes, if this is a counseling session."

"Okay, it's a counseling session. Just don't bill me for your time."

Gil laughed. "I won't. Talk to me."

"You said you didn't know who Boyd met with, so we'll have to go after this another way. Do you know if Boyd was having a problem with any of his team members?"

"Yes, he was. I'm sorry, but I can't tell you who it is."

"You have to tell me!" Hannah felt her frustration level rise. "I know about your professional ethics and all that stuff, but this could have a bearing on Boyd's murder!"

Gil held up his hands in surrender. "Hold on, Hannah. I didn't say I wouldn't tell you. I said I *couldn't* tell you. Boyd didn't give me the student's name."

"Oh." Hannah felt slightly ashamed of her outburst.

"All Boyd did was pose a hypothetical. He asked what I'd do if I were the head coach and I discovered that one of my basketball players was using steroids."

"Steroids?" Hannah was surprised. As far as she knew, there'd never been a problem of that magnitude in Lake Eden. Last year, three members of the football team had been suspended for a couple of games when they'd thrown a keg party out at the lake, but that was about it. "What did you tell Boyd?"

"I said I'd suspend the player for the rest of the season. The school rules are very clear about performance-enhancing drugs."

"What did Boyd say to that?"

"He posed another hypothetical. He asked me what I'd do if the boy's father threatened to withdraw his support from the school athletic program. I told him I couldn't let that influence my decision and I'd still suspend the boy."

"Did Boyd take your advice?"

"I think so. We talked about the best way to tell the boy's father that his son was about to be suspended. Boyd even jotted down a few notes. Then he thanked me for making his job easier. That was on Monday, Hannah. If Boyd scheduled a conference after school on Tuesday, it could have been about that."

Hannah's heart began to race as she asked the most important question. *"Did* Boyd suspend a boy from his team?"

"No, I checked on that. Either Boyd changed his mind, or . . ." Gil stopped speaking and looked a little sick again.

"Or what?"

"Or he was murdered before he had time to fill out the forms."

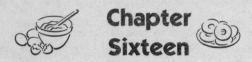

Chapter Sixteen

Lisa stood at her side with the bowl of sweetened whipped cream as Hannah sliced the Hawaiian Flan. It had turned out perfectly, and Hannah smiled as she transferred it to the cut-glass dessert bowls. She sprinkled on a bit of crushed pineapple, spooned some of the golden caramel sauce over the top, and passed the bowls to Lisa, who placed generous dollops of whipped cream on top.

Once they'd placed the dessert bowls and spoons on the serving tray, Hannah and Lisa took off their aprons and waited for the signal from the stage manager. The red light on the camera that was trained in their direction was off, and Hannah turned to Lisa with a question. "Is your dad watching?"

"He's in the audience with Mr. Drevlow. He wanted to see me live tonight. Dad thinks we have our own cooking show, and I didn't have the heart to tell him that this was only temporary."

Hannah glanced over at Rayne Phillips, who was standing in front of a blank blue screen. He was making sweeping gestures at nonexistent storm fronts and Hannah wondered how he knew where to point. Then she saw the monitor that had been set up just out of camera range, showing the computer-generated highs and lows that swirled around on a map of Minnesota. She'd never realized it before, but being a KCOW weatherman actually took some acting ability.

"Are you ready, Hannah?"

"I'm ready." Hannah smiled as she picked up the tray. "It's almost showtime. Let's knock 'em dead, Lisa."

When the stage manager gestured to them, Hannah made her way to the news desk, stepping carefully over the cables. Once Lisa had served each of the newscasters, Chuck Wilson turned to Hannah.

"What do you girls have for us tonight?"

Hannah bristled at his choice of words, but she quickly hid it with a smile. She hadn't been a "girl" for over a decade. "Pineapple custard with caramel sauce. I call it Hawaiian Flan."

"Looks great." Chuck dipped in his spoon and the camera zoomed in on him as he took a bite. He smiled, let the creamy sweetness roll around on his tongue for a moment and then swallowed. "This is a real treat, girls."

Hannah bristled again and she was about to give him a piece of her mind when Lisa stepped in. "Thank you, Chuck. I'm sure it'll be very popular with our customers at The Cookie Jar. We're expanding to desserts, and we plan to feature a different one every day."

"I'll be there for this one," Chuck promised. Then he turned to Dee-Dee Hughes. "What do you think, Dee-Dee?"

"It's heavy and light at the same time, if you know what I mean." Hannah didn't think anyone knew what Dee-Dee meant, but she managed to keep the smile on her face. "But something this yummy has got to be loaded with calories. Am I right?"

Lisa stepped in again, and Hannah breathed a sigh of relief. She'd assured Hannah that she was ready for Dee-Dee's predictable calorie-count question.

"It's certainly not diet food, but you can't eat calorie-free Jell-O every night. If you're that concerned, you can cut the sugar by half in the custard and take only a small portion of the caramel sauce. And you can substitute artificial sweetener for the sugar in the whipped cream."

"But it'll still be fattening, won't it?" Dee-Dee asked.

Hannah bit her tongue. The urge to respond was almost too strong to resist. But before she could open her mouth, Wingo Jones got into the discussion. "Dessert is a time to carb up. If you're worried about gaining weight, you should exercise to burn it off. I know I'd be willing to get out there and jog ten miles for a slice of this Hawaiian Flan."

"Me too." Rayne Phillips nodded and reached over to snag Dee-Dee's dish. "Don't worry, Dee-Dee. I'll save you from yourself. You can't get fat if I eat your dessert."

Chuck Wilson cracked up, and Hannah instantly forgave him for calling her a girl. Perhaps he wasn't such an idiot, after all. Then he turned to the camera, reminded everyone to stay tuned for the "World News," followed by the third night of the Hartland Flour Dessert Bake-Off. The music came up, the credits started to roll, and the news team pretended to be busy by shuffling papers and smiling at each other.

Dee-Dee maintained her pleasant expression until the red light on the camera went off. Then she glared at Rayne Phillips and uttered several nasty expletives that would have gotten the program bleeped off the airwaves.

Hannah was chuckling as she walked back to the kitchen set with Lisa to pack up. Lisa joined in, and they were in a fine mood as they loaded their supplies into boxes and carried them to the shelves against the back wall.

"If there's nothing else, I'm going to go and sit with Dad and Mr. Drevlow," Lisa said.

"Go ahead, Lisa. You were great tonight, and I thought your answer to Dee-Dee's question was perfect." Hannah reached into the pocket of her apron and handed Lisa an envelope. "Here. This is for you. I'm paying you for all the extra hours you put in this week."

Lisa looked surprised. "But you don't have to do that. I put in those hours because I wanted to. I like helping you, Hannah, and I didn't expect to get paid extra."

"Then call it a Christmas bonus. You earned it."

"Okay." Lisa put the envelope in her pocket. "But don't pay me any more. I'll cover for you until the bake-off's over and you're through with . . . with that *other* thing you're working on."

Hannah nodded. Lisa was the perfect employee, and maybe it was time to think about making her a partner. Between the two of them they could keep The Cookie Jar running smoothly, and they might even be able to take alternate vacations during their slowest month.

But when would that be? Hannah thought about it for a moment, her brow creased in thought. There was always a party or a social event to cater, and people ate cookies year round. Unless every resident of Lake Eden went on a low-carb diet at the same time, they'd never have a slowest month.

Hannah had just emerged from the makeup room, where the experts had touched up her lipstick and attempted to tame her flyaway red hair, when Andrea rushed up.

"There you are! Let's duck in here where we can be private." Andrea pulled her inside the ladies' room. "Lucy's not here. I've looked everywhere. I even asked Bill if she was hanging around the sheriff's station, and he told me he hadn't seen her all day."

Hannah felt her stomach drop with a sickening lurch. She'd really expected Lucy to show up at the bake-off. "Maybe she's just late?"

"Maybe." Andrea didn't look very convinced. "I've been thinking about it, Hannah. What if Lucy went home and discovered that her secret drawer was empty? If she thought the police were after her, she could have skipped town."

Hannah hadn't thought of that before. "That's possible, but it doesn't explain why she didn't keep her appointment with Norman this morning."

"You're right. It doesn't. Maybe she's just running late. How about Gil Surma? Did you find out anything interesting?"

Hannah took a moment to fill her in, and she could tell that Andrea was shocked when she mentioned the steroids. "I didn't believe it either, at first. But Gil said that Boyd was very upset about it."

"I guess it's possible," Andrea admitted. "I just don't like to think that it could happen in Lake Eden. Gil didn't know which boy it was?"

"Boyd put it in the form of a hypothetical. He never mentioned the player's name."

Andrea sighed. "Well, at least we know he's a basketball player. How many boys are on The Gulls?"

"Twenty."

"That many?"

"Yes. Gil said that basketball is Jordan High's most popular sport. Boyd had five boys on the A Team. They're the starters. And all the starters have substitutes. That's ten. Then there's a B Team and a C Team with five boys on each. We've got our work cut out for us, Andrea."

"I guess. Did you get a list of names?"

"Gil said he'd get it from Charlotte and drop it off at The Cookie Jar in the morning."

Andrea frowned as she considered how to deal with this new set of facts. "How are we going to find out which player it is? If we call them and ask, we'll get twenty denials."

"I know. Actually, I'm not even sure that this has anything to do with Boyd's murder. It could be a coincidence."

"It's no coincidence. The father of the player murdered Boyd before his son could be kicked off the team."

Hannah was surprised. Andrea sounded very sure of herself. "Do you really think that's a strong enough motive for murder?"

"Absolutely. High-school basketball is a serious sport in Lake Eden."

"But would a father go that far?"

"Of course he would. Remember that mother in Texas who killed her daughter's rival for the cheerleading squad? That wasn't even half as important as basketball."

Hannah thought about it for a moment. "The player's father could have followed Boyd home from the bake-off and tried to convince him not to suspend his son. That would explain the argument that Mr. Gessell heard."

"And arguments can escalate into full-scale fights. We know that Boyd had a hair-trigger temper. What if the player's father did, too?"

Hannah had to admit that the scenario made sense. "I guess it could have happened that way. The father could have picked up the hammer and struck out at Boyd in a rage. Maybe he didn't actually *intend* to kill him, but he did. And then, when he realized that Boyd was dead, he hightailed it out of there."

Andrea jumped up and down in excitement. "We did it Hannah! We know who Boyd's killer is!"

"Not quite yet." Hannah reached out to restrain her

overexuberant sister. "We may know why, but we don't know who. Get out there and look for Lucy. If you find her, hang on to her until after the show."

"Okay. But what if Lucy won't tell us who's in those pictures?"

Then we're up the creek, and we've wasted a lot of time, Hannah thought. But she didn't say it because that would be tempting fate. "Don't worry about that now. Just concentrate on finding Lucy. I'll get it out of her, one way or the other."

Rudy, one of the cameramen, caught Hannah as she was about to take her place behind the judging table. "Hey, Hannah. That Hawaiian Flan you made was great."

"How do *you* know?"

"Wingo got a phone call right after the broadcast and left his dish on the news desk. I snagged it before he could get back."

"Good for you." Hannah gave him a smile. She liked Rudy. He'd explained about the cameras and how she could tell when they were on. She motioned toward one of the huge cameras that were lined up on the set. "Why are these cameras different from the one you use?"

"They're line-feed. See these cables?"

Hannah spotted the heavy black cables that snaked across the floor. "Where do they go?"

"To the mobile control booth in the production truck. That's where Mason is during the show. He watches the feed from these cameras on monitors and calls for the camera angles through headsets. He's the one who decides which feed to broadcast."

"That sounds like a very difficult job."

"It is. This is a live show, and he has to make fast decisions. When he calls a shot, it's broadcast right away."

Hannah was interested. What she knew about television

production could be contained in a thimble with room to spare. "What does your camera do?"

"I shoot the montages we run during the judging. My camera's called a roving cam, and it's self-contained. It records on three-quarter-inch tape, and we edit it down later."

"Edit it down?"

"I shot four hours of footage for tonight's montage, and it'll run less than three minutes."

"That's an awful lot of tape for a couple of minutes."

"We always shoot more than we need. That way the editor can pick and choose. I shoot tape of the contestants arriving, the audience filing in, even the wrap parties out at the inn."

That information gave Hannah an idea. If Rudy shot four hours of tape every day, he could have gotten a picture of the killer and his cuff links. She still intended to get the killer's name from Lucy, but what if she'd skipped town as Andrea had suggested? They needed a contingency plan. "What happens to all the tape that isn't used?"

"The outtakes?"

"If that's what you call them. Do you throw them away?"

Rudy laughed. "At KCOW, we don't throw *anything* away. We even recycle our paper clips."

"Then you tape something else over them?"

"Yes, but not right away. We store them for a while at the station. Then they're reviewed. If Mason's sure we won't need any of the footage, we erase them and use them again."

"So all your outtakes are back at the station in storage?"

Rudy shook his head. "The tapes are still in the production truck. Why are you so interested?"

"I just find the whole process fascinating," Hannah said with a smile. "Do you think I could watch them?"

"It's a lot of tape, and most of it is pretty boring. Are you sure?"

"I'm sure." Hannah held her breath as she waited for

Rudy to answer. This could be very important. Even if she found Lucy and managed to pry the killer's name from her, seeing the man and his cuff links on tape was a way of proving that Lucy hadn't lied to them about his identity.

"If you want to be bored, it's fine with me. But I don't have the final say. You'll have to get permission from Mason."

Hannah flashed him a smile. Rudy had no idea how helpful he'd been. "Thanks, Rudy. I'll ask Mason right after tonight's show."

Hawaiian Flan

Preheat oven to 350° F.,
rack in the middle position.

1 cup white sugar
$\frac{1}{2}$ cup water
6 eggs
1 can sweetened, condensed milk *(don't use evapo-
    rated—it won't work)*
$\frac{1}{4}$ cup white sugar
1 $\frac{1}{2}$ cups pineapple juice
$\frac{1}{8}$ teaspoon salt
1 small can crushed pineapple *(well drained)*
Sweetened whipped cream topping *(optional)*

Find an 8-inch-by-8-inch square pan *(either metal
or glass)* or any other oven pan that will hold 6 cups of
liquid. Do not grease or butter it. Simply have it ready,
next to the stove top.

Combine one cup of white sugar with a half cup of
water in a saucepan. Bring it to a boil, stirring at first,
then swishing it around until the mixture turns golden
brown. *(This gets as hot as candy syrup so wear oven
mitts.)*

Carefully, pour the syrup into the pan you've chosen and tip it to coat the bottom and the sides. This is your caramel sauce. *(Be very careful. This is extremely hot.)* Run water in the saucepan you used and set it in the sink. Then set the baking pan aside while you make the custard. *(You may hear cracking noises as the caramel cools. Don't worry. It's the caramel cracking, not your pan.)*

Beat the eggs until they're light yellow and thick. *(This will take a while if you don't have an electric mixer.)* Add the sweetened condensed milk, the sugar, the salt, and the pineapple juice, and beat thoroughly.

Get out a strainer and strain this mixture into your baking pan.

Find a larger baking pan that will contain your custard pan with at least an inch to spare on all four sides. Place the custard pan inside the larger pan. Slip both pans into the oven and pour hot tap water in the larger pan, enough to immerse your custard pan halfway up the sides.

Bake one hour, or until a knife inserted in the center comes out clean.

Remove the custard pan from the water and let it cool on a wire rack for at least 10 minutes. *(This custard can be served either warm, or cold.)*

To serve, turn the custard out in a flat bowl or a plate with a deep lip. *(This is so the caramel sauce won't overflow.)* Place slices of custard in a dessert dish and sprinkle some of the crushed pineapple over the top. Then spoon on some of the caramel sauce and top with whipped cream, if you wish.

Delores prefers this custard chilled. Andrea says it's best at room temperature, and I like it warm.

Chapter Seventeen

Tonight's winner had been a man, and Hannah was glad. Baking was an equal-opportunity avocation. Once the retired army master sergeant had accepted his finalist ribbon, Clayton Hart had reminded the audience that tomorrow was the final night of the Hartland Flour Dessert Bake-Off. The show would be a full hour, and the three finalists would actually bake on camera. Each contestant would be taped live, and the tape would be shown on three giant screens that would be suspended from the ceiling, a technique that KCOW producer Mason Kimball had devised so that the audience could watch their every move.

When the show was over, Hannah turned to Edna Ferguson. "Did you mean what you said about Sergeant Hogarth's cinnamon buns?"

"I wouldn't have said it if I hadn't," Edna replied, "and I'll say it again. His cinnamon buns are even better than mine."

"And you make the best cinnamon buns in town." Hannah's stomach growled just thinking about them. She hadn't eaten since Sally's lunch buffet, if you didn't count the tiny samples of desserts she'd judged, and she was ravenous. Unfortunately, there wasn't time to eat now. She had to find Andrea to see if her sister had managed to locate the elusive Lucy Richards, and then she had to run out to the production truck to ask Mason Kimball for permission to review Rudy's outtakes.

"Are you going out to the inn for the wrap party?" Edna asked.

"Not tonight. I've got more things to do than there are hours left in the day." Hannah stood up and straightened the skirt of her new suit. It was a color Claire had called "bracken," a shade midway between a brown and an orange. Hannah had balked at even trying it on. Anything orange clashed with her hair. But Claire had insisted, and it really did look stunning on her.

Andrea was waving from the wings, and Lucy wasn't with her. Hannah headed off in her sister's direction with a frown on her face. Either Lucy had skipped town or she was . . . Hannah stopped herself in mid-thought and repeated her father's standard maxim. There was no sense in borrowing trouble. Of course, her father had lived with Delores all those years, and he didn't *have* to borrow trouble; it had resided right under his roof.

"Lucy's not here," Andrea reported as soon as Hannah was close enough to hear her, "but I can help you look for her. Bill has to go back to the station and Tracey wants to stay with Grandma again."

Hannah knew what her sister was asking. Andrea needed to be needed again. "That's great, Andrea. I could really use your help."

Andrea's face lit up with a smile. "What are we doing first?"

"I have to run out to the production truck for a minute.

You can wait for me in the lobby. Ask around about Lucy. Maybe somebody's spotted her."

"I did that already." Andrea sounded a bit petulant. "Nobody has."

Hannah reached into her purse and pulled out her keys. "All right. Then see if you can snag somebody to carry my boxes out to the truck. That'll save us some time."

"Okay." Andrea looked much happier as she grabbed the keys. "I like to be helpful."

"You're helpful, believe me. And if you want to help even more, pull around the building and park next to the production truck. That'll save us even more time."

Hannah filed her discovery about Andrea away for future reference as she headed out the back door and dashed across the parking lot to the KCOW production truck. Her sister needed to be needed, and she liked to be helpful. She just hoped that Andrea still wanted to be helpful after they'd watched four hours of Rudy's outtakes.

Mason Kimball was just coming down the metal steps when Hannah reached the production truck. He looked tired, and there were dark circles under his eyes. "Hi, Hannah. What are you doing out here?"

"I talked to Rudy before the show," Hannah told him, going into her rehearsed speech. "He told me all about how you make the montage, and I'd really like to watch his out-takes if you don't mind."

"You want to watch *all* of Rudy's outtakes? There's over twelve hours."

Hannah tried for a guileless expression. "I'd like to, but I don't have twelve hours to spare. I'm really more interested in the footage that Rudy shot on Wednesday. I thought that montage was the best."

Mason began to frown, and Hannah knew he hadn't bought her excuse. "Wednesday was the night that Boyd

Watson judged the contest. Does this have anything to do with his murder?"

"Of course not," Hannah lied through her teeth. "I'm just interested in Rudy's outtakes. I think he's very talented."

Mason's frown grew deeper. "He is, but nobody's that interested in outtakes. I think you'd better tell me what you're really after. Are you working with the sheriff's department again?"

"No, and I wasn't working with them before," Hannah declared honestly. She hadn't been exactly working with the sheriff's department; she'd been working with Bill.

"But I heard you solved Ron LaSalle's murder."

"Bill solved it, not me. I just happened to overhear something that helped him, that's all."

Mason shook his head like a dog coming out of the lake, not quite as fast, but just as definite. "No way, Hannah. I'm not getting in the middle here. If you don't tell me exactly why you want to watch the outtakes, I can't let you do it."

"Okay." Hannah sighed deeply. She wasn't about to mention the pictures that Lucy had taken of the murder and her search for the killer's cuff links, but she had to tell Mason something convincing. "Look, Mason. I know it's a long shot, but maybe there's some footage of Boyd before the contest started. Rudy told me he taped the audience coming in. If Boyd stopped to talk to anyone, Bill and Mike should know about it. Then they can interview that person and find out about Boyd's state of mind and what he said."

Mason thought about it for a minute. "Okay. I don't remember any footage of Boyd, but I didn't watch the whole thing."

"Is that a yes?"

"Sure. I don't have any objections. There's only one problem."

"What's that?"

"You'll have to watch the tapes tonight."

Hannah groaned. "Tonight?"

"I'm afraid so. Tomorrow's the final day of the contest, and we'll be so busy, I won't be able to spare anyone to help you."

"Can't I do it alone?"

"No. The engineer will have to find the right tapes for you and load them. You'll be using a sophisticated piece of equipment, and he'll have to teach you what to do. It's possible we'll need some of that footage for the final montage. I can't take the chance that you'll accidentally erase it."

"Okay. I'll watch the tapes tonight. What time does the engineer leave?"

"He doesn't. We never leave the truck unattended at night when we're out on location. There's just too much valuable equipment inside."

"Then I'll have time to run home and feed my cat first?"

"Sure. Take as long as you like. Just knock on the door when you get back here. I'll tell P.K. to expect you." Mason turned to go back into the truck but hesitated. "If you wait a second, I'll walk you to your truck. You shouldn't be out here alone at night."

"Thanks, Mason." Hannah stood at the base of the metal steps and waited for Mason to talk to his engineer. It only took a moment, then the door opened and he came back down the steps.

"You're all set. I told P.K. which tapes you wanted, and he'll have them all ready for you. Do you really think you'll find anything, Hannah?"

"Probably not, but I have to do it. And there might be some good shots of Tracey. I didn't lie to you before, Mason. I really am interested."

"If you find any footage of her, write down the time codes. The engineer will show you where to find them. We can dupe a tape of her for you. She looked great on camera."

It was snowing as they walked across the parking lot, and a cold wind whistled across the asphalt. Mason lifted his arms to turn up his collar and Hannah had all she could do not to gasp. Mason was wearing a pair of antique cuff links with ducks on them.

"Those are beautiful cuff links," Hannah said, hoping her voice wasn't shaking. "Are they antique?"

"Yes. They belonged to Ellen's grandfather. He had quite a large collection."

Hannah was almost afraid to ask, but she did. "Did Ellen's grandfather happen to have a gold pair of cuff links with horse heads on them?"

"Maybe. I know he had a couple of pairs with dogs on them, and I've got this pair with the ducks. Is it important?"

"Yes." Hannah's mind raced for a plausible excuse. She certainly didn't want to tell Mason that Boyd's killer had worn horse head cuff links. "Mother collects antique jewelry, and she's looking for a pair like that. I thought they'd make a great Christmas present for her, but I haven't been able to find any."

"I'll ask Ellen to look through her jewelry box. Would they be valuable?"

"Yes." Hannah left it at that. Mason had no idea how valuable those cuff links were. While it was true that they'd be worth a bundle on the antique jewelry circuit, they were equally valuable when it came to proving that Danielle hadn't murdered Boyd.

"I hope Ellen didn't sell them. She wanted to buy new furniture, and she sold off part of the collection about six years ago."

"To a private collector?"

"No, she placed them on consignment with one of the jewelers out at the mall."

Hannah felt her spirits plummet faster than a gunned-down goose. If the horse head cuff links she'd seen in Lucy's photo had been up for sale at the Tri-County Mall, anyone in the area could have bought them.

"Isn't that your truck?" Mason pointed to the vehicle that was rounding the corner of the building.

"Yes. Andrea's bringing it around for me." Hannah waved her arms, and Andrea pulled up next to them. Her sister slid over to the passenger's side and Mason reached out to open the driver's door for Hannah.

Hannah was pleased. Chivalry wasn't dead. She smiled at Mason, and said, "I think you're doing a great job with the show. Everyone seems to love it."

"Thanks, Hannah. The numbers are in, and we've got a lot more viewers than I thought we'd have. You're really pulling them in by doing that baking on the news."

"Good." Hannah climbed behind the wheel and waved good night to Mason. "Don't forget to ask Ellen about those cuff links. If she still has them, I'd like to buy them for Mother's collection."

Andrea waited until Hannah had pulled around the corner, then she reached out to grab her arm. "What cuff links? Mother doesn't collect cuff links."

"I know. That was just an excuse. Mason was wearing a pair of antique cuff links with ducks on them, and he said they were part of a collection that Ellen had inherited from her grandfather."

Andrea gasped. "You think that Mason has the horse head cuff links?"

"No. He told me there might have been a pair like that, but Ellen sold off part of the collection about six years ago through a jeweler at the mall. If she had them and if she sold them, anyone could have bought them. It's another dead end."

Andrea sighed. "Oh well. Nobody ever said this would be easy. Where are we going first?"

"To my place. I want to change clothes and feed Moishe.

If I don't get there soon, he'll eat my couch. Mike and I went through a couple of bags of pretzels on Wednesday night, and I haven't had time to vacuum the crumbs. One bag was garlic, and that's Moishe's favorite."

To say that Moishe had been glad to see them would have been a gross understatement. The moment Hannah had unlocked the door to her condo, he'd hurtled into her arms and licked her face. When that had been done to his satisfaction, he'd jumped down and raced to his empty food bowl to yowl pitifully.

Hannah had gone straight to the kitchen to get out his food. As she'd taken off the bungee cord that held the cupboard door shut, she'd noticed that it had been chewed almost through. She'd gotten there just in time. Five minutes more and the whole kitchen floor would have been ankle deep in kitty crunchies. She'd fed Moishe, changed into more comfortable clothes, and they'd left. And now they were in the garage, preparing to climb back into Hannah's still-warm Suburban.

"Where are we going?" Andrea asked, opening her door.

"Vera Olsen's house. I want to check with her to see if she's seen Lucy. If she says she hasn't, I'm going to ask her if we can go up to Lucy's apartment. We might find a clue to where she's gone."

"Do you really think that Vera will let us in?" Andrea sounded doubtful.

"Sure. Don't sweat the small stuff, Andrea. I'll think of some excuse when we get there."

It didn't take long to drive to Vera's house. Hannah parked on the street, and they got out of the truck.

"Lucy's not home," Hannah stated, as they walked up the sidewalk to Vera's front porch.

"What are you, psychic?"

Hannah laughed. "I wish. Then we'd know where Lucy is."

"How can you tell that she's not home?"

Hannah pulled Andrea back a couple of paces and pointed up at Lucy's windows. "There's only one light. It's the one in the kitchen over the sink, and it was on this morning. You don't think she's up there sitting in the dark, do you?"

"I guess not." Andrea opened the porch door and they stepped inside. "Have you thought about what you're going to tell Vera?"

"No, I'll let you play it by ear."

Andrea shot her a startled glance. "Me? Why *me?*"

"Because you're better with people than I am." Hannah reached out to press the doorbell that was mounted on the wall next to the heavy front door. "After all, you're a real-estate agent."

Andrea muttered something that she never would have said in front of Tracey. And then she poked Hannah as they heard footsteps coming toward the door. "Shh! Here comes Vera."

Vera Olsen pulled open the door and smiled as she saw them standing on her porch. "Hannah and Andrea. What a surprise. Did Lucy send you with my cookies?"

"Yes." Andrea responded immediately, picking up on the cue that Vera had given her. "We didn't bring them in because we weren't sure you were home. Go get the cookies that Lucy gave us for Mrs. Olsen, will you, Hannah?"

Hannah raced back to the truck as fast as she could and grabbed a bag of cookies. When she came back, she found Andrea and Vera sitting on the awful lime-colored, sectional sofas in Vera's living room, talking like long-lost friends. Hannah figured that Vera must have gotten the furniture at a massive discount. No sane person would pay retail for that color.

Vera smiled at Hannah, took the cookies, and waved her down to one of the bilious-colored cushions. "That's what I mean, Andrea. Even with all the hours Lucy's been putting in at the paper, she still remembered my cookies. Sometimes I have to complain about the mess in her apartment, but other than that, she's a real sweet girl. I figure she'll learn to be neater if I just keep reminding her."

"I'm sure she will," Andrea gave Vera her sweetest smile, "especially since she has you to teach her. She was really concerned that we bring you your cookies before you went to bed. When did you ask for them?"

"Yesterday morning. I have a sweet tooth, you know. I expected her to bring them last night, but she must have gotten home late."

"You didn't hear her come home last night?"

"No. She told me she had to take some pictures out at the inn, and the party must have lasted a long time. I didn't go to bed until eleven-thirty, and I know she wasn't home yet."

Hannah couldn't keep silent. It was just too important. "You didn't see her this morning?"

"No, she was already gone when I went up with her breakfast. I made waffles, and they're her favorites."

Hannah avoided Andrea's eyes. Both of them knew that Vera hadn't knocked on Lucy's door with a plate of waffles. Hot Stuff had climbed the inside staircase to the attic to answer the e-mail she got from Silver Wolf.

"That girl works too hard." Vera sighed. "And she never gets enough sleep. Rod depends on her for everything, you know. She writes all the big stories, and she's out taking pictures for the paper at all hours of the day and night."

Hannah bit the inside of her cheek to keep silent. The pictures that Lucy had taken certainly weren't for Rod at the paper!

Andrea shot Hannah a sharp glance, one that said, *Keep it*

zipped! Then she turned to Vera again. "Lucy asked us to pick up some film for her. Is it all right if we go up to her apartment to get it?"

"Go ahead. Use the inside staircase. Then you won't have to go out in the cold again. She gave you her key, didn't she?"

Andrea turned to Hannah. "You have it, Hannah."

"No, I don't." Hannah played it with a perfectly straight face. "I thought *you* had it."

"Never mind. You can use mine." Vera reached out, picked up a key chain from the coffee table, and handed it to Hannah. "Go upstairs and open the door at the end of the hallway. There's another set of stairs that leads up to the attic and the light's on a switch just inside the door."

Andrea thanked her and Hannah followed her up the stairs. Neither one of them said a word until they'd climbed up to the second floor and shut the hallway door behind them.

"That was brilliant." Hannah patted her sister on the shoulder as they started up the second, much narrower staircase.

"Thanks." Andrea turned to smile at Hannah over her shoulder. "But you get to wing it if Lucy's there. I've already done my part."

Lucy didn't answer their knock, and Hannah used Vera's key. She opened the door, flicked on the light, and both sisters halted, as if they'd run into an invisible wall. Someone had been in Lucy's apartment since they'd left it this morning.

"What happened?" Andrea gasped, staring at the mess in Lucy's main room.

"Somebody was searching for something," Hannah stated the obvious, "and they didn't straighten up after they were through."

The room looked as if a tornado had ripped through it. The bedding had been stripped from Lucy's bed and lay in a heap on the floor. All the drawers in Lucy's rolltop desk had been pulled out and dumped, and film canisters with strips of ruined film protruding like long, curled tongues were scattered on the rug. Lucy's computer was on and a message was flashing on the screen. It read, ALL FILES ON YOUR C: DRIVE HAVE BEEN DELETED.

"Did Lucy do this?" Andrea asked, shivering slightly.

"Not Lucy."

"How do you know?"

Hannah bent down to examine one of the gutted film canisters. "Lucy would never do something like this. It would ruin all her photos."

"The killer!" Andrea shivered, then shuddered. "He must have been searching for the pictures that Lucy took of him. And since he couldn't tell which film canister Lucy used, he destroyed them all."

"You're quick, Andrea. And you could be right. But how did the killer know that Lucy had taken the pictures?"

"Lucy must have told him. She must have tried to blackmail him, Hannah."

"That fits with what Herb told us. Lucy said that she was working on something important, and if it worked out, she'd have enough money to buy her leased car. She must have figured that Boyd's killer would cough up big bucks for those negatives."

"Lucy should have known better. I really didn't think she'd be so foolish."

"Not foolish, stupid," Hannah corrected her. *"Really* stupid."

"Do you think that the killer . . . ?" Andrea stopped speaking and steadied herself against the wall. She seemed unable to voice that possibility. It didn't matter. Hannah knew exactly what she meant.

"That's one theory, Andrea, but it's just a theory. We don't even know, for sure, that Lucy talked to Boyd's killer."

Hannah's mind went into overdrive, attempting to come up with an alternate scenario. Her gut told her that Boyd's killer had been the one who'd broken into Lucy's apartment, but Andrea wouldn't be much help if she panicked. "All this could have been done by one of Lucy's *other* blackmail victims."

A little color began to come back to Andrea's cheeks as she thought about that. "Do you really think so?"

"It's possible. They'd have a lot to gain, too. It could have been Mayor Bascomb, or Claire, or Mr. Avery."

"Mr. Avery?"

"Why not? Lucy had his money. He could have been trying to get it back."

"You're right." Andrea looked very relieved. "At least we know it wasn't Danielle. She doesn't even know about the blackmail, and she's still in the hospital. And Norman didn't do it. You gave him his letter, and he wouldn't have any reason to break into Lucy's place."

"Very good." Hannah was pleased. Andrea was starting to think straight.

"But what about Lucy's film?" Andrea asked. "Why would Mayor Bascomb, or Claire, or Mr. Avery bother to destroy it? If Lucy was blackmailing them, she had already showed them the prints. They would have been after the negatives."

Hannah sighed. Perhaps Andrea was thinking a little *too* straight. But it was a legitimate question, and she had to come up with an answer. "It could have been a new blackmail victim. Lucy might have taken some incriminating pictures last night. The new victim would figure she hadn't had time to develop her film yet."

"That makes sense. But what about Lucy?" Andrea looked nervous again. "Why is she missing?"

"You already came up with a theory about that," Hannah interrupted her, wishing that she didn't have to walk a tightrope between Andrea's hysteria on one hand and her logical questions on the other.

"You're right. I forgot about that. I said that if Lucy discovered that her evidence was missing, she'd think the police were after her and might skip town."

"That's right. And the theory still fits. If Lucy flew the coop before her apartment was vandalized, she doesn't even know about it. Let's concentrate on thinking about where she might have gone."

Andrea sighed. "That's going to be hard, Hannah. I don't even know where Lucy comes from. And I don't think she has any friends in town. Nobody seems to like her much."

"Only because she's rude, nosy, conceited, and she blackmails people. Otherwise, she's all right."

Andrea laughed, actually laughed, and Hannah knew that her sister was back on track. Now all she had to do was keep her there.

"Where shall we start, Hannah? You must have some ideas."

"Of course I do," Hannah declared, searching her mind for something that Andrea could do. "Why don't you check Lucy's closet and see if any of her clothes are missing. She might have packed a bag before she left."

"That's a good idea. What are you going to do?"

"I'll look around in the kitchen and the bathroom."

"No, don't do that." Andrea started to shiver again. "I don't want to be alone, Hannah. What if it *was* the killer? He could come back."

"Why would he? He thinks he destroyed all of Lucy's evidence. He doesn't know that we've got the film she took of him."

"That's right." An expression of relief replaced the panic that had resurfaced on Andrea's face. "Go ahead, Hannah. I'll be all right. What are you going to look for?"

"A clue to Lucy's whereabouts. It could be a map, a note

with an address, anything like that. But we have to hurry, Andrea. Vera's going to think it's weird if we're up here too long."

"Okay. You have a tape player in your truck, don't you?"

"Yes. Why?"

"When I'm through with the closet, I'm going to take out Lucy's answering machine tape. We can listen to it in your truck. Maybe somebody called her back with a reservation number or something and she'd already left."

"Brilliant." Hannah rewarded her with a smile, then headed off to search the kitchen and bathroom. She didn't think she'd find any clues, but she had to look.

There was nothing in the kitchen except pulled-out drawers and open cupboards. Hannah checked the garbage and found nothing but two tuna cans, a bread wrapper with a stale heel of bread inside, and shards of the plate and coffee cup that Andrea had broken this morning when she'd come in through the kitchen window. The worst-case scenario didn't occur to her until she'd flicked on the bathroom light and spotted the closed shower curtain. Had it been closed this morning? She couldn't remember, and she certainly didn't want to ask Andrea. Hannah reached out with shaking fingers, and then hesitated, doing her best not to think about what Anthony Perkins had done to Janet Leigh in *Psycho*.

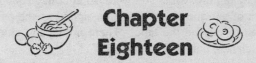

Chapter Eighteen

The shower had contained nothing but a bottle of shampoo and some rust stains near the drain. They'd double-checked Lucy's doors and windows to make sure her apartment was secure and then they'd gone back downstairs to return Vera's key. They hadn't mentioned the break-in to her, knowing that it would only cause her a sleepless night of worries about Lucy. As far as they could tell, nothing was missing from Lucy's apartment, and they'd decided to report it later, when they spoke to Mike and Bill. Then they'd driven to The Cookie Jar, pulled into Hannah's space in the back, kicked up the heater so that they could huddle close to the vents, and listened to the answering machine tape.

There had been Norman's call, the one that had told them Lucy wasn't at his office, several calls from Rod to ask where she was, a slew of messages about Lucy's overdue credit-card balances, and one from a telephone solicitor who'd read his whole pitch on the tape. The only call that was even remotely interesting was from Delores. She'd wanted to know whether Lucy was more interested in necklaces or earrings.

"What was all *that* about?" Hannah asked, when they'd played Delores's message.

"Oh, Mother's probably angling for another article in the paper. They ran one while you were off at college about her collection of antique clocks." Andrea sighed as she pressed the button to rewind the tape. "There aren't any clues on here, Hannah. What shall we do next?"

Hannah shrugged. They were getting nowhere fast. "Let's drive back over to Lucy's place. Vera said she was going straight to bed. If her lights are off, we'll check the garage to make sure Lucy's car is gone."

"What good will that do? It's got to be gone if Lucy is."

"Not necessarily." Hannah backed out of her parking spot and headed down the alley. "Lucy could have left town with someone."

"Who?"

"I don't know, but we should still check. Investigating is a process of elimination. You have to explore all the possibilities, and whatever's left, no matter how implausible, has got to be it."

"I never thought about it like that before." Andrea sounded impressed. "You've really got a good head for this, Hannah."

"It's Sir Arthur Conan Doyle's head. I read it in a Sherlock Holmes book. I probably misquoted it, but it's essentially what he said."

"Maybe I should buy Bill a set of Sherlock Holmes for Christmas." Andrea sounded thoughtful. "Do they have them on tape?"

"Yes, if you're talking about the PBS series."

"Not television, audio. Then he could listen to them on his way to work."

"It's only a ten-minute commute. He'll get so interested, he'll probably sit out in the parking lot until the end of the chapter and get docked for being late." Hannah drove around the corner. "Here we are, Andrea. Check to see if Vera's still up."

Andrea peered out her window as Hannah drove slowly past her house. "It's all dark. She must have gone to bed."

"Good." Hannah cut her lights and turned into the alley. She didn't want any of the neighbors to spot her. Vera's garage was an old-fashioned, freestanding structure that sat on the rear corner of her lot. Hannah parked at the side of the alley and shut off her engine. "We're here."

"If Vera ever listed her house on the market, we'd call that a two-car garage," Andrea said, sounding amused. "Can you imagine two cars fitting in there?"

Hannah flicked off the dome light so that it wouldn't shine when she opened the door. "Two little sports cars, maybe, but that's about it. Come on, Andrea. Grab those flashlights in the back and let's check out the garage."

"Do you really need me for this?"

Andrea's voice had started to shake again, and Hannah turned to her in surprise. "What's the matter?"

"I've got cold feet."

Hannah knew her sister wasn't referring to the fact that the heater in her truck wasn't putting out much hot air. "Why now?"

"Because the last time we searched a garage, we found a dead body."

"The last body we found wasn't in the garage, and this is a different situation. We're not even sure that Lucy is missing, much less dead. She could be out chasing down a hot story."

"Do you *really* believe that?"

Hannah sighed. She didn't like to lie. "Not really."

"I don't believe it, either. And I have a really bad feeling about this. I think we should call Bill and Mike."

"And tell them what?" Hannah asked. "Do you want Bill

to know that we broke into Lucy's apartment and stole her stash of evidence?"

"No."

"Okay, then buck up. If I have to break in, I'm going to need you to hold the flashlight."

"Break in?" Andrea sounded shocked. "You didn't say anything about breaking in!"

"I said *if.* The first thing we'll do is look through the window. If the garage is empty, there's no point in breaking in. Besides, you told me you like to be helpful."

Andrea groaned, but she retrieved the flashlights and handed one to Hannah. "All right. But if Lucy's car is there, I'm not going in."

"Deal."

Hannah got out of the truck and waited for Andrea to join her. They walked around the side of the garage and Hannah pressed her flashlight up against the windowpane before she clicked it on. She peered through the dusty pane, spotted Lucy's car, and gave a little groan.

"What is it?" Andrea's whisper was loud in the quiet night.

"Lucy's car," Hannah whispered back. "And that means I go in."

"Why?"

"Because she could have left something inside that'll tell us where she's gone."

Andrea thought about it for a moment. "All right. Are you going to break the garage window?"

"Not unless the door is locked. It's the old kind that doesn't have an opener. I can see the mechanism." Hannah snapped off her flashlight and stuck it in the pocket of the parka.

"Do you think it'll be unlocked?"

"There's a good chance. Most people don't lock their garages in Lake Eden. There's practically no crime."

"If you don't count murder."

Hannah gave an appreciative chuckle as they retraced her steps to the front of the garage. At least Andrea had recovered enough to crack a joke. She bent down to grasp the handle on the door, turned it until it clicked, and then pulled. The door slid up smoothly. Either Lucy or Vera must have greased the track before the first snowfall.

Andrea gave her the high sign and squared her shoulders. "I changed my mind. I'm going in with you. I'd never forgive myself if something bad happened to you and I wasn't there."

That comment struck Hannah as funny and she bit back a giggle. Andrea seemed to think it would be terrible if something had happened when she wasn't there, but everything would be okay if she was. It didn't make sense, but Hannah was glad to have her company all the same.

After they'd stepped in, Hannah reached up to lower the door. Andrea gasped and she stopped. "What is it?"

"Do you have to close the door? It's so dark in here."

"I guess not, but don't turn on your flashlight. Vera's neighbors across the alley might see it. Just inch your way along the side of Lucy's car and don't trip over anything. I'll go first."

Both sisters inched their way forward until Hannah had reached the driver's door. She reached into her pocket, pulled out her flashlight, and pressed it up against the window. "Okay, Andrea. I'm going to look to see if I can spot anything."

"Okay. Hurry, Hannah. I'm freezing."

Hannah snapped on her flashlight, took one look, and snapped it right back off again. "Do you have your cell phone with you, Andrea?"

"Of course I do. I'm a real-estate agent, and I never go anywhere without it."

"Where is it?"

"It's in my purse in your truck. Why?"

"I want you to go back to the truck and call Bill. Tell him to come over here right away."

Andrea gasped as the implication of Hannah's request sank in. "Lucy's *in* her car?"

"That's right."

"Is she . . . uh . . . dead?"

"As a mackerel."

"But are you sure?"

"I'm sure." Hannah fought to keep her voice steady. The sight she'd captured with the beam of her flashlight had completely eliminated the necessity for an ambulance, and she wasn't about to share the details with her sister. "Just do it, Andrea. Right now. And after you've called, eat a couple of cookies. It's going to be a long night."

The county cruiser pulled up in record time, and Hannah was relieved to see Bill and Mike. At times like this, the presence of two officers who'd been trained to deal with the aftermath of death was very reassuring.

Mike got out of the cruiser and came straight up to Hannah. "What happened?"

"It's Lucy Richards. She's in her car and she's dead."

"You're sure?"

"I'm positive. Get Bill and come with me. I'll show you."

The garage had a light with a pull string. Hannah reached up to turn it on, but she stopped before her fingers could touch the cord. "Should I touch this? There could be fingerprints."

"Go ahead. We can't get fingerprints from that." Mike motioned for her to pull it. "Did you touch anything else before you found Lucy?"

"The side of the car and the garage handle, but Andrea and I were both wearing gloves. That's it."

"How about the handle on the passenger's door?" Bill asked.

"I didn't open it. I just looked through the window with my flashlight. It was . . . uh . . . pretty obvious that she was dead."

"How about Andrea?" Bill looked concerned. "Was she with you when you found Lucy?"

"Yes, but she didn't see anything. I snapped off my flashlight and told her to go back to my truck and call you. I said that Lucy was dead, but that's all she knows."

Bill looked relieved, and he gave her a hug. "Thanks, Hannah."

"You can go back to your truck, but don't leave." Mike took her hand and squeezed it. "We'll talk to you later."

She'd been dismissed and Hannah was glad. She really didn't want to view Lucy's body again. Lucy Richards had been shot in the back of the head, execution style, and the sight wasn't pleasant. Hannah took a couple of deep breaths of the frigid night air to clear her head. It smelled like pine needles and aromatic wood. Someone must have a fire in their fireplace. Then she climbed back into her truck.

Andrea turned to Hannah as she slid in under the wheel. "Is Bill really mad at me?"

"No. He even thanked me for keeping you from seeing Lucy."

"Oh, good." Andrea gave a sigh of relief. "What did they ask you?"

"They wanted to know if we'd touched anything. That was about it. They're coming back here to talk to us later."

"Are we going to tell them that we were in Lucy's apartment?"

"Yes, but only the second time. Vera knows we were there, and there's no reason to lie about it. It'll explain why we looked in Lucy's garage."

"It will?"

"I'll say we could tell that someone had broken in and were worried about Lucy, since no one had seen her all day. We came out to the garage to see if her car was gone."

"Okay, but why didn't we tell Vera about the break-in?"

"We figured she'd get hysterical, and we didn't know, for sure, that anything bad had happened to Lucy. We were going to go back inside later, when we knew more about what had happened."

Andrea still looked apprehensive. "And we won't have to tell them about breaking in this morning?"

"Not unless they ask us directly, and it's in an official capacity."

"Good. Are you going to show them the pictures of the murder?"

"I think I have to," Hannah answered, and her voice was grim. "Those pictures could be the reason why Lucy was killed."

"But how are you going to explain how you got Lucy's film?"

Hannah dropped her head in her hands. Andrea was asking too many questions. "I'll think of something when the time comes. Hand me a couple of those Cocoa Snaps, Andrea. I really need a lift. And take a couple for yourself. If your mouth is full, you won't ask so many pesky questions."

The two sisters munched in silence. After a few minutes, Hannah began to feel better. She was more alert, her mind seemed clearer, and she was ready for more questions.

"Okay, Andrea." Hannah turned to her sister. "Shoot."

"Shoot what?"

"Ask me all those questions you wanted to ask before."

"Are you sure?" Andrea's brows knit in a worried frown. "You said my questions were pesky."

"They were, but I've recovered."

"From what?"

"A chocolate deficiency. You wanted to know what I was

going to say when Bill and Mike asked how I got Lucy's film?"

"Yes."

"I'm not going to go into details. I'm just going to say I ran across the film this morning, and I asked Norman to develop it for me."

"But they'll want to know where you found it."

Hannah shook her head. "No, they won't. When they see the prints and realize that they're pictures of Boyd Watson's murder, they won't look a gift horse in the mouth. It's like this, Andrea. If Bill and Mike know we did something illegal to get that film, it can't be used as evidence against the killer. But if they *don't* know, they can use it."

"I get it. But will Bill and Mike be smart enough to figure that out?"

"I'll give them a big hint." Hannah glanced out the windshield and spotted Mike and Bill coming out of the garage. "Here they come. Open the glove compartment and hand me the pictures of Boyd's murder. They're in a separate envelope."

"You don't want all of them?"

"No. Leave the other ones there. And try to pretend you're still too upset to talk much and take your lead from me."

Andrea opened the glove compartment and handed her the murder pictures. Hannah had just stashed them in her parka pocket when Bill walked over to the passenger door and pulled it open. He hugged Andrea with one arm, and asked, "Are you all right, honey?"

"I . . . I think so. I just feel kind of . . . of shaky."

Hannah breathed a sigh of relief. Andrea was trembling again, even though, a second earlier, she'd been as calm as could be. It was too bad she couldn't nominate her sister for an Academy Award. Andrea deserved it.

"Hannah?" Mike opened Hannah's door. "I need to ask you some questions."

"Okay." It was a good thing she didn't have to pretend to be too rattled to answer. Andrea was a much better actress than she was. "Your place, or mine?"

Mike grinned at that, but his grin faded fast. Murder was serious business. "Come back to the cruiser. It's a lot warmer than your truck. Aren't you ever going to get that heater fixed?"

"It's fixed. It's just not very efficient." Hannah got out of the Suburban and motioned to Andrea. There was no way she was going to take the chance that her sister would confide in Bill if she left them alone in the truck. "Come on, Andrea. We're all going back to the cruiser to warm up and spill our guts."

Chapter
Nineteen

The moment Mike opened the back door of the cruiser, Hannah shoved Andrea in and followed on her heels. Bill and Mike had no choice but to get in the front, and that was the way Hannah had wanted it. Since her sister was in the back with her, it would give Hannah the opportunity to nudge Andrea if she *really* started to spill her guts.

Mike turned around in his seat to look at Hannah. "You knew Lucy. Why do you think she was murdered?"

"I don't know," Hannah answered quite truthfully. She didn't know. All she had was an educated guess.

"How about you?" Bill asked Andrea. "Can you think of anyone who had a reason to kill Lucy?"

"I . . . I'm not sure. Maybe. You tell them, Hannah."

"She's talking about the person who ransacked Lucy's apartment," Hannah rescued her sister. "We just came from there. All the drawers were pulled out, and everything was dumped on the floor. It looks like somebody broke in to search for something. That's why we came out to the garage. We wanted to see if Lucy's car was gone."

Bill's eyes narrowed, and Hannah knew he was remembering the night they'd broken into Max Turner's house. "How did you get into Lucy's apartment? Or shouldn't I ask?"

"You can ask," Hannah answered quickly, before Andrea could even think of opening her mouth. "Vera Olsen gave us her key."

Bill looked confused as he turned back to Andrea. "But why did you go up to Lucy's apartment?"

"Because we hadn't seen her all day. I even asked you if you'd seen her, remember? And . . . and we were worried about her."

"You told me you wanted to ask Lucy about the pictures she took of Tracey."

"I did." Andrea shivered slightly. Hannah knew she had to be acting, because the heater of the county cruiser was running full-blast and the backseat was on the warmer side of toasty. "At least that's the way it started out. And Hannah needed to talk to her, too."

"Why did *you* need to talk to Lucy?" Mike asked Hannah.

Hannah seized the opportunity and ran with it. She knew she'd never have a better chance. "I wanted to ask her about my suspicions."

"What suspicions?"

"Suspicions about Boyd Watson's murder. But a *trained professional* like you wouldn't be interested in anything I just happened to *stumble across,* would he?"

Mike winced, and Hannah knew her barb had hit its mark. He'd remembered the words he'd used when he'd warned her not to meddle in his case.

"Maybe I shouldn't have been quite so hard on you," Mike admitted. "Would it help if I offered to eat my words?"

"Not really." Hannah shook her head. When a person like Mike ate his words, it was recycling. She'd just hear them again, in a slightly different form.

"Come on, Hannah." Mike reached back to pat her arm. "I really need your help on this. Can't you just forget what I said and tell me what you know?"

Hannah knew that it was about as close to an apology as she'd get and decided to accept it. "All right. But how about if I show you instead of telling you?"

"Show me? Did you stumb . . ." Mike cut himself off, and it took him a moment to rephrase what he'd been about to say. "Did you uncover some evidence?"

Mike was learning, and Hannah decided to reward him. She handed him the three prints of Boyd's murder. She'd see what he thought before she gave him Norman's blowup of the killer's cuff link. "I don't know if it's evidence or not, but it could be the reason Lucy was murdered. Take a look and see."

Mike snapped on the dome light, Bill slid over for a closer look, and they examined the photos together. Then Mike asked, "Did Lucy take these pictures?"

"They were taken with her camera." Hannah repeated what Norman had told her. "I don't know the exact time, but I've narrowed it down to between Wednesday at five and Thursday morning at daybreak."

"Do you think they're pictures of Boyd Watson's murder?"

"Definitely."

Bill looked doubtful. "It's not exactly definite. The time frame fits, but they're so dark, it's impossible to tell for sure."

"That's right," Mike agreed. "They'd never stand up in court, Hannah. If you have the negatives, our photographer might be able to lighten them up."

"He can't." Hannah shook her head. "This is as good as it gets, Mike. Norman developed the film for me, and he's great in the darkroom. Your guy can try, but he won't be able to do any better."

Bill's eyes narrowed. "Wait a minute. When did Norman have time to develop this film?"

"This morning. It was right after I found it. That's all you want to know."

"You gave Lucy's film to *Norman Rhodes?*" Mike sounded shocked.

"That's right. I didn't know what was on it, and I knew you'd ask a lot of questions if I brought it out to the station. It was easier to take it to Norman."

"But how did you manage to . . ." Bill stopped himself, just in time. "Do we want to know how you found Lucy's film?"

"No. That's not important."

Bill looked a little nervous about her answer, but he didn't press it. "And you think that Lucy shot this film?"

"I'm ninety-nine percent sure, but I didn't find her in time to ask her. This is just a hunch because I'm not a . . ."

"Trained professional," Mike interrupted her before she could use that particular phrase again.

"That's right. Do you want to know my theory?" Both men nodded, and Mike leaned closer, over the back of his seat. Hannah felt vindicated. He'd progressed from warning her not to meddle to valuing her opinion in the space of a few minutes. "I think that Lucy was there in the alley on the night that Boyd was murdered. She saw the whole thing and took those pictures. They're dark because she didn't dare use her flash."

"That makes sense," Mike said. "And you think the killer discovered that Lucy took pictures of him?"

"Of course. That's why she ended up dead. Lucy knew who he was, and he had to get rid of her before she could talk."

"Do you know *when* Lucy was killed?" Bill asked.

"I can only guess."

"Guess." Mike flashed her a smile. "So far, you're the best guesser we've got."

That made Hannah feel good, and she smiled back. "Dick Laughlin told me that Lucy left the inn last night at midnight. And she didn't keep her seven o'clock dental appointment with Norman this morning."

"So it was between midnight and seven?"

"That's my best guess. Lucy didn't call to cancel, and Norman said she'd never been late before. I've got to assume that she was already dead by that time."

"Okay." Mike took out his notebook and jotted down the times. "Maybe Doc Knight can narrow it down even more than that. Let's think about the logistics for a minute. Boyd's killer murdered Lucy between midnight and seven, then he went up to her apartment to search for the film she took?"

Hannah nudged Andrea to keep her silent. There was no way she wanted to admit that they'd been in Lucy's apartment at seven this morning. "That's not quite right. I think he killed her and fled the scene. Maybe one of Lucy's neighbors turned on a light or something and he panicked. He came back later to search for the film."

"How do you know he didn't kill Lucy and go right up to her apartment to . . ." Mike stopped as Bill gave him a nudge. "I shouldn't ask?"

"That's right. You'll just have to take my opinion on it, Mike."

Mike looked as if he wanted to press her for details, but he managed to curb his curiosity. "Okay. Do you know when the killer came back to look for the film?"

"After seven-forty-five this morning and . . ." Hannah turned to Andrea. "What time did Vera give us her key?"

"Nine. I looked at my watch right before we went up the stairs."

"I just thought of something." Bill looked alarmed as he

turned to Hannah. "Is there any way the killer could know that you've got Lucy's film? I mean, if Lucy said anything before he killed her, you could be in big trouble!"

"Relax, Bill." Hannah smiled to reassure him. "The killer doesn't know that I have it."

"You're sure?" Mike sounded equally worried.

"I'm positive. The killer assumes he found it and destroyed it. He pulled all of Lucy's film out of their canisters. You'll see that when you get up to her apartment."

"Wait a second." Bill looked confused again. "Wouldn't the killer take Lucy's film and develop it to make sure he had the right pictures?"

"Not unless he's got his own darkroom. Think about it, Bill. There's no way he'd take an incriminating piece of evidence down to Lake Eden Neighborhood Pharmacy and send it off for processing."

"You've got a good point," Mike said.

"Of course I do. And I have another piece of the puzzle if you want to see it."

"You said *see*." Mike picked up on her word immediately. "Is it another picture?"

Hannah handed him her final print. "It's a blowup Norman did from the last shot on Lucy's roll, the one where the killer is raising his arm. It's the killer's cuff link, and it's clearer than the rest of the picture because it was glittering in the moonlight."

Mike stared at the last print for a moment and then he handed it to Bill. "It's a horse head, and it looks like an antique."

"It's also rare," Andrea informed them. "I dashed over to Mother's this afternoon and looked it up in one of her auction catalogues. The last pair that went on the block sold for seven thousand dollars."

Hannah turned to Andrea in surprise. She hadn't known

that her sister had done that particular piece of legwork. "When did you find time to do that?"

"Right after John and Wendy bought the farm."

"Don't say *bought the farm.*" Hannah started to laugh. "Especially not with a killer on the loose."

Mike cracked up, and so did Bill and Andrea. It felt good to laugh, and it relieved the tension. For a few moments, all of them managed to push the brutality of the two murders out of their minds, but then they saw headlights at the mouth of the alley as Doc Knight's Explorer pulled in. It was a tangible reminder that violent death lay only a few feet away, and their laughter ended abruptly.

"There's one other thing you should know," Hannah said quickly, before Mike could get out of the cruiser.

"You can tell me in a minute." Mike opened his door and motioned for Bill to do the same. "Just stay right here. We'll fill Doc in, and I'll be right back."

"What are you going to tell him?" Andrea asked, the moment they were alone.

"Something new," Hannah said. She didn't want to go into the story of Rudy's outtakes for Wednesday's montage and that it would take four hours to watch them. "I'll tell you both when Mike gets back."

That seemed to satisfy Andrea because she smiled. "You were really something, Hannah. You told Bill and Mike just what they had to know, and you didn't even have to lie about the rest. You just . . . well . . . what's the right word?"

"Evaded. I evaded telling them the whole truth."

"That's it. You evaded, and it worked out just fine. You know, Hannah? Maybe I shouldn't say this, but I think you'd make a great real-estate agent."

"Aren't you happy, Hannah?" Andrea asked as they drove down the snowy streets to the school.

"Happy?"

"Yes. Mike finally agreed to let us do some real detective work. He gave us his permission to watch the outtakes."

"Right." Hannah pulled into the lot. There was no need to burst Andrea's bubble by telling her that Mike and Bill might have had an ulterior motive. If she and Andrea watched the outtakes, they'd be saving the *real* detectives four hours of work, and they'd be safely in the KCOW production truck with the night engineer. Hannah suspected that it was Mike's way of keeping them out of trouble, but perhaps she was being uncharitable. "Are you sure you don't mind watching the tapes with me?"

"I don't mind. There could be some pictures of Tracey. Wasn't it nice of Mason Kimball to offer to make me a copy if we found some?"

"Yes, it was." Hannah thought about Mason's antique cuff links and made a mental note to ask him if he'd talked to Ellen about any with horse heads on them. It probably wouldn't do any good, but it couldn't hurt to follow up. Even if they'd been sold, the jeweler in the mall might have kept records of something that valuable. It was a long shot, but not impossible.

"Bill said he'd be at least another two hours," Andrea said. "He'll pick me up here when he's through. I hope he's late. I'd really like to see the whole tape."

"Maybe he will be." Hannah pulled around the building and parked next to the production truck. "Okay, Andrea. Let's go. Reach in the back and snag some cookies. I still haven't eaten, and my stomach is growling."

"Oh-oh." Andrea held up the empty bag of Cocoa Snaps. "I just ate the last one. Do you want to make a trip out to the Quick Stop and get some snacks?"

Hannah considered it for a brief moment, but driving out to the Quick Stop would take at least fifteen minutes, and it was already close to eleven. "Never mind. It won't kill me to go without food for another couple of hours. I'll catch something later, when I get home."

"Moishe."

"What?"

"You'll catch *Moishe* when you get home. I thought it was really cute when you unlocked your door and he jumped right up in your arms. He must really miss you when you're gone all day."

"All Moishe misses is a full food bowl," Hannah said, even though she didn't really believe it. Moishe did seem to miss her, and that made her feel good.

They climbed up the metal steps to the production truck, and Hannah knocked. She heard footsteps approaching, and then the door opened to reveal a bearded man with a ponytail and a diamond stud in his left ear.

"Hannah Swensen?" the engineer asked.

"That's right. Mason Kimball gave me permission to watch Rudy's outtakes for Wednesday. I brought my sister, Andrea, to help me."

"No problem." The engineer took one look at Andrea and started to smile. "Come in, and I'll set you up. I'm P.K."

Hannah wondered what P.K. stood for, but it didn't really matter. They followed him down a hallway to a door near the end of the truck. P.K. opened it and gestured for them to go inside.

"This is Mason's screening room. He said you could use it. Sit down, and I'll get you the tapes."

Hannah was impressed. The small room was like a den with two swivel chairs and a table between them. A television set was pulled out from the opposite wall and a rolling cart with a large VCR was set up right next to it.

"Not bad," Andrea said, taking a seat in one of the swivel chairs. "It would look a lot better with wallpaper instead of that dark paneling, but it's cozy."

"Cozy?" Hannah stared around at the perfectly bare walls. "I thought cozy meant chintz and teddy bears."

"Not in real estate. A small room is cozy, a large room is spacious, and a kitchen is a gourmet's dream."

In a few moments, P.K. came back with four tapes in black boxes. They were bigger than the tapes Hannah had for her home VCR, and she figured that they were the three-quarter-inch kind that Rudy had mentioned. He opened one of the boxes and slid the tape into the VCR. "I'll start it for you and teach you how to use the remote. Have you ever used a VCR?"

"Yes," Hannah answered, "but the one I have isn't three-quarter-inch."

"The controls are pretty much the same. The tape's a different size, that's all."

"I have a VCR at home, too." Andrea smiled at him as he perched on the edge of her chair, and Hannah suspected that her sister had made another conquest. She looked good in her tight black slacks and fuzzy pink sweater, and men had never been able to resist Andrea.

"Then you'll be able to handle this one just fine." P.K. held out the remote so that Andrea could see it. "There's play, stop, fast-forward, rewind, freeze-frame, pause, and the search buttons."

Hannah almost hooted. Andrea always let Bill set the VCR, and she'd probably never held a remote in her life. But she nodded knowledgeably, and P.K. seemed satisfied.

"Just don't touch that circle in the middle," P.K. warned. "That's for something you don't need. Do you know about time codes?"

Andrea shook her head and turned to Hannah. "Do you?"

"Mason mentioned them. He said we should write them down if we wanted him to dupe a tape of something."

"Okay." P.K. tore his eyes away from Andrea and turned to Hannah. "Time codes are a bunch of numbers that advance at the bottom of the screen. The cam puts them on automatically. It's distracting at first, but you'll learn to ignore it."

P.K. turned on the tape, and they saw a picture of the school. There were numbers at the bottom of the screen, just as P.K. had told them, and the fractions of seconds clicked by so fast, Hannah barely had time to read them.

"When you find something you want, press the freeze-frame." P.K. held up the remote and demonstrated. "Then all you have to do is back up the tape with the reverse search and freeze-frame it again to read the number."

"Okay. I can handle that," Hannah said. "We write down the number at the beginning?"

"And at the end. Bracket the section of the tape for me with time codes. That'll tell me what footage you want and how long it lasts." P.K. demonstrated again and handed Andrea the remote. "I'll get you a couple of notepads and pens from Mason's office."

"Thanks," Andrea smiled up at him. "I'm sorry we're so much trouble."

Hannah waited until P.K. had left and then she turned to her sister. "You're sorry we're so much *trouble?* "

"I had to say something." Andrea shrugged. "He's being very nice."

"He might be getting a little *too* nice. And you're flirting with him."

"I always flirt. Bill doesn't mind. He knows that I'd never actually *do* anything. And he understands that flirting makes it easier for me to get what I want."

Hannah had never heard it put quite that way before, but at least Andrea was being honest with herself. "Okay. What do you want from P.K.?"

"Coffee. If I smile a couple more times and happen to mention how cold I am, he's bound to offer to bring us some."

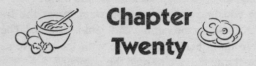

Chapter
Twenty

Viewing the outtakes was exciting at first, especially when they saw their friends appear on Rudy's tape. Hannah and Andrea kept their eyes glued to the monitor, pens poised to write down the time codes. Then the novelty began to wear off. Since the footage Rudy had shot was especially for the montage, and that had been designed to be set to music, there was background noise but no clear comments. Occasionally, they heard Rudy's voice giving information on the location and the people in the scene he was taping, but no one spoke directly to the camera.

During a long sequence that Rudy had shot on Wednesday morning as he followed the contestants' cars from the lot at the Lake Eden Inn to the Jordan High auditorium, Andrea gave an impatient sigh. "It's just cars, Hannah. And the camera's not close enough to pick up the drivers."

"Mason warned me that this would be boring," Hannah reminded her.

"You told me. I just didn't think it would be *this* boring. How long do we have to go?"

Hannah glanced at the time code flashing on the bottom of the screen. "Three and a half hours."

"Can you fast-forward through this part?"

"I'd better not. We might miss something."

Andrea took another sip of the coffee that P.K. had brought them. "I guess you're right," she conceded. "Which car is Mr. Avery driving?"

"The dark blue Ford, but we've already eliminated him as a suspect."

"We have?"

"Yes. Both Sally and Dick said he was at the wrap party with his wife at the time Boyd was killed. Just to make sure, I confirmed it with Jeremy and Belle Rutlege."

"Okay, he didn't kill Boyd. But that doesn't mean he couldn't have killed Lucy. After all, she blackmailed him. Lucy's killer could have been any one of her blackmail victims. They could have been trying to get even with her or recover the evidence she used against them. They didn't know that we had all of her pictures and negatives."

Hannah shook her head. Andrea just wasn't thinking clearly. "How about the film her killer destroyed? Why would one of her other blackmail victims do that?"

"I don't know." Andrea thought about it for a moment. "Maybe her killer was trying to keep her from blackmailing anyone else."

"Lucy was already dead by that time. Her killer knew that it was impossible for her to blackmail anyone else."

"That's right." Andrea rubbed her eyes again. "Are you sure the same man killed Boyd and Lucy?"

"Sure enough."

"And you're sure you shouldn't turn over Lucy's other blackmail pictures?"

"Yes, I am." Hannah was very definite. "Lucy's victims have been hurt enough, and we know that none of them killed her."

Andrea didn't look convinced. "Tell me your reasons again."

"We know it wasn't Claire because it's a man in the pictures with Boyd Watson. It's not Mayor Bascomb, he's much taller than the man in Lucy's photo, and we've already eliminated Mr. Avery because he has an alibi. It can't be any one of them."

"You're wrong Hannah. We forgot about Norman. I don't think for a second that he killed Boyd or Lucy, but we haven't eliminated him yet."

"Yes, we have. I gave his evidence back. There was no reason for him to kill Lucy and search her apartment, especially since he knew we'd already done it. And it was Norman's idea to enlarge the killer's cuff link. He wouldn't have suggested it, if the cuff links were his."

"You're right." Andrea sighed deeply. "I guess I'm just tired and not thinking straight."

"Have some more coffee." Hannah reached out and filled her sister's cup from the carafe that P.K. had brought them.

"This coffee's like tar." Andrea made a face. "Even my instant is better than this."

"I know, but it'll keep you awake until you can go to sleep. Try to concentrate. They just pulled up in front of the school."

Both sisters watched as the contestants went into the auditorium and their families drove away. There was a series of shots as Herb checked their name badges, asked them for their signatures on the sign-in sheet, and unlocked the doors so that they could enter the kitchen sets.

"This isn't going to do any good, Hannah." Andrea sighed. "They're all women, and we know Boyd's killer was a man."

"Right. Let me fast-forward through this part. When you see a man, holler out."

"All right. Whatever you say."

Hannah could hear the dejection in Andrea's voice and she fought against the same feeling. She knew the chance of spotting the killer's cuff links on tape was slim, but there was no way she'd give up without watching Wednesday's footage all the way through to the end. "Keep alert, Andrea. When we get to the part where the audience arrives, there should be some shots of Tracey. You're probably there, too."

"I forgot about that. Okay, Hannah. I'm watching."

Andrea sounded much more alert and Hannah's lips twitched as she hid a smile. She knew there wouldn't be any shots of Tracey and Andrea until they'd watched another two hours or so of outtakes, but there was no need to tell Andrea that.

"Thanks for your help, Andrea." Hannah put the tape on pause to say good night to her sister. "I'll call you in the morning."

"Not before eight."

"Of course not. I know what happens to people who call you early."

It took Andrea a minute, but then she gave a reluctant smile. "If you're referring to Lucy, that wasn't very nice."

"I know. I never said I was nice. Go home, Andrea. I still have two hours to go."

"Good luck." Andrea started for the door, then turned back. "Do you want us to stop somewhere and bring you back something to eat? Speedy Burger isn't that far from here."

Hannah was sorely tempted. Visions of greasy burgers, milk shakes, and onion rings danced through her head and made her mouth water. But Andrea looked exhausted and it wasn't fair to take advantage of her. "That's okay. I can hold out until I get home."

"Good night then."

Andrea went out the door, and Hannah hit the play button. Her stomach was complaining and the fact that the footage was of Sally's happy hour buffet didn't help. The platter of stuffed mushrooms was almost her undoing. Hannah knew that Sally used a sausage and cheese mixture that was incredibly delicious. Her stomach growled, and she took another sip of coffee, but it was a poor substitute for food.

Something on a man's shirtsleeve glittered as he helped himself to Sally's smoked salmon appetizer. Hannah's heart raced and she hit the pause. She backed up the tape very slowly and sighed as she realized it was only a button on his cuff that had caught the light. She sighed and started the tape again. If she nodded off and missed any of the footage, she'd have to watch it all over again, and once was more than enough.

Hannah stopped the tape four more times during the happy hour buffet sequence. The first time it turned out to be a copper bracelet that was supposed to ward off arthritis, the second time it was a gold button on the sleeve of a blue blazer, and the third and fourth times were only wristwatches. She was seeing cuff links behind every bush.

There was nothing else of interest for several minutes, which seemed as long as hours. Hannah wondered how time could go so slowly. Then there was another drive to the auditorium as the contestants left the Lake Eden Inn for the contest. Hannah fast-forwarded through that section, telling herself that cars following cars wouldn't yield any antique cuff links. She watched the contestants get out of their cars when they arrived at the school and filed into the auditorium, but nothing caught her eye.

Once the contestants had gone inside, Rudy had trained the camera on the parking lot again, for footage of the audience, which was just arriving. This was more interesting, and Hannah didn't have to fight so hard to stay awake. Delores and Carrie drove up and Hannah grinned as Carrie chose a spot and parked. The space was perfectly adequate, but it still took Carrie several attempts to straighten out her wheels and pull in.

Bill's car was next, and Hannah stopped the tape to write down the time code. Andrea looked gorgeous, as always, and Tracey was smiling in Rudy's direction. She gave a little hop and a skip as Bill and Andrea took her by the hands and they walked to the entrance. At least Hannah had managed to accomplish one thing tonight. Andrea would love having a copy of this footage.

Once she'd bracketed the footage of Tracey by time codes on her notepad, Hannah started the tape again and concentrated on the other members of the audience. She recognized Betty Jackson's little Honda as it pulled into a spot, and she watched as Betty emerged from her car. Actually, Betty was quite adept at sliding out, an amazing feat for someone so large. Hannah spotted Phil and Sue Plotnik, her downstairs neighbors, without baby Kevin. Either they'd dropped him off at Sue's mother's place, or they'd called in a baby-sitter. Several of Bertie Straub's older ladies walked up to the entrance, their hair carefully protected by scarves. Hannah suspected they'd just come from appointments at the Cut 'n Curl. Sheriff Grant was next, looking official in full dress uniform, and then Mayor Bascomb and his wife.

Hannah watched as various Lake Eden residents filed in. They were all smiling and looked as if they were anticipating the night's entertainment. There were a few faces she didn't know, people who'd driven in from other Minnesota towns. She paid close attention to them, but she didn't spot any cuff links on the men.

Rudy moved into the auditorium lobby with his camera, right after the last person had filed in. Hannah spotted Claire, who was exchanging a few words with Marge Beeseman and doing her best to ignore the fact that the mayor and his wife were standing only a few feet away. Hannah watched for a moment and then she sighed. If she'd seen this tape a week ago, she wouldn't have batted an eyelash, but it was amazing how a little hindsight could change things. Now that she knew about Claire and Mayor Bascomb, she could see the guilt on their faces in the way they studiously avoided each other's eyes.

Two figures arrived at the back of the line. It was Boyd Watson and his sister, Maryann. He turned to speak to Father Coultas, who'd also come in late, and Maryann spotted several friends and waved at them. Hannah stared at Boyd intently, but he didn't seem any different than usual. He was smiling and relaxed as he turned back to Maryann, and it was clear that he had no premonition he'd be dead in a few short hours.

The next shots were taken backstage, and Hannah winced as Rudy's camera caught her from behind as she walked onto the kitchen set. Her hair flamed orange under the lights and her rear looked a lot larger than she'd thought it was. She thanked her lucky stars that this was an outtake and some kind soul had cut it from the montage. And then she reminded herself that she had to work harder to lose those extra ten pounds.

There was a shot of the newscasters arriving and taking their places behind the news desk. Dee-Dee Hughes was arguing with Rayne Phillips about something, Hannah could see that by their expressions, but there was no sound on that portion of the tape. Rudy had caught another shot of her, placing a slice of her cake on a dessert plate. She didn't look fat, and Hannah gave a grateful sigh. Perhaps it had merely been the angle on Rudy's first shot and she didn't have to lose weight, after all.

There was a shot of several people in makeup chairs and Hannah watched for Tracey. When she spotted her niece, looking adorable in a makeup cape that covered her all the way down to the tips of her shoes, she bracketed the segment by time codes for Andrea. As she wrote down the numbers, she sighed with relief. Only an hour to go.

"Hannah?"

Hannah turned toward the door at the sound of her name and saw P.K. standing there. "Yes?"

"If you're okay here, I thought I'd run out to the Quick Stop and pick up some snacks."

"I'm fine," Hannah assured him. "I found some shots of my niece."

"Just give me the time codes before you go and I'll dupe a tape for your sister. How about you? Do you want anything?"

"Just the tape for Andrea."

"Not that. I mean from the Quick Stop."

"Oh. Sure." Hannah started to smile, but then she remembered her diet. She rummaged in her purse, pulled out a five-dollar bill and handed it to him. "I'd like a large Diet Coke and as many chocolate candy bars as you can get for this."

"Chocolate candy bars and a *Diet* Coke?" P.K. asked, sounding amused.

"I need the endorphins from the chocolate," Hannah explained, with what she thought made perfect sense, "but there's no sense in adding empty calories."

P.K. quirked his eyebrows, but he didn't comment on that reasoning. He just waved and ducked out the door.

After he'd left, the huge truck seemed much less friendly. Hannah settled back down to watch the tape, but she felt uneasy. An icy wind had kicked up, and the metal walls of the

truck creaked and groaned with each gust. She wasn't the
type to be frightened at nothing, but Hannah couldn't help
thinking about what would happen if the killer had found out
that she was searching Rudy's outtakes for the sight of his
cuff links. Perhaps he'd murdered Coach Watson in the heat
of anger, but Lucy's execution had been cold-blooded and
calculated. If the killer thought that Hannah was closing in
on him, he could be waiting for an opportunity to get her
alone and then . . .

It took some real effort on Hannah's part to calm her
nerves. She told herself that the killer couldn't possibly
know what she was attempting to do. Only six people knew
that she was viewing the outtakes. There was Mason
Kimball, who thought she was watching them to spot anyone
Boyd had talked to in the audience. He knew nothing about
her *real* reason, and since he didn't know, he couldn't tell
anyone. Then there was Rudy, who thought she was just curious about how much footage had gone into making up the
montage, and P.K., who'd assumed that they were looking
for shots of Tracey. Andrea and Bill knew, but they'd gone
home, and neither one of them would mention it anyway.
Then there was Mike, and Hannah knew she was safe on that
score. No one could pry any information from Mike.

Hannah sat back and picked up the remote control. She
was safe. There was no reason to worry. If she was a little
jumpy, she could attribute that to the caffeine in P.K.'s extra-
strong coffee and her overactive imagination. She pressed
the play button and sighed as she noticed the time code on
the screen. An hour to go, and it couldn't be over soon
enough to suit her.

She suffered through a close-up of her at the judging
table and groaned. She could almost see her hair frizz under
the lights. There were close-ups of the other judges, too, and
that made her feel a bit better. None of them were movie star
material. Then Boyd came into the frame, and Hannah

leaned forward to scrutinize his face. He looked excited at being chosen as a judge, but he certainly wasn't nervous, and there was no sign of fear on his face. Boyd conferred with her for a moment, Rudy had caught their off-camera dialogue on his roving cam, and Hannah could hear her own voice faintly in the background as she told Boyd how to rate the four desserts and enter his scores on the score sheets.

Boyd looked vital and healthy, a man in the prime of his life. Even though she fought against it, Hannah felt a slight pang of sadness. Boyd had been a brute to Danielle, and nothing would change that, but he'd died horribly, and the person who'd taken his life deserved to be caught and punished.

Rudy's camera shifted to shots of the contestants, who were putting the final touches on their desserts. Hannah grinned as she noticed how the contestant who'd baked the winning lemon tart looked back and forth from the judging table to the samples of dessert she'd prepared. She straightened a slice on the plate, wiped the edge with a clean dish towel, then stood back and drew a deep breath. Hannah could see how nervous she was. There was no way, at this point, that she could know she'd end up winning and advancing to the finals.

The next shot made Hannah laugh out loud. It was a rear shot of Mr. Hart, as he bent over to pick up a note card he'd dropped. It wasn't at all flattering, and she heard Rudy's voice saying, "Don't use this shot. We'll all get fired." Then the stage manager motioned the contestants forward, and Rudy taped them delivering their entries to the judging table.

A montage had run during the judging. Hannah half expected Rudy to have trained his camera on the giant screen that the audience had watched. It would have been a bit like *Pyramus and Thisbe,* Shakespeare's play-within-a-play in *Midsummer Night's Dream,* but Rudy had avoided that particular self-indulgence and panned the audience instead.

Hannah could hear the music from the montage faintly in the background as a shot of Mr. Avery appeared. He looked extremely nervous, on the edge of panic, and Hannah knew why. He'd tried to bribe Jeremy Rutlege the day he'd arrived, and Lucy had caught him in the act.

There was a shot of Maryann sitting next to Boyd's empty seat. She was smiling at Boyd instead of watching the montage, and she looked very proud that her baby brother had been chosen to be one of the judges. The audience was quiet, except for a few scattered coughs from winter colds, and almost everyone was gazing up at the giant screen.

Suddenly, out of nowhere, there was a loud crash. Hannah leaned forward to stare at the monitor, but Rudy's tape was still running, and nothing seemed to be wrong. Then there was a second crash and Hannah hit the pause button. The noise hadn't come from the sound track. There was someone outside in the parking lot.

Heart pounding fast, Hannah jumped up from her chair. Someone was trying to get into the production truck, and she had to find some kind of a weapon. She grabbed the first thing she saw, a folded light stand that was heavy enough to serve as a club, and raced down the hallway toward the door.

The door was locked, but it didn't look very secure. Hannah was about to copy a technique from a movie she'd seen and grab a desk chair to shove up under the knob. Then she realized that the door opened out. A chair would do no good.

Hannah swallowed hard, attempting to push down the tide of panic. Her ears were on full alert, listening for the sound of footsteps on the metal stairs. The only sound was the wind and the creaking of the truck as the icy gusts hit the sides.

There was no way that Hannah could move. Her legs were shaking too hard. The killer could be standing on the other side of the door, preparing to break it down. When nothing happened for several minutes, she crept quietly to a position near the door, where she could watch the knob. If the killer broke in, she wasn't going down without a fight. She stood there trembling, her adrenaline racing and her makeshift club at the ready, praying that it was only the wind, rattling the lids on the Dumpsters, and knowing in her heart that it wasn't.

Chapter
Twenty-One

Hannah knew she couldn't stand there forever, waiting for something to happen. Why had she told P.K. that she'd be all right alone? She should have said she'd ride with him. They could have locked up the production truck for a couple of minutes and right now she'd be standing at the counter of the Quick Stop, paying for her own Diet Coke and chocolate candy bars. Instead, she was all alone, about to face the killer who'd bludgeoned Boyd Watson to death and shot Lucy in the back of the head.

Hannah's mind whirled, going into overdrive. She had to call for help. But the phone was on the desk right in front of the window and the slats on the venetian blinds were open slightly. If she used that phone, the killer could see her. She'd be a perfect target for one quick shot through the window.

The moment she thought of it, Hannah hit the light switch next to the door and doused the lights. Being in the dark would be to her advantage. Then she crept to the desk and lifted the receiver, preparing to punch out 9-1-1. But there was no dial tone. The gusts of wind must have snapped the temporary telephone lines they'd run to the production truck.

Then another, even more frightening thought occurred to Hannah and her fingers shook as she replaced the receiver in the cradle. The phone lines ran on the outside of the truck. The killer could have cut them.

Heart beating in panic mode, Hannah moved to the window and peeked out through the slats of the blinds. Nothing was moving except gusts of snow that kicked up with each blast of wind. They rattled up against the metal walls of the truck like snare drums. They reminded Hannah of the muted snare drums in *The Private Life of Henry VIII,* right before the blade had severed Anne Boleyn's head.

That kind of thinking made Hannah shudder, and she pushed the visual image from her mind. It was snow, only icy snow that rattled against the walls, and the gusty winds gave her another advantage. It was windchill. The actual temperature was in the low teens, but wind robbed heat from a person's body. If you added in the windchill factor, the loss of heat would be comparable to a reading of twenty below. The killer would be wearing fur-lined gloves to keep his fingers from freezing, and that meant he'd have to pull off his gloves before he fired his first shot. Perhaps it would only give her an extra second or two, but it was something.

Hannah gazed out at the parking lot, her eyes alert for any movement. The longer the killer stayed out there, the colder he'd get. She didn't hear any car engines running in the silence between the gusts of wind. At least he wasn't sitting inside his car with the heater going full-blast to thaw out his trigger finger.

There was a light in the parking lot, an overhead fixture that gave everything a strange pinkish orange glow. The banks of snow looked as if they were made from the mango slush machine at the Quick Stop. She could still see an indentation on the surface of the snow-covered asphalt where

P.K.'s car had been parked only minutes ago, but the winds were filling it in fast. Her Suburban sat right next to it, looking more orange than candy-apple red.

Hannah thought of the crowbar in the back, right next to the spare tire. It would be a better weapon than the aluminum light stand, but she wasn't about to venture out to get it. She was safer here by a long shot.

She winced at the phrase "a long shot." Would the killer just start shooting up the production truck, trying to kill her from a distance? Should she duck for cover under one of the metal desks, hoping the thin panels would protect her? But the killer wouldn't dare fire too many shots. There were neighbors across from the school. One of them would hear and call the sheriff's station to report the gunfire. He would have to make his first shot count and that meant he'd have to come inside.

As Hannah stared out between the slats, her eyes aching from the strain of not blinking, she had a sudden thought. Where was the killer's car? It had to be parked on the other side of the truck. If she could see it, she could write down his license plate number. She could leave it for Mike and Bill just in case . . .

Hannah stopped herself in mid-thought. She wasn't going to consider the worst-case scenario; it would only slow her down. She felt her way to the other side of the truck, gripping her light stand, for what it was worth. Then she wiggled behind the cabinet that held the fax machine and the copier, and crept up to the window.

There was nothing there. Absolutely nothing. The parking lot was completely deserted. But the killer had to have driven here, unless . . .

Hannah's eyes moved to the street on the other side of the school, the block where Danielle lived. Several cars were parked there, but it was too far away to see their license plates. They were just snow-covered lumps under the streetlight. The killer could have parked there. There were no lights in any of the houses. All of Danielle's neighbors had turned in for the night. With the gusty winds outside, none of them would have heard a car pulling up and parking.

He could also be parked in front of the auditorium, in the lot that was reserved for the audience. There was no night watchman at the school. The students at Jordan High were a pretty good bunch and loved their school. It had never been vandalized, and there was no need for nighttime security.

Hannah jumped as she heard another crash, coming from the side of the truck she'd just left. She ran back to that window and looked out in time to see a large shape disappearing around the far side of her Suburban. A dog? No, the shape had been too big for a dog. A man in a bulky coat, crouched and running, afraid that someone might spot him? That was much more likely.

The winds howled again, rocking the production truck, and in the interval between the gusts, Hannah heard a loud thump. Someone had hit the side of her Suburban with a lot of force. Was the killer trying to break into her cookie truck? Did he think she was hiding in there? And when he found out that she wasn't, would he come to the production truck to kill her?

There was a second thump that was even louder than the first, what sounded like an enraged growl, and then Hannah saw headlights come up behind her Suburban. A spotlight flashed from the side of the car, illuminating the whole area, and Hannah watched in openmouthed astonishment as a huge black bear emerged from the far side of her truck. It froze for a second in the light, then tore across the parking lot at a faster pace than she'd known bears could run. She watched as it disappeared into the bushes that led to the woods at the far side of the athletic field, and then she sat down hard in the desk chair.

"Hannah?" There was a knock at the door. "Open up, Hannah. It's Mike."

"Coming." Hannah got to her feet on legs that still felt weak. She opened the door, saw Mike standing there, solid and reassuring in the pinkish orange light, and did the first thing that came into her mind. She threw her arms around his neck and hugged him as hard as she could.

"Hey, there's a shot of your mother," Mike said, pointing to the monitor. "She looks really good. You've got a gorgeous mother, Hannah."

"I'm glad you think so. It's very important." Hannah started to grin. They were munching chocolate bars and watching the footage that Rudy had shot of the audience as they'd left after the show.

"Why is it important?" Mike gave her a puzzled look.

"They always say that if you want to know what a daughter will look like, all you have to do is meet her mother." Hannah sneaked a glance at Mike and noticed that he looked very uncomfortable. It was obvious he wasn't sure whether he should agree with her or argue the point. Hannah's grin grew wider, and she reached out to pat his arm. "Never mind. I'm just kidding around. Andrea and Michelle take after Mother. I don't."

"Yes, but you're still beautiful. You're just not like your mother, that's all."

Now Hannah was uncomfortable. She hadn't been fishing for compliments, but Delores had taught all three of her daughters that when a man paid you a compliment, you were supposed to merely thank him and leave it at that.

"Thank you," Hannah said, fighting her urge to say anything further. But the silence hung between them and she was too uncomfortable not to break it. "And thanks for running off that bear. He had me pretty scared."

"That bear was a she, and you were right to be scared.

She was big, and she was hungry. That's a dangerous combination."

"Hungry?" Hannah seized the new direction their conversation had taken and ran with it. "How do you know that?"

"Most bears are hibernating about now. Something rousted her out, and she came down here to search for food. She got some from the cafeteria Dumpster. It was tipped over on its side, and garbage was scattered all over the place. I figure she'd had her dinner and she was going for dessert."

"Dessert?"

"Your truck. It probably smells like cookies inside."

"She would have been disappointed. Andrea ate every one I had left." Hannah caught something on the screen, and she reached out for the remote control. "Hold on, Mike. I saw something."

Hannah backed up the tape and they stared at the screen as she started it again, freeze-framing at the critical moment. It was another false alarm, only a shiny button on a man's coat sleeve that Hannah had glimpsed as he'd unlocked his car.

"Here comes Boyd Watson." Mike sat forward on the edge of his chair.

Hannah watched Boyd as he walked toward his car, her domed cake carrier in his arms. He handed it to Maryann so that he could unlock and open the passenger door for her, took it back while she got in, and handed it to her again. Once he was sure that Maryann was settled, he closed the door and walked around to the driver's side of the car.

"Polite, isn't he?" Mike commented, his brows knit in a frown.

"Of course he is. People might be watching." Hannah couldn't keep the sarcasm from her voice. She'd also seen Boyd being very solicitous of Danielle when they'd attended public functions.

"Maryann doesn't know, does she?" Mike asked.

"No." Hannah knew exactly what he meant. "She wouldn't believe that her brother was a wife beater unless you showed her proof. And if you did that, she'd tell everyone that Danielle had done something to bring it on."

"It's a sick world."

"Not all of it." Hannah shook her head. "There are some really good people out there. You're at a disadvantage because you're a cop. You don't get to deal with the good ones very often."

Mike turned to look at her, then started to smile. "You're just what I need, Hannah. You're an optimist."

"Maybe." Hannah smiled back. "Right now I'm optimistic that there's one of those candy bars left."

Mike glanced down at the sack on the table and crunched it down with his hand. "You were too optimistic. I just ate the last one."

"Oh, well." Hannah sighed, and then she had an idea. "Why don't we finish this tape and drive out to the Corner Tavern? They've got great steak and eggs, and they're open all night. I'll even pay for your breakfast for saving me from that hungry bear."

"Sounds good. I haven't been treated to breakfast by a beautiful woman in years. If you keep this up, you might make an optimist out of me yet."

"You're right." Mike cut off a slice of his steak and eyed it with satisfaction. "They do a great steak here. It's cooked just the way I ordered it."

Hannah glanced down at the hunk of meat on his fork and snapped her mouth shut. How anyone could eat well-done beef was beyond her. Her steak was blood rare, just the way she liked it. She'd given her order the standard way, *Thirty seconds on one side, thirty seconds on the other side and slap it on the plate. If you can't do that, bring it to me raw with a book of matches.*

"We need to talk, Mike," Hannah told him, dipping the corner of her toast into the egg yolk on her plate. "I know some things about your case."

Mike swallowed and his eyebrows shot up. "More than you told me in the squad car?"

"Yes. I'll tell you, but you have to promise not to accuse me of meddling."

Mike thought about it for a minute. "Okay. I won't mention the word. What is it?"

"It's not it. It's a whole series of things. Let's finish breakfast before our eggs get cold, and I'll tell you everything I think you should know."

Mike dropped his fork and stared at her. "You'll tell me everything you *think* I should know?"

"Right. Some of it's confidential and doesn't have anything to do with the murders. You'll just have to trust me on that. Is it a deal?"

Mike picked up his fork and stabbed another piece of steak with more force than he needed. He thought about it for a moment as he chewed and swallowed, then sighed. "Okay, Hannah. I can't say I like it, but it's a deal."

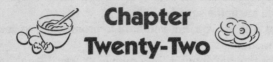

Chapter
Twenty-Two

When the alarm clock went off at six the next morning, Hannah rolled over and shut it off. She performed that act by feel, not even bothering to open her eyes. Then she rolled over again, pulled up the covers to her chin, and went back to sleep.

A bit later, Hannah became aware of something tapping her cheek. She happened to be dreaming of homicidal woodpeckers at the time, a huge flock of redheaded birds who were swarming around Lucy's garage, pecking at the door to get inside. She startled awake, her arms flailing to ward off their needle-sharp beaks and managed to upend Moishe, who had been trying to wake her by batting at her face. He yowled at her rude response to his efforts, leaped to the table by the side of the bed, and stood there staring at her accusingly.

"Sorry, Moishe," Hannah mumbled, sitting upright. She glanced at the clock and made a face. Six-thirty. She'd overslept. Someone ought to pass a law to make mornings illegal.

Twenty minutes later, Hannah was sitting at the kitchen table, showered, dressed, and on her second cup of coffee. Moishe had forgiven her for strong-arming him the moment after she'd filled his food bowl. Now he was crunching his breakfast and purring loudly.

Hannah glanced out the window. It was ten minutes to seven, and the sky was as dark as night. They were closing in on the shortest day of the year. On December 21, the sun would shine for less than nine hours, and most Lake Eden residents would drive to and from work with their headlights on.

Sitting here thinking about day and night in the northern hemisphere wouldn't accomplish much. Hannah drank the rest of her coffee and pushed back her chair. It was time to get to work, figure out what she wanted to bake on camera tonight, and call Andrea to cue her in on what she'd told Mike last night at the Corner Tavern.

Hannah got into her parka, grabbed her car keys and her garbage, and groaned as the phone rang. Delores. Should she answer it, or pretend she'd already left? Of course it could be Mike. Or Bill. Or any of a hundred other people. Hannah stood there and listened as the answering machine picked up.

The outgoing message played, and she heard her mother's voice. "Hannah? Pick up if you're still there. I've got something important to tell you about The Gulls."

Hannah raced for the phone. The Gulls were Jordan High's basketball team, and there was a chance that Delores might have heard something about the player who used steroids.

"I'm here, Mother." Hannah shrugged out of her parka and tossed it over the back of a chair. Delores didn't know how to have a short conversation. If she wore her coat for the entire call, she'd drop from heat exhaustion. "What about The Gulls?"

"It's what Mason Kimball did. Isn't he a wonderful man?"

"I guess so." Hannah collected her coffee cup from the sink and filled it with the last from the carafe. It would take a while to get any pertinent facts from her mother. "What did Mason do?"

"I know you don't have much time, so I'll make it fast," Delores promised.

"Thanks, Mother," Hannah said, instead of *Oh, sure. Fat chance.*

"Carrie and I drove out to the inn for the party last night, and while we were there, we ran into Mason. Sally certainly does a nice buffet, doesn't she?"

"Yes. What about Mason?"

"He was talking about The Gulls and how upset the boys were, now they'd lost their coach. Gil Surma is filling in temporarily, but he admits he doesn't know that much about basketball. You know Gil, don't you, dear?"

Hannah took a big gulp of her coffee. "Yes, I know him. What else did Mason say?"

"He told us that he arranged for a professional basketball coach to take over until the school could hire someone new."

"Really?" Hannah was surprised. "I didn't know the school had a budget for things like that."

"They don't. That's why I said that Mason was such a nice man. He's paying for the coach out of his own pocket."

"That's very generous." Hannah thought about it for a moment, then she began to frown. "Why would Mason do something like that?"

"Because he has a real interest in Jordan High's basketball program. His son plays for The Gulls. You know Craig Kimball, don't you, dear?"

It took Hannah a moment, but then she placed him. Craig had come into The Cookie Jar a couple of times to pick up cookies for the team. "Sure, I know him. He seems like a good kid."

"He is. Mason said Craig took Coach Watson's death hard. And he's very concerned about the college recruiters that are coming to watch the game with the Little Falls Flyers next weekend. Craig was afraid that Gil might make strategic mistakes, and that's why Mason hired a professional coach to take over the team."

Hannah started to smile. She finally had most of the picture. "Craig's up for an athletic scholarship, and Mason wants him to look good on the court?"

"That's what I said, dear."

Hannah started to grin. Delores hadn't said that, but she might have if Hannah had given her another twenty minutes or so. "Is Craig a good player?"

"He is now. Craig sat on the bench for most of last year, but he's improved a lot since then. This year he's The Gulls's star player."

Hannah's senses went on full alert. Steroids enhanced a player's performance. "Why do you think Craig improved so much?"

"Mason sent him to basketball camp over the summer. They have professional coaches and trainers, and the enrollment is limited to twenty boys. Each boy has his own personal mentor, and most of them go on to make names for themselves in college basketball."

Hannah's suspicions died a quick death. Summer basketball camp could easily account for Craig's improvement. "A camp like that sounds expensive."

"It was. Mason didn't tell me how much, but he said it was worth every penny. Craig already had most of the skills, but the camp really built up his self-confidence. Just a couple of weeks ago, he broke the school record for scoring the most points in a game. The other boys elected him team captain this year, and Mason says they're always asking him for advice."

"Thanks for telling me, Mother." Hannah jotted Craig Kimball's name on her notepad. Perhaps she should talk to him. If he knew which of his teammates was using steroids, he might tell her, especially if she convinced him that they were dangerous and the player who used them would need medical help to wean him off the drug. "I've got to run, Mother. I'm already late."

"Just one more thing. I ran into Rod Metcalf at the party last night, and he told me that Lucy Richards wants to do an article on my antique jewelry collection. He's going to send her over at eleven to take pictures and I need your advice on which pieces to display. I thought I'd put them out on a piece of blue velvet and . . ."

"Don't bother," Hannah interrupted her. "Lucy's not coming."

"How do you know that?"

Hannah sighed. She really didn't want to go down that particular road, but she couldn't let her mother get out every piece in her jewelry collection for pictures that no one would take. "Lucy's not coming because she's dead."

"Dead?"

"Yes, Mother. Lucy was murdered."

"But it hasn't been on the radio yet! I've been listening. There's no way you could know, unless . . ." Delores stopped speaking, and Hannah knew that her mother was gathering herself to ask the obvious question. "Hannah? Tell me you didn't . . ." Delores paused to clear her throat, and when she spoke again, she sounded very tentative. "Did you?"

"I'm afraid I did, Mother. I found Lucy last night."

"Hannah! You've simply got to stop doing things like this!"

"It's not like a scavenger hunt, Mother. I don't go around

looking for murder victims on purpose." Hannah realized she sounded defensive and she tried to moderate her tone. "It just happened. And I had to report it."

"I suppose you're right. But I do wish you'd be a little more careful, Hannah."

Hannah laughed. She couldn't help it. What did being careful have to do with finding bodies?

"It's no laughing matter," Delores chided her.

"I know." Hannah bit back another chuckle. "You're right, Mother. I promise I'll do my best not to find any more bodies."

"Good. Tell me what happened."

"I don't have time, Mother. Listen to the radio if you want the details. The news should break any minute now. I've got to get to work."

Before her mother could object, Hannah hung up and drew a deep breath. She glanced down at Moishe, realized that he was staring up at her expectantly, and got out the kitty crunchies to refill his food bowl. Then she slipped into her parka for the second time, picked up the garbage for the second time, and felt to make sure her car keys were still in her pocket. "See you tonight, Moishe," she said. Then she hurried out the door before the phone could ring again.

A blast of frigid air greeted Hannah as she rushed down the outside stairs to the garage. The stairs were snow-free, thanks to the Minnesota construction firm who'd designed them. They were open stairs made of textured cement slats with a sloping roof above them. The roof kept off the rain in the summer, and the snow and ice in the winter.

Once Hannah had dropped her garbage bag into the Dumpster that sat in what looked like a little concrete bunker in the garage, she unplugged her truck, wound the cord around her bumper and climbed in under the wheel. She fired up the engine, flicked on her headlights, drove up the ramp and exited her condo complex on automatic pilot. As she turned onto Old Lake Road and drove toward town, she thought about Craig Kimball again. She'd approach him as a friend who could help him. If Craig knew who was using steroids and he was wrestling with the problem alone, he might welcome an adult's help.

What would she do about Mike? Hannah started to frown. If Mike knew that she intended to talk to Craig Kimball about steroid use, he'd want to come along. Mike was a good guy, but he'd end up tying her hands. Not only was he a relative newcomer to Lake Eden, Mike was a cop. Craig wouldn't say boo about steroids in front of a cop. She had to talk to Craig alone and leave Mike out of it until she needed him.

Hannah hit the brakes and swore as a car passed her on the left and pulled back into her lane much too fast. The car was sporting Florida plates and was obviously owned by a person who knew nothing about winter driving conditions. Hannah felt like pulling up beside him and giving him a piece of her mind, but that would take time, and time was one thing she didn't have.

A cookie would help to improve her mood. Hannah reached in the back before she remembered that Andrea had eaten them all. This was starting off to be a very bad day. She'd only had a couple of hours of sleep, she was late to work, Delores had called, she'd almost had an accident on the road, the heater on her truck was putting out even less hot air than usual, and there were no breakfast cookies. If she hadn't had a tendency to sunburn in thirty seconds flat, she'd seriously consider hopping the first plane to Hawaii and chucking it all for a weekend on the beach.

"Hi, Hannah." Lisa greeted her with a sunny smile as she blew in through the back door, and Hannah immediately felt better. "Take off your coat, and I'll pour you a cup of coffee."

"Cookies?" Hannah asked, hanging her coat on the rack.

"The Chocolate Chip Crunches are still warm. Do you want a couple?"

"More than a couple," Hannah answered, pulling a stool up to the work island. "Bring me four to start."

Lisa was efficient at baking as well as serving, and a few moments later Hannah was smiling as she sipped hot coffee and munched cookies. If chocolate were a mandatory part of breakfast, people wouldn't be so grouchy in the morning.

"You asked me to think about what we should bake tonight," Lisa reminded her. "How about cookies? You haven't done them yet, and you're famous for your cookies."

Hannah's eyebrows shot up. "You're right! Which ones should we bake?"

"Molasses Crackles. Everybody loves them, and they look gorgeous when they come out of the oven."

"Perfect. Will you have time to mix up the dough? I've got something I have to do this morning, and it has to chill before we bake."

Lisa gave a smug grin. "I'm way ahead of you. I mixed it up last night, and it's in the cooler. I even baked a test sheet this morning, to make sure they were perfect."

"Were you so confident that I'd take your suggestion?"

"Not really. I figured that if you wanted to make something else, I'd bake the cookies and freeze them for the children's Christmas party. They look really nice if you pipe green frosting around the edge and put on a red frosting bow, like a wreath."

Hannah winced. She'd promised to bring ten dozen cookies to the Lake Eden Community Center for the party and forgotten all about it. But Lisa hadn't forgotten. She was already planning out what to bake. Lisa was a lot more than an assistant, and it made Hannah even more convinced to offer her some kind of a partnership.

"I'll prepare your box of ingredients for tonight. I've got plenty of time to do it before we open. Do you want more coffee? I'll get it."

"That's okay. My legs aren't broken," Hannah said with a grin. She got up and walked through the swinging door to the cookie shop and blinked in astonishment. Not only had Lisa finished the baking, set up the tables, filled the large glass cookie jars behind the counter, and written the day's cookies on the menu board, she'd also found time to decorate the shop for Christmas.

Definitely a partnership, Hannah thought, as she took in the clever pinecone-and-candy-cane centerpieces on each table, the miniature Christmas lights that framed the plate-glass window, the Christmas stockings that were tacked to the top of the wainscoting that ran around the walls, the wreath on the front door, and the Christmas tree that Lisa had set up in the corner. *If I paid Lisa what she's really worth, I'd be broke in no time flat.*

Hannah walked over to the tree for a closer look and just shook her head. Lisa had outdone herself. The Christmas tree was perfect. It was decorated with miniature lights, a glittering tinsel garland, and ornaments that looked like real cookies.

"I wanted to surprise you." Lisa stood in the doorway, a happy smile on her face. "I know I should have asked you first, but you've been so busy, I didn't want to bother you. Do you like it?"

"Are you kidding? Everything's gorgeous, especially the tree. Are those cookie ornaments real?"

Lisa nodded. "I shellacked them. I followed the instructions in a craft book, and it said they should last for years."

"I believe it." Hannah chuckled as she touched one of the cookies. "They're as hard as rocks."

"Then you're not upset that I just did it without asking?"

"I'm not upset, I'm impressed. The Cookie Jar's never

looked so good. Last year I just hung a string of lights, and that was it." As Hannah gazed around her, she thought about Lisa's abilities. Not only was she reliable and loyal, she baked like a dream, she was good with the customers, she could decorate cookies even better than Hannah could, and she'd decked out the shop for Christmas like a pro. It was time to make a move before someone else in Lake Eden discovered just how talented Lisa was. Hannah turned, walked over to Lisa and shook her hand. "Good work, partner."

Lisa's face was a study in contrasts. It was clear she hoped she'd heard Hannah right, but she was almost afraid to ask. Finally, she gulped and asked, "Partner?"

"Partner," Hannah repeated it and smiled. "It's the least I can do when you're doing most of the work. I'll work out the details with Howie Levine and have him draw up the papers before Christmas. There's no way I'm going to chance losing you, Lisa."

Lisa shook her head. "You won't lose me. I love working here. You don't have to make me a partner to keep me."

"Bad move, Lisa." Hannah couldn't resist teasing her a little. "When someone offers you a partnership, you're not supposed to try to talk them out of it. Just say 'no thanks,' or 'I accept,' and that's all there is to it."

Lisa nodded, and Hannah noticed that her eyes were shining. "You're right, Hannah. I accept."

After a quick phone call to Charlotte Roscoe, Jordan High's secretary, Hannah headed for the school. She'd learned two things. Mike had called Charlotte and she'd faxed him a complete roster of The Gulls basketball team, and Craig Kimball was spending his first period, from eight-forty-five to nine-forty, in the library, where he would be studying for his midterm in English literature.

As she parked her truck in the section of the teachers'

parking lot that was reserved for visitors, Hannah remembered that she'd intended to bring her box of ingredients for tonight's baking. She got out of her truck with a frown on her face. Why did she always remember things after the fact? She had the test sheet of Molasses Crackles that Lisa had baked. At least she'd remembered to take them. She'd give them to Craig to soften him up for her questions.

A yellow school bus was parked at the entrance as Hannah walked up. It was filled with elementary-school students, a teacher, and three parents. It was obviously a field trip of some type and as Hannah passed, several bus windows lowered and kids leaned out to wave at the Cookie Lady. Hannah waved back and hid the test batch of Molasses Crackles under her coat, wishing she had more cookies to give them.

The lobby of the school was quiet, and Hannah realized that classes must have started. It smelled the same as it always had, a combination of sweeping compound, warm bodies, and chalk. Hannah had always loved that smell. It meant that brains were at work. She walked down the hall past the principal's office and waved at Charlotte, who had her nose deep in a filing cabinet and didn't see her.

The library was in the same place it had always been, at the rear of the school and adjacent to the covered walkway that connected the high school to the elementary school. Hannah remembered walking from the elementary school to the high school when she was in fourth grade, clutching a note from her teacher, Miss Parry. The high-school library had been her favorite place, and Miss Parry had given Hannah permission to visit it every time her assignments had been completed early.

The main part of the library was exactly as Hannah remembered it. The only change was the computer lab that had been added after her graduation. She glanced at the long oak tables that were placed around the room and spotted Craig at a table near the stacks. He was alone, and Hannah thanked her lucky stars for that. At least she wouldn't have to pull him away from his friends.

"Hi, Craig." Hannah spoke softly, a habit the librarian, Mrs. Dodds, had instilled in her on her first visit. Mrs. Dodds had retired several years ago and Hannah had noticed that a very young-looking woman, surely too young to be a librarian, had taken her place behind the old curved desk at the front of the room. "Do you have a minute?"

"Sure." Craig looked surprised to see her, but he pulled out a chair for her.

Hannah sat, the smile still on her face. She'd start with a little flattery and go from there. "Congratulations on breaking the school single-game scoring record. I brought you a dozen Molasses Crackles."

"Thanks, Miss Swensen." Craig grinned as he reached out for the bag. "I didn't know you came to our basketball games."

"Every chance I get." Hannah told a little white lie. She'd never been a big basketball fan, not even in high school, and the last basketball game she'd attended had been over a decade ago. "I need to talk to you about The Gulls, Craig."

"Okay." Craig placed a pencil in his book to hold the place and closed it.

Hannah managed to keep the smile on her face with difficulty. It was a good thing Mrs. Dodds had retired. She would have had heart palpitations if she'd seen Craig use a pencil for a bookmark. Her favorite phrase had been, *A book is your friend, and you don't break a friend's back.*

Craig looked at her expectantly. "I don't mean to be rude, Miss Swensen, but I've only got a few minutes. I still have to study for a test."

"English lit?"

"That's right. How did you know?"

"I called Mrs. Roscoe to find out your class schedule, and she told me. What does your test cover?"

"Nineteenth-century English poets." Craig made a face.

"Maybe I can help you cram for that test." Hannah slid her chair closer. "You hit my field, Craig. I was an English lit major in college."

"You were?" Craig looked at her with new respect. "Do you know about . . . uh . . . Byron?"

"*Lord* Byron. His most famous poem was *Childe Harold's Pilgrimage,* and he limped all over the Lake District looking soulful while the girls chased after him."

Craig's eyebrows shot up. "Lord Byron limped?"

"Yes," Hannah said. Perhaps she would have made a good teacher after all. "He was born with a deformed foot, but that didn't turn anyone off. He couldn't go anywhere without groupies following him."

"So he was like a rock star?"

"As close as you could get in nineteenth-century England. He married very briefly, had a daughter, got divorced, and left the country. He caught a fever in Greece and died."

"From a fever?"

"Yes. People died from things like the flu or a really bad cold back then. They didn't have any of the medicines we have now."

Craig was clearly surprised. His literature teacher had obviously failed to set the scene. "Not even aspirin?"

"Only in the form of willow bark. When people got sick, there wasn't much a doctor could do. Either they got better on their own, or they died."

"It sure doesn't say all that in here." Craig tapped his literature book. "It makes Lord Byron's life a lot more interesting, just like in a movie."

"I know." Hannah could sympathize. A list of dates and

titles didn't do it for her either. "You can remember a lot better if you know some personal facts."

Craig leaned forward. "Say . . . do you know stories like that about Shelley and Keats?"

"You bet I do." Hannah took Craig's book and flipped it open, glancing at the list of poets who were covered. "And I can tell you all the dirt on Coleridge, Wordsworth, and Southey."

Craig looked dubious. "I read about them. They're pretty boring guys."

"That's because you don't know anything about their personal lives. Coleridge got disowned by his family for fighting in the French Revolution, Wordsworth said that he wrote his best poetry when he was stoned, and Southey went crazy and died insane. That's not boring, is it?"

"I guess not!" Craig shook his head.

Hannah rummaged through her purse and pulled out a pen. It was the one that P.K. had given her last night, a gold-plated Cross that had some engraving on the side. She'd forgotten to return it, but that was easily fixed. Right after she finished with Craig, she'd run out to the production truck and give it back.

"Okay, Craig. Here's the deal." Hannah prepared to outline her plan. "Take out a pen, open your notebook, and I'll tell you all about the poets in your book."

"Okay, but I got to warn you. I'm not very good at taking notes."

"You don't have to be," Hannah assured him. "Just write down things to jog your memory."

"Like what?"

"Write down *Lord Byron* and underline it. And then write down things like, *Bum Foot, Groupies,* and *Died in Greece.* I'll jot down all the other stuff for you. Just give me a blank page from your notebook."

"Here you go." Craig tore off a blank page and handed it

to her. "But what about The Gulls? You said you wanted to ask me something."

"We'll talk about it after I help you cram for your test." Hannah knew she was doing the right thing. Once she'd helped Craig, he'd be more inclined to help her. "Let's start with John Keats. Did you know that he was almost a surgeon instead of a poet?"

Craig leaned forward, his pen at the ready and the Molasses Crackles forgotten. Hannah smiled. Perhaps she should think about starting an English lit study group down at The Cookie Jar.

Molasses Crackles

Do not preheat oven yet.
Dough must chill before baking.

1 ½ cups melted butter *(3 sticks—³/₄ pound)*
2 cups white sugar
½ cup molasses *(use Brer Rabbit green label or a very dark molasses)*
2 beaten eggs *(just whip them up with a fork)*
4 teaspoons baking soda
1 teaspoon salt
3 teaspoons cinnamon *
1 teaspoon nutmeg *(freshly ground is best)*
4 cups flour *(there's no need to sift it)*

* I use 2 ½ teaspoons cinnamon and ½ teaspoon cardamom when I want a deeper, richer flavor.

Melt butter in a large microwave-safe bowl. Add sugar and molasses and stir. Let it cool slightly. Then add the beaten eggs, baking soda, salt, cinnamon, and nutmeg, stirring after each addition. Add flour in one-cup increments, stirring after each one. The dough will be quite stiff.

Cover and refrigerate for at least 2 hours. *(Overnight is fine too.)*

Preheat oven to 350 degrees F., rack in the middle position.

Roll the chilled dough into walnut-sized balls. Put some sugar in a small bowl and roll the balls in it. Place them on a greased cookie sheet *(12 to a standard sheet)*. Press them down just a little so they won't roll off when you carry them to the oven.

Bake for 10–12 minutes. They'll flatten out, all by themselves. Let them cool for 2 minutes on the cookie sheet and then move them to a wire rack to finish cooling.

Molasses cookies freeze well. Roll them up in foil, put them in a freezer bag, and they'll be fine for 3 months or so. (You'd better lock your freezer if you want them to last that long.)

These were Dad's favorite cookies. He used to ask me to bake them on Sunday morning, so he could eat them while he read the paper. Mother is also crazy about them, even though they don't have chocolate.

Chapter Twenty- Three

Hannah walked around the side of the building shaking her head. Craig would do well on his midterm. She was almost sure of that. But he had given her zilch in return. The minute she'd mentioned steroids and The Gulls, the friendly team captain had turned anxious and edgy. He'd denied knowing anything about a suspension in the works or about any kind of drug use, performance-enhancing or otherwise, but Hannah had seen the barely concealed panic in the depths of his eyes. She was positive that Craig knew which player was using steroids. She was equally positive that no power on earth could make him tell her. Craig had wanted to confide in Hannah, but his peer loyalty had won out.

There was a note taped to the production truck door, and Hannah climbed the steps for a closer look. *Staff meeting— back soon,* it read. Hannah knocked on the door, just in case someone had come back and forgotten to take down the note, but no one answered the door. She'd struck out twice, once with Craig and once with returning the pen.

Hannah was about to leave when she had a thought. Perhaps she could leave the pen with Herb. He could give it to a member of the production staff, and they could return it to P.K. She reached inside her purse, pulled out the pen, and immediately discarded that idea when she read the inscription that was written on the side. The gold Cross pen belonged to Mason Kimball, and it had been presented to him when he'd won an award for the best short documentary in a student film contest. It was a keepsake, and Hannah didn't want to take the chance that someone would misplace it.

She thought of Craig Kimball and sighed. If she'd taken the time to read the inscription when she'd been with Craig in the library, she could have given the pen to him to return to his father. But perhaps that wouldn't have been wise. If Mason knew that his night engineer had appropriated his pen, P.K. could wind up in trouble. The best thing to do was give it directly to P.K. so that he could return it to Mason's office.

Hannah glanced at the note again. *Back soon* could mean a few minutes, or an hour, and she didn't have time to wait. She'd catch P.K. when she came back for the contest tonight, and that would have to be soon enough.

Turning on her heel, Hannah walked down the metal steps and across the snowy parking lot, heading for her truck. She'd wasted most of the morning, and her mind was spinning. What she needed right now was to get back to The Cookie Jar for a second dose of chocolate.

"So what did Craig say?" Andrea asked, leaning across the surface of the workstation. She'd dropped in at lunch to find out what had happened since she'd left Hannah at the production truck, and she'd already gotten the full story of the bear, the fact that Hannah had located some shots of Tracey, and her morning cram session with Craig Kimball.

"Nothing."

"You mean he refused to answer your questions?"

"No. He answered them, but he didn't tell me anything. He said he didn't know anyone on The Gulls who was using steroids or any other kind of drugs."

Andrea shrugged. "That's about what I'd expect him to say. He wouldn't be very popular if he ratted on his teammates. Do you think he knew and just didn't want to tell you?"

"Exactly. At least he seemed to realize how serious it was. He said he'd learned about steroids at basketball camp, and I have the feeling he'll talk to his teammate and try to get some help for him. That's good, but it doesn't help us."

"How about Mike? Do you think he's learned anything from the roster?"

Now it was Hannah's turn to shrug. "I don't know. I haven't talked to him since we split up after breakfast at the Corner Tavern."

"Breakfast?" Andrea gave Hannah a sharp look. "You spent all night with Mike?"

Hannah knew exactly what her sister was asking, and she laughed. "Most of it, but it's not what you're thinking. We finished the tapes, we had steak and eggs, and then we went home . . . separately."

"Oh." Andrea looked a little disappointed. "What are you going to do next?"

"I'm going to run home, feed Moishe, and grab my clothes for tonight. If I'm lucky, I might even get in an hour's nap."

"But how about the killer?"

"He'll wait. I'm fresh out of ideas, and I can't think when I'm this tired. I've got to go recharge my batteries."

"Okay. I'll run over to Lucy's neighborhood and pass out

some fliers. I got some good information the last time I did it."

"If anyone can do it, you can." Hannah stood up and walked over to retrieve her parka. She was so tired, it took her a couple of attempts to get her left arm into the sleeve hole. "Call me at home if you learn anything important."

"I thought you were going to take a nap."

"I am." Hannah yawned widely. "But I'm willing to wake up for that."

When Hannah woke up at three-fifteen, she felt ninety percent better. She padded into the kitchen, put on the coffee, and sat down at the table to wait for it to drip down into the carafe. Moishe went straight to his food bowl and seemed surprised to see that it was still full. He'd chosen to take a nap with her, rather than scarf down his kitty crunchies.

"It's not morning, Moishe," Hannah told him. "It's afternoon."

Moishe cocked his head to stare at her. He looked puzzled, and Hannah laughed. "Never mind. Time is a difficult concept. I'm not sure I understand it either."

The coffee was ready and Hannah got up to pour herself a cup. She inhaled the steam and felt the remaining ten percent better, bringing her up to a hundred percent. There was nothing like a cup of coffee when you woke up in the morning, even if the morning was actually afternoon.

By the time she'd finished her third cup, Hannah was ready to face the remainder of the day. There wasn't much left. It was overcast, and the sky was already darkening outside her kitchen window.

"I've got to go, Moishe," Hannah said, and as if on cue, the phone rang. Delores? Andrea? Mike? Hannah wanted to let the answering machine get it, but she was too curious to wait through her outgoing message. She shoved back her chair, lifted the receiver, and answered.

"Hannah?" It was Mason Kimball's voice. "We've got a problem, and I need you on the set early."

"Okay. What's the problem?"

"We're changing the format for the show tonight, and I need to go over some things with you."

"When do you want me there?"

"Ten minutes ago. This could take a while. You'd better bring your outfit for tonight and you can change in Dee-Dee's mobile dressing room. How soon can you get here?"

Hannah glanced at the clock. It was three-thirty. "I'm leaving right now. I have to stop at the shop to pick up my box of ingredients for tonight, then I'll drive right over. I should be there by four-fifteen."

"Good. Come straight to the set. No one's there right now, and it's my only chance to check out camera angles with you."

Hannah said good-bye and made quick work of gathering up her things and leaving the condo complex.

Traffic was light, and Hannah made good time. She breezed in the back door of The Cookie Jar at three-forty-five and pushed through the swinging door to tell Lisa that she was back.

"Hi, Lisa." Hannah caught her new partner in the act of draping the mirror behind the counter with a garland made of pine branches. "That looks nice."

"Thanks, Hannah. Dad made it in one of his craft classes at the Senior Center. Are you here to stay?"

Hannah shook her head. "No, I'm just passing through. Mason Kimball called, and he wants me on the set early. I just stopped by to pick up the box of ingredients for to-night."

"It's on the counter next to the sink. Just take the one box. I'll bring the chilled dough, and Dad can carry in the one with the pans and the bowls."

"Your dad's coming to see you again?"

"Mr. Drevlow can't make it, but Mrs. Beeseman offered to sit with him while I'm up there helping you on the set."

"Really?" Hannah tried not to sound as surprised as she felt. Marge Beeseman usually sat with her own group of friends.

"Herb asked her. Dad told him how much he wanted to go, and Herb said he'd arrange it."

Hannah started to smile. Things must be getting serious between Herb and Lisa if he'd asked his mother to do a favor for her.

"After the show, we're all going out to the inn for the party. Dad says he's going to ask Mrs. Beeseman to dance. He's still a real good dancer. And she promised Herb that if Dad asked her, she would."

Hannah's smile grew wider as she pictured the unlikely double date. "I've got to run, Lisa. I'll see you later, at the school. If Mike calls before you leave, tell him I don't know any more than I did last night."

"I will." Lisa stepped back and eyed the pine garland critically. "I think it needs some red-velvet bows."

"You're my decorating expert. If you want to buy bows, take some money out of the register. Get a receipt and leave it in the tax box under the counter."

"Red-velvet bows are tax deductible?"

"Stan Kramer does our taxes. And with Stan, everything's a tax deduction."

Hannah glanced at her watch as she pulled into the school parking lot. She was ten minutes early, and that was a miracle. It would give her time to return the pen before she met Mason on the set.

As she drove around the building and prepared to pull up next to the production truck, she saw P.K. standing on the metal steps, smoking. Hannah rolled down her window and called out to him. "I've got the pen you let me use last night. Wait a second, and I'll give it to you."

P.K. walked over to her truck as she parked. Hannah left the garment bag hanging from the hook in the back. She could get it later, after she finished talking to Mason on the set. P.K. took her box of ingredients, and they walked toward the production truck together.

"I can let you in, but I've got to take off," P.K. informed her, setting the box on the top step and unlocking the door. "I have to run out to the station to pick up some things. Do you want me to put this box on the set for you?"

"I can take it. I have to go there anyway. Do you want me to put the pen in Mason's office?"

"Yeah. There's a penholder on his desk. Just stick it in there and make sure you lock up when you leave."

"I will," Hannah promised, stepping aside so that P.K. could descend the narrow steps. She gave a little wave as he headed off to his car, then she opened the door and stepped inside the production truck.

Mason's office was at the far end of the hall, in the very back of the truck. Hannah passed the room where she'd watched Rudy's outtakes and stopped with her hand on the knob of Mason's closed door. She knew he wasn't here, but she knocked anyway, just in case someone else was using his office and Rudy hadn't known about it. When there was no answer, she opened the door and stepped in.

The room was a lot smaller than Hannah had thought it would be, just a cubbyhole with a desk, a swivel chair, and bare walls devoid of pictures. For a moment, Hannah wondered why no one had bothered to decorate the boss's office, but then she remembered that this was a mobile production truck. Pictures would have fallen off the walls and broken in transit.

There were pictures on Mason's desk. Hannah noticed them as she slipped the keepsake pen in the holder. He probably kept them in a desk drawer when the truck was moving, but since it was parked for the duration of the bake-off, he'd taken them out and arranged them on the top of his desk. There was one of Ellen in a gold frame, smiling at the camera and looking ten years younger. There was another of Mason and Craig, and Hannah could tell that it was a recent photo. Father and son were both beaming, and together, they were holding up a silver trophy. It was a cup with a silver basketball at its base and both of them looked proud and happy.

She stared at the picture for a moment. It must have been taken at the award ceremony that Delores had mentioned, when Craig had broken Jordan High's scoring record. Craig was dressed in his basketball uniform and Mason was wearing a blue blazer with a white shirt and . . .

Hannah gasped as she noticed something shiny on Mason's shirtsleeve. The sleeve of his blazer had pulled up as he'd lifted the award with Craig and his cuff link was exposed. She picked up the photo for a closer look and almost dropped it as she realized that Mason's cuff link was shaped like a horse head with a diamond for the eye.

She stood there for a moment, her knees shaking and her heart racing with the awful realization. Mason had lied to her about the cuff links. He'd had them all along.

And that meant Mason was the killer.

Hannah froze as she heard footsteps outside, approaching the production truck. Someone was coming, and she had to get out of Mason's office right away. She couldn't let him know that she'd seen the picture and guessed his secret.

For one frightening moment, Hannah's feet refused to

obey her command to flee. Then panic took over and she dashed out of Mason's office in a flash, rushing down the hall and heading straight for the phone on P.K.'s desk. She had to call Mike right away and tell him that Mason Kimball was the killer.

Hannah had just grabbed the phone when she heard heavy footsteps on the metal stairs. And then the door opened and Mason came in. He was wearing a smile that made Hannah shudder as the phone dropped from her nerveless fingers.

Chapter
Twenty-Four

"There you are, Hannah." Mason gave her his chilling smile. "I believe we have an appointment?"

Hannah took a deep breath. She had no choice but to brazen it out. Perhaps Mason didn't know she'd realized that he was the murderer, and it was only her own fear that was playing tricks with her mind.

"You're right. Let's go, Mason." Hannah brushed past him and headed for the door. "I was just returning a pen that I borrowed from P.K. last night. Don't let me forget to lock the door behind us."

Mason didn't say anything, but Hannah could feel his menacing presence behind her as she reached for the door-knob. She had to get outside. They were alone in here, but there might be people in the parking lot. She'd be safe around other people.

Her hands were trembling so hard, she couldn't turn the doorknob. Hannah tried once and failed. Then Mason reached forward, around her waist, and Hannah had all she could do not to scream out in terror.

"I'll get it," Mason said, turning the knob and pushing the door open. But instead of letting her walk past him, he blocked the exit with his arm and turned around to face her. "Why are your hands shaking like that?"

"Because I'm freezing." Hannah said the first thing that popped into her mind. If Mason thought she was afraid of him, he'd know she'd guessed the truth. "The heater on my truck went out."

Mason smiled again. "Very good, Hannah. If I didn't know better, I might believe you."

"What?" Hannah tried for her most innocent expression.

"I know you figured it out. It's right on your face."

Hannah felt her hopes die but she gave it one last shot. "Figured out *what*, Mason?"

"It's too late to play games." Mason gave a bitter laugh. "You tipped your hand when you asked me about the cuff links. I knew you'd seen the pictures Lucy took. But I figured no one would connect the cuff links with me and even if they did, they couldn't prove anything. Then Craig came out to the truck this afternoon to tell me you were asking about steroids, and I knew it wouldn't be long before you put the pieces together. It's a pity you figured it out, Hannah. Now I'll have to kill you."

Hannah swallowed hard, attempting to dislodge the lump of panic that filled her throat. "You can't kill me here. P.K. will be back any minute."

"No, he won't. I waited until he left before I came in. But you're right, Hannah. Someone could drive by and hear the shot." Mason reached out and grabbed her arm. "Come on. We're going to the kitchen set. When they find your body on the news tonight, it'll give the ratings a real boost."

Hannah dug in her heels and refused to budge. Mason

was strong, but so was she. If she could shove him away and pull the door shut, she could call Mike for help.

"Forget it, Hannah." Mason pulled a gun from his pocket and slammed the barrel up against her side. "I'll kill you here, if you leave me no choice."

Mason was serious. Hannah could see that from the determined expression on his face. He *would* kill her here, but if she cooperated and walked to the kitchen set with him, it would give her time to think of a way to escape.

"You win, Mason. I'm coming." Hannah wasn't about to argue with a loaded gun. As they walked down the steps, she spotted the box that P.K. had left on the steps and her brain kicked into gear. If it was still there when P.K. came back, he'd take it to the kitchen set for her. If she could delay Mason long enough, P.K. might arrive in time to save her.

"What's this?" Mason kicked the box with his foot.

Hannah thought about lying, but she knew he wouldn't buy it. "It's my box of ingredients."

"Take it with you," Mason ordered, but then he changed his mind. "No. Hold it right there. What's in it?"

"Butter, sugar, eggs, molasses, flour, soda, and spices," Hannah rattled off the ingredients.

"Pick it up."

Hannah picked up the box. She glanced inside and sighed as she realized that Lisa had put everything in soft plastic containers. She'd been hoping to swing the molasses bottle at Mason's head, but the molasses was in Tupperware, and wasn't much of a weapon.

"Walk."

Mason prodded her with the gun barrel in his pocket and Hannah walked. She felt like a prisoner walking to her execution until she remembered that Herb would be on duty in the auditorium. Perhaps she could give him some sort of signal that Mason wouldn't catch, some trick phrase that would make him call Bill and Mike at the station. She was still trying to think of what it could be when Mason opened the auditorium door and pushed her inside.

Herb was gone. The sight of his empty chair made Hannah's hopeful heart drop down to her toes. She should have expected it. Mason had planned all this out. He would have sent Herb on some fool errand, just as he'd done with P.K.

"This is a bad idea, Mason." Hannah did her best to sound reasonable. She had to buy herself some time, think of some way to delay him. P.K. could return and come into the auditorium, Herb could come back from his errand, Mike could call Lisa and track her down at the school, Mr. Purvis could come in to check on the condition of the stage floor, practically anyone could happen along. That wouldn't do much good if she was already dead, but she was still alive.

"It's a very good idea. I made sure nobody would disturb us."

Mason gestured toward a sign that was posted on the auditorium door. It read, *CLOSED SET—NO ADMITTANCE,* in black block letters, and below it was a note in Mason's handwriting, *Hannah—I have a staff meeting at 4:45. Join me at the production truck at 5.*

"When they find your body, they'll assume you ignored the sign and went in to drop off your box. They'll also assume that the killer followed you onto the set and killed you," Mason said, sounding very proud of himself.

Hannah's mind started to slow down in fear, but she made herself concentrate. Mason wouldn't kill her, not if she could think of a way to stop him. "You goofed, Mason. They'll suspect you when you don't show up for the staff meeting."

"I'll be at the staff meeting. It's four-thirty-five now. I've got ten minutes to make it, and killing you won't take more than a minute or two. Open the door, Hannah. I'm on a tight schedule."

Hannah thought about whirling around and attempting to hit Mason with the box, but she knew she couldn't move faster than his trigger finger. She opened the door, stepped into the auditorium, and walked down the aisle to the steps that led to the stage.

"You first." Mason prodded her with the gun barrel. "I'll be right behind you."

Hannah went up the steps and headed for the kitchen set she'd used on the other three shows. As she approached, she noticed that Rudy had left his roving cam on the counter. Maybe she couldn't stop Mason from shooting her, but she could leave evidence for Bill and Mike. If the roving cam had tape and if the batteries were charged, she could turn it on.

"Oops!" Hannah pretended to trip on one of the heavy cables that snaked across the floor. She grabbed at the counter to steady herself, and the box flew out of her hands. Mason glanced down at the box and in the few seconds his attention was diverted, Hannah flicked on the roving cam. By the time he looked up, her hands were back down at her sides.

Mason pointed the gun in her direction again. "Pick everything up and put it back in the box. Hurry up."

Hannah did exactly what he said, kneeling and putting the containers back in place. As she picked up the flour, she remembered how her great-grandmother had always kept a bowl of flour by the side of her bed, planning to throw it in the face of anyone who broke into her house. As far as Hannah knew, Great-Grandma Elsa had never put it to the test, but it was better than nothing.

Flour didn't seem any match for a gun, but Hannah put the container on top. If she couldn't think of anything else, she'd try it. The important thing was to keep Mason talking, and that wouldn't be easy. "I've got a question, Mason."

"What?"

Mason motioned her over to the counter next to the sink, and Hannah put down the box. She managed to pry up the lid on the flour and ease it off the container. "Did you mean to kill Coach Watson?"

"If I'd meant to kill him, I would have brought my gun." Mason frowned. "I just wanted him to agree not to suspend Craig."

"But if it was a fight that got out of hand, why didn't you tell the police? You could have claimed self-defense."

"I would have had to tell the police why we were fighting, and I couldn't do that. Once Craig gets on a good college team, he'll go all the way to the pros. But if the college recruiters find out that he's using steroids, he can kiss his athletic scholarship good-bye."

"Won't they test him for steroids before they offer him a scholarship?" Hannah reached behind her to grip the container of flour, waiting for the perfect moment.

"Of course, but nothing will show up. The drug I got for him is so new they don't have a test for it yet. Everything would have been fine if Craig hadn't gotten worried about some minor side effects. After all I'd done for him, he blabbed the whole thing to Coach Watson and begged him for help."

Hannah felt sick. Mason had gotten steroids for his son and forced Craig to use them. And then, when Craig had tried to get help, Mason had killed the one person who might have actually helped his son. But feeling revulsion for what Mason had done was gaining her nothing. She had to keep him talking. "Did Lucy Richards know about the steroids?" she asked.

"Of course not. Once I got rid of Coach Watson, that leak was plugged."

Hannah shivered. Even though she hadn't liked Boyd Watson, he had been a living, breathing person, not some leak that a plumber might plug. "Then why did you kill Lucy?"

"She said she had pictures of me with Coach Watson." Mason looked highly amused. "Would you believe she actually had the nerve to try to blackmail me?"

Hannah wasn't quite sure if she should nod or shake her head in denial. Instead of reacting, perhaps in the wrong way, she asked another question. *"Did* she have pictures?"

"Who knows? She gave me a story about not having time to develop the film, and she offered to sell me the roll."

"But you didn't fall for that."

"No. Her apartment keys were on her key ring. I went back the next day and took care of all her film."

"Why didn't you do it right after you killed her? Someone else could have found it and developed it."

"Who?" Mason grinned, as if he were enjoying a very funny joke. "Lucy didn't have any friends, and nobody ever visited her. I knew it would be a while before anyone noticed that she was missing, and I had time to take care of any loose ends. And speaking of time, yours is running out."

Hannah tried to think of another question, but absolutely nothing occurred to her. Mason was going to kill her. He'd planned it all out.

"See that tarp?" Mason gestured toward the floor, which was covered with a blue-plastic tarp. "Purvis is so prissy about his stage floor, I didn't want to stain it. I think that's pretty considerate of me, don't you?"

Hannah shuddered. She knew exactly which type of stains Mason meant. He was talking about bloodstains, *her* bloodstains. She knew she had to say something, and she latched on to the first thing that popped into her mind. "You're more considerate about the stage floor than you are about Lisa. Think about how awful she's going to feel when she finds me."

"It can't be helped." Mason shrugged. "It's too bad about Lisa. She's a bright girl and I've always liked her, but I have to think about the ratings."

Hannah felt her anger peak. Mason was a monster, and if she had a gun stashed in her box of ingredients, she'd have no compunction about plugging him right between the eyes. But all she had was a plastic tub of flour.

"It's getting late." Mason glanced at his watch, the opportunity that Hannah had been waiting for. "Guess you won't be baking any more of those overrated cookies. It's time for you to . . ."

Hannah waited until Mason glanced up, then threw the flour in his face. He let out a yell, his hands flew up to his eyes, and Hannah hurtled forward to grab his gun arm.

Mason was strong, but Hannah was fueled by pure rage. He'd hooked his own son on steroids, he'd killed Boyd Watson and Lucy, he'd intended to pump up his ratings by letting poor Lisa find her body on camera, and he'd called her cookies overrated. Hannah didn't know which of his sins bothered her the most, but she was spitting mad.

The struggle seemed to last forever. Mason tried to jerk the gun down and point it at her, but Hannah had watched enough detective movies to know a few street-fighting tricks. She brought her knee up hard, right where it would do the most good. And while Mason was attempting to recover from that unexpected assault, she shoved him back with the full weight of her body and hammered his wrist up against the handle of the oven.

His face turned white. Hannah knew he was in pain, so she did it again, and again. She heard a snap the third time his wrist hit the stove handle, and the gun flew out of his fingers and skittered across the floor.

Mason let out an agonized howl, but Hannah didn't feel a shred of sympathy for the man who'd tried to kill her. While he was writhing on the floor, grasping his wrist and moaning loudly, she retrieved the gun and plunked herself down on the middle of his back.

"Move and you're dead meat," she threatened, "and don't think that wouldn't give me a whole lot of pleasure."

"Hannah! Are you all right?"

It was Mike's voice, and Hannah looked up to see Mike and Bill racing up the aisle. Help was almost here, but she kept the gun pressed tightly to the back of Mason's head.

"Hannah?"

Mike was climbing up the steps and Hannah gave him the best smile she could muster. "I'm fine, but Mason's in big trouble. He killed Boyd, and he killed Lucy. I've got his whole confession on videotape."

"You *what?*" Mike fairly flew across the stage floor with Bill on his heels.

"I'll tell you later." Hannah jammed the gun against Mason's head a little harder. "Just cuff him and get him out of my sight before I do something illegal, will you?"

Chapter
Twenty-Five

Hannah rolled dough balls and dropped them into the bowl of sugar that Lisa held. She knew she looked calm, but that was only because she was still in shock. Mason had come very close to killing her, and only Great-Grandma Elsa's flour defense had saved her. But she didn't dare think about that now. She had to put the dough balls on the cookie sheets and pop them into the oven.

"Are you all right?" Lisa whispered, as Hannah arranged twelve dough balls on a cookie sheet and pressed them down slightly, so they wouldn't roll off when she carried them to the oven.

"Fine," Hannah whispered back.

"You still look a little shaky. Do you want me to carry those?"

"I can do it." Hannah smiled as she remembered the old theater maxim. "The show must go on."

After Hannah had opened the oven and slipped the two sheets of Molasses Crackles inside, she caught sight of the yellow crime-scene tape that the deputies had stretched across the entrance to the fourth kitchen set. Sheriff Grant had decided that the contest could go on, but no one could use that kitchen set. It really didn't matter because there were only three finalists, the winners from Wednesday, Thursday, and Friday nights. All the same, the empty kitchen set with Hannah's flour still scattered over the plastic on the floor was a tangible reminder that she had almost ended up as dead as Boyd and Lucy.

It struck Hannah then, with full force, and she steadied herself against the counter. If she hadn't been able to pry the lid from the container of flour, or if Mason had decided to shoot her right there in the production truck, or if . . .

Later, Hannah told herself. *You can think about it later. Right now, you have to bake cookies and smile.*

Wingo Jones was giving the sports news, all about teams who had trounced, clobbered, whipped, and thrashed their opponents. Hannah glanced out at the audience and saw her mother sitting with Carrie Rhodes. Marge Beeseman and Lisa's father were a few rows ahead. The crime-scene tape was below eye level, and the audience was completely oblivious to what had occurred less than two hours ago on the fourth kitchen set. The sheriff's department wouldn't release the information until tomorrow morning, and then she'd become a local celebrity. It wasn't a status that Hannah sought. If she had to become a celebrity, she'd much rather gain fame as the Cookie Lady.

Doc Knight had set Mason's broken wrist, and he was in custody at the county jail. Mike had removed the cassette she'd taped on Rudy's roving cam, and it would be used as evidence at the trial. When that was over and Mason had been convicted, he'd spend the rest of his life behind bars, where he couldn't hurt anyone, ever again.

The timer on the oven beeped just as Rayne Phillips got up to do the weather. Hannah removed the pans from the oven and carried them over to Lisa, who would transfer them to a wire cooling rack. She was right on schedule, and all she had to do was deliver the cookies to the news team and judge the contest. When all that was done, this perfectly gruesome day would be over.

Hannah glanced over at Rayne Phillips, who was standing next to his blue screen, pointing at something that only the television audience could see, and telling them all that the weather would be cold with occasional snow flurries. Of course it would be cold. This was winter in Minnesota. And of course it would snow. It always did.

Lisa moved closer to Hannah and patted her on the back. "You're a hero, Hannah. They never would have caught Mason without you."

"Heroine," Hannah corrected her, and then she thought about it. Lisa had a valid point. She was the one who'd found the pictures of Boyd's murder. If she hadn't taken the film to Norman to develop, Mason might have found it and destroyed it the way he'd destroyed all of Lucy's other film.

While Rayne Phillips talked on about International Falls and how it was the coldest spot in the nation again, Hannah thought about the other clues she'd discovered with Andrea. Mrs. Kalick hadn't told Bill or Mike about the third car. Andrea had gotten that information from her. And Danielle hadn't mentioned the phone call to Mike or to Bill. She hadn't thought it was important. Norman hadn't gone to the sheriff's station to report Lucy's extortion. He'd confided in Hannah because he'd trusted her to keep it confidential. And since Mike and Bill hadn't known about Boyd's parent-teacher conference, they hadn't questioned Gil Surma about it.

The fact that Mike and Bill had arrived at the auditorium in time to arrest Mason had been a stroke of luck. Hannah had laid the groundwork, showing them the pictures that Lucy had taken of the murder and cueing them in about Gil's reference to steroids. Mike and Bill had spent the morning interviewing the boys on The Gulls. When one player had mentioned that Craig had really buffed up over the summer, they'd driven to the school to ask Mason about it. And when they'd noticed Hannah's truck parked next to the locked production trailer, they'd come to the auditorium to ask her if she'd seen Mason. Mike and Bill would have arrested the right man eventually, they were both good cops, but Hannah and Andrea had provided some very critical pieces of the puzzle and accelerated the process.

"Are you all right?"

"Yes, I am." Hannah turned to give Lisa a big smile. It was a darned good thing she'd interfered in Mike's investigation. If she hadn't, Mason would still be out there, forcing Craig to take steroids and ruining his future.

"It's time, Hannah." Lisa gestured toward Rudy, who was motioning to them. Rudy was managing the news and the bake-off tonight, and the original stage manager had taken over Mason's duties in the production truck.

Hannah picked up the plate of cookies and winked at Lisa. She was back to normal and raring to go. If Dee-Dee Hughes said one word about calories when Lisa passed out the Molasses Crackles, Hannah planned to retaliate by mentioning the half-eaten box of chocolate creams she'd found in Dee-Dee's mobile dressing room.

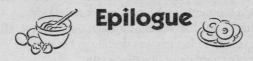

Epilogue

The bar at the Lake Eden Inn was packed with people, and the final wrap party was turning out to be a rousing success. The winner of the Hartland Flour Dessert Bake-Off was holding court at the center table. It was the same lady who'd made the lemon tarts the first night of the contest, and all of the judges had agreed that her entry tonight, a mouth-watering apple pie, was the best they'd ever tasted.

Just after the party had started, Mr. Hart had announced that he planned to make Lake Eden the permanent site of the Hartland Flour Dessert Bake-Off. Now he was sitting with Mayor Bascomb and Rod Metcalf at the far end of the bar, and Hannah suspected that they were talking about how to make the most out of the publicity.

Claire Rodgers was at a table with Reverend Knudson and his grandmother. Hannah had pulled her aside, before the party had started and given her an envelope with Lucy's incriminating photos and negatives. Neither the reverend nor Priscilla was known for scintillating conversation. Perhaps Claire was doing penance for past misdeeds. But she looked happier than she'd looked in months, and Hannah suspected that she'd broken it off with the mayor.

Mr. and Mrs. Avery were sitting with a crowd of other bake-off contestants. Hannah had returned the money, along with Lucy's prints and negatives, to them. Mrs. Avery had told her that they were donating the cash to charity, and Mr. Avery hadn't objected. As Hannah watched, Mrs. Avery reached out to pat her husband's hand. Apparently, all had been forgiven, but Hannah was willing to bet that Mr. Avery wouldn't make a mistake like that again.

Danielle was still in the hospital. Hannah had dropped by to see her on the way to the party and together, they'd torn Lucy's evidence into pieces and flushed them away. No one would ever know about Boyd's problem unless Danielle chose to talk. Hannah didn't think that she would. Boyd's students still idolized him, and it was a shameful thing that was better kept secret.

Hannah was sitting alone at a four-person table. Mike and Norman had gone back for seconds from the huge buffet that Sally had put out for the guests. She picked up one of the bar cookies she'd baked in Sally's kitchen to celebrate the fact that Mason Kimball was behind bars, and tasted it. It was a recipe she'd just perfected, and she'd named her creation Chocolate Highlander Cookie Bars. The bars had a shortbread crust with a creamy, dark chocolate topping, and they were so delicious, Hannah decided to add them to her menu at The Cookie Jar.

Norman and Mike were laughing as they helped themselves to Sally's Lasagna Verde, and Hannah smiled as she watched them. They were a study in contrasts. Mike was so handsome, he could have played the lead in any romantic movie. Norman wasn't. His appeal didn't come from the outside, but Hannah found his solid stockiness and his receding hairline endearing. While Mike was so sexy her stomach went thump, Norman was safe and comforting, like a favorite teddy bear. If she were a magician and she knew how to combine the two of them into one perfect man, she'd take her mother's advice and get married tonight.

"Hi, Hannah." Lisa walked past Hannah's table, carrying an empty dessert plate. "Dad and Mrs. Beeseman asked me to get some more of your bars, but they're all gone."

"There's a second pan in the kitchen. Just go help yourself."

Lisa headed for the kitchen, and Hannah took another sip of her wine. Mike had ordered it especially for her as a way of saying thank you for helping them solve the murder case. Hannah knew it was a good vintage and very expensive, but she still preferred her green gallon jug.

Herb came over to her table, looking distracted. "Where's Lisa? Her dad just asked my mother to dance, and she won't want to miss it."

"She'll be back any minute. She just ducked into the kitchen to get more bars." Hannah grabbed his arm so he couldn't leave. "Sit down for a second, Herb. I need to ask you a favor." Hannah waited until he'd taken the chair next to her, then leaned close, so she wouldn't be overheard. "Do you still go to those cowboy weekends, Herb? The ones where they have shooting competitions?"

"Every chance I get. Why?"

"I need to learn about handguns. Do you think you could teach me?"

"No problem. My shooting club has a range. I'll take you out there some Sunday. Are you planning to buy a handgun for home protection?"

"Not exactly." Hannah glanced around, but no one was listening. "Did Lisa tell you about how I pinned Mason down with his gun?"

"Yes."

"It's like this, Herb. I know how to shoot a shotgun. My dad taught me. But this wasn't a shotgun and I . . . uh . . ."

"You didn't know how to use it?" Herb interrupted her with a guess.

"That's right. Of course I knew where the trigger was. Any fool would know that. But I wasn't sure if I had to do anything first, before it would fire."

"I'll bring out my collection of handguns and teach you how to use them. Once you know the basics, you'll be fine. I taught Lisa, and she took second place in our last cowboy shoot."

"Good for her." Hannah started to smile. It seemed Lisa had talents that she didn't even know about.

After Herb had left, Norman came back to the table. They were sitting there talking about the computer program he'd just installed so that they could design their house for the contest, when Mike came back.

"Hi, Mike." Hannah gave him a smile, then she turned back to Norman, to answer his question. "I don't think we can get along with less than three bathrooms. We'll need one that's a part of the master suite, one between the kids' rooms upstairs, and one downstairs for the guests."

"How about one in the basement, next to the recreation room? We could put it in under the stairs."

"Good idea," Hannah agreed, and then she happened to glance at Mike. He was staring at her in shock. "What is it, Mike?"

"You and Norman are buying a house together?"

"No, we're *designing* a house together," Norman corrected him. And then he clamped his lips shut and didn't say another word.

Hannah stared from one to the other, reading the expressions on their faces. There was a gleam of triumph in Norman's eyes. He was enjoying the fact that Mike was sweating. And Mike looked a little like the rancher who'd come out to his stable in the middle of the night to find a horse thief leading off his best mare.

Hannah knew she should explain before the situation could worsen, but she'd had an exhausting day. She'd almost been killed, and the fact that Norman's and Mike's collective noses had been pushed out of joint seemed rather unimportant in the giant scheme of things.

"Is there something you want to tell me, Norman?" Mike asked in a belligerent tone.

"No. Is there something you'd like to tell *me,* Mike?"

Hannah didn't stick around for the answer. Andrea would know exactly what to do in a situation like this, but Hannah decided she'd had it with jealous men. She pushed back her chair, rose to her full height, and faced them both. "I have to leave. I've got someone at home, warming up my bed for me."

Mike stared at her in astonishment, and Norman looked equally shocked. For a moment, neither of them spoke, and Hannah had an almost-uncontrollable urge to laugh.

"Who?" Norman asked, breaking the silence. He looked extremely upset.

"Yeah, who?" Mike echoed his question, and Hannah noticed that he didn't exactly look happy either.

Hannah thought about the old childhood taunt, *That's for me to know and you to find out,* but she didn't repeat it. Just because she'd reduced them to junior-high level didn't mean that she had to reply in kind. She merely smiled sweetly and turned to walk away, but her conscience prodded her before she could take more than a step. She turned back and grinned. "Moishe. Who did you think I meant?"

And then she walked across the floor toward the door, making an exit that was almost worthy of her screen idol, Katharine Hepburn.

Chocolate Highlander Cookie Bars

Preheat oven to 350° F.,
rack in middle position.

1 cup softened butter *(2 sticks, ½ pound)*
½ cup powdered sugar *(make sure there's no big lumps)*
¼ teaspoon salt
2 cups flour *(no need to sift)*

4 beaten eggs *(just whip them up with a fork)*
1 cup melted butter, cooled to room temp. *(2 sticks, ½ pound)*
1 cup white sugar
1 teaspoon baking powder
¼ teaspoon salt
½ cup flour *(don't bother to sift)*
2 ½ cups chocolate chips *(measure BEFORE they're melted)*

⅓ cup powdered *(confectioner's)* sugar to sprinkle on top of the pan

FIRST STEP: Cream butter with ½ cup powdered sugar and salt. Add flour and mix well. Pat it out in a greased 9-inch by-13-inch pan with your fingers. *(That's a standard cake pan.)*

Bake at 350 degrees F. for 15 minutes. That makes the shortbread crust. Remove from oven. *(Don't turn off oven!)*

SECOND STEP: Mix eggs with melted butter and white sugar. Add baking powder, salt, and flour, and mix thoroughly. *(A hand mixer will do the job if you're tired of stirring.)*

Melt the chocolate chips in a small double boiler, a pan over hot water on the stove, or nuke them for 3 minutes in the microwave on high. *(Be sure to stir—chips may maintain their shape even after they're melted.)*

Add the melted chocolate chips to your bowl and mix thoroughly.

Pour this mixture on top of the pan you just baked and tip the pan so it covers all of the shortbread crust. Stick it back into the oven and bake it for another 25 minutes. Then remove it from the oven and sprinkle on additional powdered sugar.

Let it cool thoroughly and cut into brownie-sized bars. You can refrigerate these, but cut them before you do. *(They're pretty solid when they're cold.)*

Andrea said these were so rich, no one could eat more than one. (I watched her eat three at the wrap party.)

Index of Recipes

Please turn the page for
an exciting sneak peek at Joanne Fluke's
next Hannah Swensen mystery:

BLUEBERRY MUFFIN MURDER

Now on sale wherever mysteries are sold!

Hannah's headlights cut two converging tunnels through the darkness to illuminate the stop sign at the corner of Main Street and First Avenue. She was early, an hour ahead of her normal schedule, but she felt good about giving Lisa the morning off.

Nothing was moving as Hannah drove through the silent business district of Lake Eden. Norman's dental clinic was locked up tight, Hal & Rose's Café was dark, and there was only a dim security light shining through the front plate glass window of the Lake Eden Neighborhood Pharmacy. The town was still slumbering, but Hannah was alert and ready to go to work. This was the opening day of the Winter Carnival, and the cookies they'd baked yesterday wouldn't last through the day. She had to bake more and deliver them to the warm-up tents.

Instead of driving down the front of her block, Hannah turned into the alley and passed the back of Claire Rodger's dress shop, her neighbor to the north. Claire had mentioned that she planned to open Beau Monde Fashions early this morning, but early for Claire was a whole lot later than early for Hannah. No one would want to buy designer dresses or Winter Carnival wear at five-thirty in the morning.

Hannah frowned as she turned into The Cookie Jar parking lot, and her headlights flashed across the rear of the building. The back door of her shop was slightly ajar.

The fact that her door was unlocked didn't set off warning bells in Hannah's mind. Everyone in Lake Eden knew that she emptied the cash register before she went home, and

314   *Joanne Fluke*

there wasn't much else to steal. If some homeless person had jimmied the back door to secure a warm place to sleep, Hannah couldn't really blame him. It had been a bitterly cold night. She'd just give the unfortunate soul a hot cup of coffee and a bag of cookies and send him on his way.

Hannah parked in her usual spot, plugged her extension cord into the strip of outlets on the white stucco wall, and walked closer to examine her door from the outside. The lock was intact and the door showed no sign of pry marks. Janie had simply forgotten to lock it when she left with Connie Mac. Thanking her lucky stars that the gusty winds hadn't torn her door off its hinges and caused a massive jump in her heating bill, Hannah pushed it open and flicked on the lights.

At first glance, her startled mind refused to believe what was right in front of her eyes. Then her mouth opened in a soundless gasp of shock. A bag of cake flour was on the floor, its contents scattered over the tiles like super-fine snow. Stainless steel mixing bowls filled with dried cake batter covered every inch of the work island, and sticky spoons and spatulas stood up inside them like miniature flagpoles. Several cartons of eggshells and dirty utensils were piled on the counter near the sink, and next to them was Hannah's industrial mixer with cake batter glued to its beaters.

Hannah fumed as she surveyed her usually immaculate kitchen. Janie never would have left this incredible mess. She must have gone back to the inn early, and Connie Mac just hadn't bothered to clean up before she left.

Uttering a string of expletives that would have made her mother run for the soap, Hannah stepped inside. It would take her at least an hour to clean her kitchen, and she didn't have any time to waste. She had just started to wipe off the counters when she realized that there was a sickeningly sweet, charcoal-laden smell in the air. Something was burning!

Hannah raced to her oven, opened the door, and jumped back as a cloud of black smoke rolled out. Through the smoke, she could see several charred, smoldering lumps that had once been layers for the official Winter Carnival cake.

With lightning speed Hannah turned off the gas and hurried to her second oven. Smoke was beginning to leak out the door, and she didn't have to look to know that there were similar lumps inside. She turned it off, ran to the windows to yank them open, and flicked the exhaust fan on high. Coughing slightly from the smoke and the exertion, she ran out the back door and propped it wide open behind her.

Hannah was livid as she paced back and forth in the parking lot, kicking up snow with the toes of her boots and waiting for the smoke to clear. Connie Mac had waltzed out of The Cookie Jar with cakes in the ovens, and if Hannah hadn't come to work early, The Cookie Jar might have burned to the ground!

After ten minutes of pacing and fuming, Hannah approached the doorway and took a tentative sniff. There was still a trace of smoke in the air, but it no longer made her eyes water. She stomped into her kitchen with a scowl on her face and headed straight for the sink. There was no time to waste. She had to clean up the mess and begin mixing her cookie dough for the day.

Hannah swept the egg cartons and shells into the nearly overflowing trash can and turned on the hot water to fill the sink with soapy water. Once she'd set the dirty dishes to soak, she carried out the trash and lined the can with a new plastic bag. She was gathering up her cake-batter-encrusted mixing bowls from the work island, preparing to move them to the counter by the sink, when she noticed something that made her stop cold.

Connie Mac's leather handbag was sitting on top of a stool. She must have forgotten it, unless . . . Hannah swiveled around with a frown on her face. Connie Mac's sable coat was still hanging on a hook by the back door. It had dropped down below zero last night. Connie Mac must have been in a real rush to leave if she hadn't taken the time to grab her coat.

Suddenly, the pieces clicked into place, and Hannah glanced around her uneasily. Janie had left early. That much was obvious. Her car was gone, and so was her coat and purse. Connie Mac had been here alone, and someone or something had frightened her away.

A glimmer of light caught Hannah's eye. The pantry door was open a few inches and someone had turned on the light. Hannah grabbed the first weapon she could find, the heavy pot she used to make boiled frostings. If the person who'd frightened Connie Mac away was hiding in her pantry, she'd get in a few good licks before she turned him over to the sheriff!

Once she had moved silently into position, Hannah inched the door open with her foot. She glanced inside, and what she saw caused the pot to slip from her nerveless fingers. Her earlier assumption was wrong. Connie Mac hadn't left last night.

The Cooking Sweetheart was facedown on the pantry floor, her arms and legs sprawled out like a kid who'd hit the surface of Eden Lake in an ungainly belly dive. She had been struck down by a massive blow to the head in the act of sampling one of Hannah's Blue Blueberry Muffins.

Shock rendered Hannah immobile for a moment, but then she knelt down to feel for a pulse. The biggest celebrity ever to set foot in Lake Eden would never star in another episode of her television show or pose for pictures in her magazine. Connie Mac was dead.

ABOUT THE AUTHOR

Like Hannah Swensen, Joanne Fluke was born and raised in a small town in rural Minnesota but now lives in sunny Southern California. Readers are welcome to contact Joanne at the following e-mail address: Gr8Clues@aol.com.

Get More Mysteries by Leslie Meier

Tippy Toe Murder 1-57566-392-9	**$5.99**US/**$7.99**CAN
Mistletoe Murder 0-7582-0337-3	**$6.50**US/**$8.99**CAN
Trick or Treat Murder 1-57566-219-1	**$5.99**US/**$7.99**CAN
Wedding Day Murder 1-57566-734-7	**$6.50**US/**$8.99**CAN
Back to School Murder 1-57566-330-9	**$5.99**US/**$7.99**CAN
Turkey Day Murder 1-57566-685-5	**$5.99**US/**$7.99**CAN
Valentine Murder 1-57566-499-2	**$5.99**US/**$7.99**CAN
Christmas Cookie Murder 1-57566-691-X	**$5.99**US/**$7.99**CAN
Birthday Party Murder 1-57566-833-5	**$6.50**US/**$8.99**CAN
Father's Day Murder 1-57566-835-1	**$6.50**US/**$8.99**CAN
Star Spangled Murder 1-57566-837-8	**$6.50**US/**$8.99**CAN

Available Wherever Books Are Sold!

Visit our website at **www.kensingtonbooks.com**

Enjoy These Mysteries from Laurien Berenson

HUSH PUPPY	1-57566-600-6	**$5.99**US/**$7.99**CAN
DOG EAT DOG	0-7582-1317-4	**$6.99**US/**$9.99**CAN
A PEDIGREE TO DIE FOR	0-7582-0854-5	**$6.50**US/**$8.99**CAN
UNLEASHED	1-57566-680-4	**$5.99**US/**$7.99**CAN
WATCHDOG	0-7582-1344-1	**$6.99**US/**$9.99**CAN
HAIR OF THE DOG	0-7582-1345-X	**$6.99**US/**$9.99**CAN
HOT DOG	1-57566-782-7	**$6.50**US/**$8.99**CAN
ONCE BITTEN	0-7582-0182-6	**$6.50**US/**$8.99**CAN
UNDER DOG	0-7582-0292-X	**$6.50**US/**$8.99**CAN
BEST IN SHOW	1-57566-784-3	**$6.50**US/**$8.99**CAN
JINGLE BELL BARK	1-57566-786-X	**$6.50**US/**$8.99**CAN
RAINING CATS AND DOGS	0-7582-0814-6	**$6.99**US/**$9.99**CAN
CHOW DOWN	0-7582-0816-2	**$6.99**US/**$9.99**CAN

Available Wherever Books Are Sold!

Check out our website at **www.kensingtonbooks.com**